The Lies She Wore

C.C. Hansen

Dancing Willows Press

For my grandmother—if I become one tenth the woman she is, I will have far surpassed my wildest dreams.

"It is during our darkest moments that we must focus
to see the light."

Aristotle

Chapter 1

Cathryn's Diary

I've been an adult since I was seven. At five, I noticed things: my father smiled with clenched teeth; my mother flinched before high fives; our neighbors whispered behind my father's back but didn't speak to his face. At six, I realized those things weren't normal. Other mommies ran toward their husbands. At seven, my childhood took a fatal blow.

Now I am sixteen, an adult playing dress-up as a child. Tomorrow, another school year begins. I will giggle about boys who don't interest me and nod my way through conversations about clothes I can't afford. As much as I tire of hiding beneath long sleeves, it's worth it. Learning is my escape. With every report card, I prepare myself for a future that may never exist, but still I dream.

Maybe this time we'll succeed.

* * *

Jeans and a long-sleeved shirt covered most of Cathryn's secrets; the rest required makeup. Her appearance was a lie she wore instead of spoke, another strand of falsehood in the rope that strangled the truth. Still, leading a double life beat staying home.

Cathryn stood at her bathroom sink and rubbed the sleep from her eyes. The nightmare had been a poor beginning, but if a bad

1

dream was the only trouble she faced today, she wouldn't complain. A few brush strokes turned her night-owl grogginess into morning-person cheer. A couple more transformed her nightmare into a normal teenage life. Cathryn examined her handiwork by the dingy light. She couldn't afford mistakes. Not today. Not this year.

She took a single step into her room and stumbled over the secondhand blankets and saggy pillows that littered the floor. With practiced efficiency, she collected her mother's makeshift bedding and stacked it near her bed's iron footboard. The drab colors atop the bedspread's faded lavender flowers created a mournful garden.

Her stomach growled as the scent of breakfast reached her, but she scolded it into submission. It should know by now those eggs weren't for her.

"You're up early." Cathryn's father strode into her room. Stubble still shadowed his chin, but his dark hair dripped from the shower.

"It's the first day of school." Cathryn faced him, careful not to glance toward the panel at the back of her closet. All her hopes rested on his never discovering it.

Her father's face lit with the smile that made women sigh and men offer him beer. "Can't I lock you in a little box so you can't grow up?"

Cathryn lost all desire for food, but her father's face maintained its creamy coloring. His arms dropped lazily from his shoulders, waiting like yawning hounds. Amusement danced in his eyes. He was joking.

Cathryn's forced chuckle emerged more like a hen's nervous cluck. "I don't think that would work."

He pulled her into a straitjacket-tight hug. "You sure you don't want to play hooky and spend the day with me?"

Cathryn's eyes flitted to the door. "You work anyway. I'll be home before you are."

"Guess you're right." She refrained from wincing as his affectionate pat on the back hit a bruise. He released her with another smile. "I love you, sweetie."

Cathryn pushed her facial muscles into a smile as though molding the expression from dry clay. "I love you too, Dad."

She waited until his footsteps thudded down the stairs before grabbing her books. The scent of old paper, dust, and ink filled her lungs and eased the tightness in her chest. She ran her finger over the bent spines—organized in alphabetical order by author—before loading them into her backpack. She tugged its frayed strap to test her repair work. It should last the year.

Over the weekend, Cathryn and her mother had scrubbed the house clean and completed what repairs they could manage. Their efforts were akin to giving crutches to someone with no legs, but they never took chances with the first day of school. The telltale sound of her father's car struggling to life signaled his departure and their success.

Cathryn hesitated at the top of the stairs. The fourth step down moaned like a ghost with indigestion when stepped on. Last night, she dreamed it collapsed, and she tumbled through endless darkness. She didn't consider herself superstitious, but she skipped the stair anyway.

Her mother stood at the kitchen sink, the pale skin on her arms reddening from the hot dishwater as she washed one pan, one plate, and one fork.

"Need any help, Mom?"

"No." She frowned, moved her dirty-blond ponytail out of the way, and blew on the stove's only working burner. Satisfied the gas was off and the flame dead, she returned to the dishes. "You don't want to be tardy."

"I know. 'Don't make trouble and don't attract attention.' It's a normal year." *As if our lives have ever been normal.*

Her mother dropped the sponge and wrapped Cathryn in a hug. Her wet hands left dark puddles on the back of her shirt. "We can do this, right?"

Cathryn hugged her back, feeling more stable with her mother's warmth around her. "Of course we can. We'll just follow Francis of Assisi: 'Start by doing what's necessary, then do what's possible, and suddenly, you are doing the impossible.'"

"That's my girl." Her mother squeezed her once more before pushing her toward the door. "Have a good day at school."

The ridiculous normality of that statement followed Cathryn into the crisp fall morning. The trees' leaves shivered in a breeze, but they were still green. *Maybe they're in denial about winter.* Cathryn shook off her musings. She had her own winter to worry about.

Just get through this year.

* * *

Brooks High contained the drama of a paperback romance and the testosterone-directed posturing of a wrestling cage match. Like a visiting anthropologist, Cathryn ensured she blended into the atmosphere with the scents of sweaty gym clothes and dollar-store perfume. She slipped around joyful reunions and overdue gossip sessions en route to her junior-year locker assignment, but a pair of shouts brought her to a halt.

"What'd you call me?"

"Requesting you shift your position hardly constitutes ridicule."

Cathryn recognized the first speaker: Tony Giordani. Judging by his red face, he'd changed little since she'd last seen him. Her stomach churned at the thought of spending a year as locker neighbor to the raging bull. *What if I carried my books?* No. The mended strap on her backpack wouldn't last more than a week of that, and she couldn't afford a new one. Not this year. This year, every penny counted.

Cathryn examined Tony once more. Despite his clenched jaw, his eyes hadn't yet attained the animal-like glare of a man consumed by rage. She took the risk.

"He wasn't insulting you, Tony. He was asking you to move. His locker must be under yours." Her conciliatory tone had its intended effect. Tony's muscles no longer threatened to tear through the white T-shirt stretched over his stocky frame, and his skin faded to a more muted ruddy tone.

The second speaker whirled to face her, blue eyes wide in his pale face. "You understood me?" His sharply articulated syllables contrasted with the long o's and eh's of a typical Minnesotan.

"You speak just fine," Cathryn said, "but your vocabulary is a bit . . . formal."

"Vocabulary schmabulary. Show some respect, or I'll punch your face in." Tony stalked away with the swagger of a sailor.

The tall boy observed Tony's departure with an expression more annoyed than intimidated. His perfect posture exuded an air of confidence that suggested Tony would have a harder time punching his face in than he believed.

"I won't speculate on how he concluded I was mocking him."

"Tony talks tough, but he won't bother you if you stay out of his way." Cathryn opened her locker, annoyed that its placement would put her repeatedly "in his way." *One problem at a time.* "I'm Cathryn, by the way."

"Gustaf Hein." The boy turned the combination on his locker, which was indeed below Tony's.

Cathryn's sleeve slipped as she put away her books, revealing a purple splotch on her forearm. She yanked her sleeve to cover it and checked if anyone noticed, but her classmates focused on the newcomer. The guys' eyes filled with jealousy; the girls' lingered on Gustaf's lean muscles as he tried and failed to open his locker.

A brunette flounced her glossy curls and left the cluster of admirers. "Scooch, Caitlyn." She pushed Cathryn aside and tapped Gustaf's shoulder with a manicured fingernail. "I'm Belinda, the junior class president. I'd love to get you connected with student council."

Gustaf's scowl could have curdled milk. "No thank you."

Belinda's smile froze. "The student council—"

"Is a pubescent mimicry of civil service led by a simpleton who can't recall the names of her constituents."

Belinda's face transitioned from polished mannequin to toddler having a tantrum. "What?"

Gustaf looked over her shoulder at Cathryn. "Unless I misheard, her name is Cathryn, not Caitlyn." Like the toddler whose expression she mimicked, Belinda stomped her foot and left them in a cloud of her jasmine perfume. Gustaf clicked a button on his watch and raised his eyebrows at Cathryn.

Cathryn shrugged. "I voted for Faduma."

Gustaf returned his gaze to his watch in lieu of responding. "Three point seven seconds."

"Three seconds to what?"

"The average time elapsed before a girl realizes (a) she doesn't understand a word I say, and (b) I will not mount a white horse and whisk her away to a castle filled with roses."

"You calculated the average time it takes a girl to lose interest in you?"

"If I must endure their insipid chatter about lip gloss, I may as well collect data of interest." A grunt of frustration punctuated his last words as the locker continued to deny him entry.

"You have to hit it."

Gustaf paused his battle with his locker long enough to give her an acidic sneer. "Applying force to the door will not release the lock."

Cathryn smacked the locker with the side of her fist, and like an obedient dog, it opened.

He glared at the open door and muttered, "Thank you."

"What's your first class?"

Gustaf's scowl deepened. "As you seem determined to raise the average beyond four seconds, allow me to be explicit. I have no interest in friends. My only goal is a scholarship to whatever university is farthest from here."

His rudeness would have offended Cathryn had she not been honing her ability to read emotions since childhood. She knew every signal for anger—flared nostrils, pulsing veins, tense shoulders—but she sensed only frustration in Gustaf. Whatever his situation, he wanted out. Cathryn empathized. *No. You have bigger things to worry about than a disgruntled genius. Stitch up your bleeding heart and focus.*

As a good-looking new guy, Gustaf had already attracted their classmates' attention. Cathryn pinched the bruise beneath her sleeve to remind herself why, this year especially, that attention was dangerous. *Just get through this year.*

Gustaf's sigh echoed her thought. A hint of despondency broke through the hardness of his scowl as he collected his folders. Cathryn pinched her bruise again, but the pain wasn't enough to prevent her heart from hijacking her tongue.

"'In the middle of difficulty lies opportunity.'" She closed her locker. "I like quotes. That one's from—"

"Albert Einstein."

Cathryn nodded, unable to keep from smiling at his recognition. "And Isaac Newton said, 'Men build too many walls and not enough bridges.'"

Gustaf's eyes narrowed as he reassessed her. He consulted the half sheet of paper containing his schedule. "My first class is Honors Chemistry, room 304B. If there is any logic to this building's design, it will be in that direction." He gestured down the hall with his books.

Cathryn chuckled. "It may have been logical in 1889, but they've renovated it into an architectural Frankenstein's monster since then. The original building looked was more classic, but they designed the later additions without windows because of student unrest during the Vietnam War. The newest rooms have windows, but the art wing lost its skylight after a heavy snow in 1996."

Gustaf fixed his stony gaze on her as he closed his locker. "Does your encyclopedic knowledge of the building include a map?"

Cathryn's cheeks burned. "Sorry. If I like quotes, I love history." His expression didn't reveal whether he found her insightful or insane. "If you prefer, I can switch to insipid chatter about lip gloss."

Gustaf coughed out what might have been a laugh had he not choked on it. "Shall we?"

* * *

As far as his classmates were concerned, Gustaf may as well be speaking Martian. Fortunately, he shared his honors courses with Cathryn, who translated with the naturalness of a bilingual.

He examined the girl as they walked toward the cafeteria. From the faded long-sleeved shirt to the patched jeans that were two inches too short, nothing in her appearance marked her as the single bastion of intelligent life in this school. Even the way she walked suggested a rabbit skittering to avoid a predator's eye.

"So, are you from Germany?" Cathryn glanced his direction and returned her gaze to the floor. She had an irritating habit of doing that, as if she were asking the floor's forgiveness for speaking.

"Why do you ask?"

She fidgeted with the end of her dirty-blond ponytail. "You, uh, don't speak like a local."

Probably because the locals' combined IQ is less than 50. "I was born in New Jersey but attended boarding school two hours north of Los Angeles," Gustaf said, though he certainly felt as if he were in a foreign country. "I inherited my name from a German scientist who refuted Nazi falsehoods." *How far we've fallen from his legacy.*

"What brings you to Minnesota?"

"It is a long story."

"I enjoy long stories as much as long words."

Gustaf glimpsed eyes of a color somewhere between hazel, gray, and green, but the eyes weren't what caused him to halt in the middle of the hallway. The smile Cathryn flashed radiated the warmth of a fireplace. His explanation flew out as though she were a magnet for words.

"My parents' colleague accused them of grant fraud. The colleague was . . . romantically involved with the university's president, which assured their termination." *At least, that's their version.* His mother used stronger words than "romantically involved."

"Sounds like the plot of a soap opera."

"If only it were fiction. An eccentric sponsor offered them positions at the University of Minnesota provided I attend his alma mater." *As if this asylum for imbeciles qualifies as a school.*

Cathryn shifted her books to her other arm. "If it helps, I'm glad I met you. Teddy Roosevelt said, 'Do what you can, with what you have, where you are.' Perhaps you'll find unexpected opportunities here."

Despite the unnerving effects, Gustaf wished she would maintain eye contact so he could see her smile better. *I'm sure there is a whole field of psychology related to such expressions.*

"I'm meeting my friend Minh for lunch. You're welcome to join us." She smiled again, and despite his commitment to avoiding friendships, he followed her into the cafeteria.

* * *

To locate Minh in a crowd, Cathryn simply looked for the ripple that arose from people getting out of her way, like a river diverting around a particularly stubborn rock. Had her parents not so detested swearing, the Asian artist would have painted BITCH ON WHEELS across the back of her wheelchair. Unlike Cathryn, no one forgot Minh Jones's name.

Cathryn chewed the inside of her cheek as she scanned the cafeteria. *I didn't think this through.* Living in Minh's shadow helped her stay invisible, but Gustaf was an unknown variable. Their personalities might prove volatile when mixed.

I can't just uninvite him. Then she'd have to explain why. Before Cathryn could spin an acceptable lie, Minh arrived.

"Sorry I'm late," Minh said, lunch tray resting on her lap. "Art is in Timbuktu, and the elevator is worse than my dad's old Chevy." She nodded toward Gustaf. "Who's the walking statue?"

"And people say *I* lack decorum," Gustaf said dryly.

Minh raised a graceful eyebrow. "Cat, I like that you're being more social, but are you sure you want to start collecting misfits?"

"Misfit? Says the girl with ink stains on her hands," Gustaf said.

"What's wrong, you afraid of a little pen puke?" Minh wiggled her fingers as though casting a spell.

Shoot. Less than ten seconds and they were already arguing. *Find a place to sit.* Her best hope was to contain their argument to the lunch table, but the bench seats meant Minh could only pull her wheelchair up to the ends.

"There, by the vending machine." She pointed to an empty table.

They weaved around a trash bin full of stale pizza and crusted milk cartons, pressed through the crowd of wide-eyed freshmen, and took their seats. Cathryn made formal introductions as she opened her water.

Gustaf watched her hands. "You're ambidextrous."

Minh snorted. "As if she could pick sides."

Cathryn ignored the jibe and addressed Gustaf. "How did you know?"

"Your ponytail is a few centimeters left of center, suggesting you used your left hand. This morning you turned the combination of your locker with your right hand but reached for your books with your left. Now you are eating with your left hand, but it lacks the lead smudges typical of a left-handed writer."

"That's amazing." Her hand stiffened around her water bottle. *What else has he noticed?*

"Do us a favor, Sherlock: keep your amazing to yourself," Minh said.

"This guy bothering you ladies?" Tony's question was more of a pronouncement as he set his tray next to Gustaf's. Apparently, he too was joining her collection of misfits. *So much for not attracting attention.* Cathryn shifted to the edge of her seat, grateful the table lay between her and the hulky newcomer.

"We're fine," Minh said. "Gus, the boy genius, was just strutting like a rooster in front of an ambidextrous hen." Minh's smile had the edge of an assassin's dagger.

"Well, if he does, you say the word, and I'll punch his face in." Tony threatened Gustaf with his plastic spork.

Gustaf transferred his glare from Minh to Tony. "You underestimate me. I am well-versed in martial arts."

"What, like *Karate Kowabunga?*"

"What?" Gustaf looked to Cathryn, who lowered her gaze.

"I don't watch TV." Her father was king of the remote, reason enough to avoid it.

"Neither do I," Gustaf said, his tone approving.

Minh shook her head as she chewed, eyes wide as though observing something disturbing but unable to tear her gaze away.

"You should try lacrosse," Tony said around a bite of his sandwich. "I got a cousin who plays, says they need tall guys like you."

"I'll consider it." Gustaf's tone suggested he wanted nothing more to do with Tony, much less his cousin.

"Have you ever thought of going by Gus?" Cathryn asked, hoping Minh's unintended nickname was a safer topic.

"No."
"It might help you fit in."
"I'm not sure I—
"Too late," Minh declared. "Gus it is."

Chapter 2

After last night, Laurel Ostergaard needed retail therapy. The headache she'd nursed all morning disappeared as she searched the shelves for a loaf tin. She'd never liked the way her banana bread turned out in the glass pans she'd inherited from Mark's grandmother. Until now, she'd been too afraid of hurting his feelings to buy a new one. Not today. Today was a new-loaf-tin day. *Serves him right.*

"Are you albino?" The voice belonged to a girl at Laurel's hip. She couldn't have been over four.

"What do you mean?"

"My brother Jeremy said our cat is albino 'cause she's all white. You wear a scarf on your head, but your skin is white, not brown. Are you albino?"

"Oh, no, sweetie, that's not how it works." *She must have seen someone wearing a hijab.* Most Muslims in Minneapolis were Somali. Laurel was neither. She had other reasons to cover her hair. "Where's your mother?"

"April!" A red-faced woman took the girl's hand. "How many times have I told you not to wander off while Mommy is shopping?" She turned to Laurel. "I am so sorry."

Laurel put on her well-practiced smile. "No problem." The little girl waved over her mother's shoulder as she was carried away. The ache that plagued Laurel's head arose anew in her heart.

"They're cute at that age," said a woman who was restocking the shelves nearby. Her name tag read BEATRICE BANKS.

"Yeah."

"My daughter Cathryn was the same way, only she liked to eavesdrop on people speaking other languages. I learned to say *lo siento* pretty quickly." She added a pan to the stack. "Do you have little ones?"

Laurel set the loaf tin back on the shelf in slow motion. "I wanted to."

"I'm sorry. I didn't mean—"

"It's fine." She took the longest strides she could to get away before the clerk noticed her tears. She left without the loaf tin.

* * *

The gravel road home from work grated against Beatrice's aching feet, but she resented the woods more. Even if the "woods" were just a tangle of trees around the cul-de-sac, they hid secrets.

The trees might want to isolate her, but the roar of the 35W and 94 interstates reminded her she lived in downtown Minneapolis. Across that interchange lay Cedar-Riverside, or "Little Mogadishu," home to an influx of Somali immigrants fleeing a civil war. To the west was the neighborhood Cathryn dubbed "The Encyclopedia of Spanish Dialects," and a shortcut south through the woods led to the Lewis Library.

Not the worst place to live. Not the best either.

Beatrice stepped around a rusty bicycle and knocked on the door of her only remaining neighbor. Last winter, he contracted a nasty case of pneumonia, and since then checking on him had become part of Beatrice's weekly routine. The frail man waved from a couch that appeared to have gone through a shredder—twice. Beatrice didn't even know the old man's name. She only knew he spent his time growing "recreational" plants.

She averted her gaze as she passed the remains of their previous neighbors' house. She'd tried to erase her memories of the Maldonado family—Diego's square glasses, Joaquín and Cathryn's Spanglish chitchat, fresh-baked *conchas* and pantomimed chats with

Luciana—but the wreckage stood as a monument to what happened, to what would happen again if their plans failed.

Beatrice hurried to her own front door. She fumbled with three different keys as she unlocked the knob, lower lock, and middle lock. The upper lock was for nights. She didn't have a key to that one. She didn't have a key to the ones outside the bedroom doors either.

Once inside, she relocked the doors, knowing the consequences should Jedidiah find them unlocked. Cathryn sat on their sky-blue couch, bent over a book the size of a dictionary. Beatrice thanked God they lived within walking distance of the library. Otherwise, Cathryn's drug of choice might have been something other than books.

A twinge of remorse accompanied the surge of pride she felt at the sight of her daughter. She may not have her daughter's brain, but she would never forget the look on that customer's face as she fled the store. The woman covered her hair with a scarf, but nothing could cover her sorrow.

Beatrice locked the feeling in her heart as she approached her only child. "Don't tell me they gave you homework already?"

"You're late."

Someday our lives will be normal enough to talk about homework. "I cashed the check." Beatrice followed her daughter upstairs to her room, careful to avoid the one loose step. Both of them feared it would give way, but they knew better than to ask for repair money.

Cathryn slid a panel out from the back of her closet and put Beatrice's work uniform inside. She pulled out a toolbox and wiggled the rusted latch open.

"How much more do we need?" Beatrice tried not to hover.

"Depends. If we run far away, we'll need money for travel. If we stay close, we'll need to lie low until the search dies down. Between that and the new social security cards and IDs, it'll be a while."

"You're sure this Javier guy is trustworthy?"

"He's helping us commit a federal crime, Mom—of course he's not trustworthy. But he and I used to play capture the flag in the woods. We bonded over the fact that we both sucked."

"Is there no way besides identity theft?"

Cathryn shook her head. "We've been over this, remember? You don't have a credit card, so the first thing the police will do is run your social. Even if they don't believe Dad when he claims you've kidnapped me, they'll still look, and he'll find a way to follow them to us. We need a number no one can track, and the social security administration won't issue you a new one without formal evidence."

"What about Minh's dad?"

"And have her family end up like the Maldonados?"

Beatrice shook her head. "Lord help us; this is crazy."

Cathryn placed a hand on her forearm, the one that healed crooked. "Has he gotten better or worse?"

Beatrice saw the answer in the bruise under her daughter's sleeve. "How much longer until we have enough?"

Cathryn checked the account sheet. "Between your income and what Mr. Zabinski pays me . . . at the earliest, November of next year."

"No. I don't want you missing school. We go this spring, hide out over the summer, and enroll you in a new school in the fall. Next time—" She stopped at Cathryn's expression. Evidently, her daughter hadn't thought of starting over at a new school. "Cathryn? We can still back out."

Cathryn shook her head. "At least this way I might graduate."

Beatrice took her daughter's face in her hands. "More than graduate. We're getting out of here, and you're going to college. I won't fail you this time. When you go to the library tomorrow, ask Pilar if she can get me into her night job."

"You'll never get out of the house."

"I'm not that old. I've done my fair share of sneaking out windows. You handle your father's breakfast, and I'll sleep in. I'll get home from my dayshift at the store in time to nap before dinner."

"But what if he . . . calls for you?" At Beatrice's raised eyebrows, Cathryn said, "They teach sex ed in school, Mom."

"Your father is only interested in that after the news and before he heads to the bars." Jedidiah never drank at home. He said some things belonged in a man's world. "You know how rigid he is, like clockwork. I'll be fine."

"Mom, I—"

Gravel churned beneath wheels. Beatrice checked her watch. Six p.m. Clockwork. Cathryn stowed the toolbox as Beatrice dashed downstairs to the kitchen. She lit the stove and mangled open two cans of chicken noodle soup. Two. More wasted money, less dishonored his hard work. Either miscalculation led to bruises. Cathryn set the table. She was reaching for the bag of dinner rolls when the locks clicked open.

"Where are my favorite girls?"

"Here, Dad. Let me take your lunch bag."

Beatrice cranked up the heat. Jedidiah had thrown out their microwave four years ago after it started throwing sparks like a defunct spaceship. "Why do we need a microwave when we have a perfectly good stove?" he'd said. Beatrice made rapid figure eights with the spoon and willed the soup to heat. Even on high, it wasn't near warm enough.

A pair of arms constricted around her waist. Jedidiah worked moving boxes at a shipping warehouse. He could break her in half if he wanted.

"Soup tonight?" he said over her shoulder.

Beatrice nodded, smelled salami in his breath. "Just a few minutes."

The arms squeezed tighter.

"I made a new cushion for your chair, Dad. Come try it."

Good stall, Cathryn. A chair scraped against the floor as Cathryn pulled it out for her father. Beatrice had taught Cathryn to patch clothes, but she had no idea whether Cathryn had really made a new cushion.

At last, the soup simmered. Simmering. Not too cold, not too hot. Once, she'd boiled it, and Jedidiah threw it at her.

"Soup is ready." She kissed him on the cheek. "Thank you, darling, for working hard so I don't have to."

"Thank you, Dad, for always being home to have dinner with your family." Cathryn recited the litany with surprising devotion. *When did she become an actress?*

Jedidiah picked up his spoon. "No bread?"

Cathryn's head snapped up, her eyes wide. She dashed to the counter and grabbed the bag of dinner rolls. "You came home just as

I was setting them out. I—"

"You're old enough to know how to set a table." Cathryn winced as Jedidiah gripped her wrist.

Beatrice clenched her fists in her lap. "You're right, Jed. It's time Cathryn took on more responsibilities around the house. Maybe she ought to make your breakfast from now on." She held her breath.

Jedidiah released his grip and smiled the smile that used to make Beatrice go weak at the knees. "Right. Cathryn, from now on you're in charge of breakfast. I—"

"Two eggs, one sausage patty, and one piece of whole-wheat toast, but not the fancy bread from the bakery, the normal kind. Toasted just enough to melt half a pat of butter. Not dry."

"And no bacon because?"

Cathryn swallowed before answering. "Sausage has more meat for the money. Bacon is a rich person's way of getting fat."

Jedidiah flashed another dazzling smile and pinched Cathryn's cheek. "See, all those smarts do come in handy."

Beatrice bit her tongue until she tasted blood. *You say that now.* "Why don't you eat before it gets cold, darling?"

Beatrice and Cathryn waited, heads bowed, wedged between Jedidiah's slurping and the clock's ticking. They'd learned years ago the best way to placate the beast was to feed it. An empty stomach was better than a bruised face.

Jedidiah ladled seconds. Then thirds. *Thirds. Bad day.* He was more likely to "call her," as Cathryn put it, on a third-helping day.

After gulping down the third bowl, Jedidiah slouched into their couch and turned the TV to the news. Beatrice checked the pot. Half a bowl of soup left.

"Cathryn, you eat." She kept her voice low to avoid disturbing Jedidiah.

"I get a free lunch at school, remember? I always eat a lot, just in case." Before Beatrice could protest, Cathryn poured the rest of the soup into her bowl and went to the sink to start the dishes.

The Banks house had three rules: break nothing, spend as little as possible, and have dinner ready by six. As long as they followed those rules, nobody got hurt, but a misstep by one meant bruises for both. Beatrice spooned the now-cold soup into her mouth.

Spring couldn't come soon enough.

* * *

Cathryn's Diary

I need not attend church to learn about hell. It walks through my door every night at six p.m. Last time I went to church, the pastor preached as though hell were confined to a distant under-realm in an indeterminate future. He was wrong.

Hell is here, hidden behind false smiles and unsaid words. Though the truth burns, I contain it, cover it, coax it into submission to the lie that I'm okay. That is hell: a truth that when released destroys you from the outside, but when bound in chains of lies destroys you from the inside.

* * *

Cathryn may have slept in a house on Maple Leaf Avenue, but the Lewis Library was home. The books were closer than siblings, and if she'd had her choice of grandfathers, she would have selected the head librarian, Mr. Zabinski. Here among the bookshelves, she existed in her natural habitat.

When she was five, her father screamed at her for dropping her mug of hot chocolate. In a panic, she'd packed a backpack full of books and run to the one place she felt safe—the story circle. Of course, Mr. Zabinski called her mother, who was beside herself. Her father banned her from the library for months. From then on, Cathryn strove to separate him from this place. That way, she could at least escape for a couple hours.

Cathryn shook off her reflections. Today, she'd have to briefly merge her two worlds when she asked for Pilar's help. She still had a few minutes before the kids—including Pilar's sons—arrived for Story Time, so she grabbed a cart of returned books and headed for the shelves.

"You know, as of last month, we have officially doubled the size of the *libros en español* section." Mr. Zabinski smiled at her from the end of the row. Cathryn first met the elderly gentleman when she attended Story Time as a toddler. She'd spotted the willowy white man's scraggly gray beard and assumed Santa Claus ran out of cookies.

"Circulation increased a ton after you hired Mrs. Nelson," Cathryn said as she squeezed another book into place. "The English tutoring gets the parents through the door, and the kids check out books afterward."

"Don't sell yourself short, my dear. Starting a Spanish Story Time was your idea." He picked up a book from the cart. "What are your plans for today?"

Cathryn couldn't stop the smile from bubbling onto her face. "*The Fantastic Flying Books of Mr. Morris Lessmore* by William Joyce." Usually, she read books originally written in Spanish, but the kids had requested her favorite, and she couldn't resist sharing. Rosa María had double-checked her translation, so Cathryn knew she would do the story justice.

"I'm glad you finally agreed to let me pay you," Mr. Zabinski said. "You're money well spent." He winked and left to attend a lost-looking patron.

Cathryn's mood dampened as she finished shelving. If she'd had a normal life, she never would have accepted payment for the privilege of spending her afternoons here, but she didn't. She and her mother needed the money.

Don't forget to talk to Pilar. Cathryn burned the thought into her memory as she returned the empty cart and took her place in the story circle. The children trickled in, and their smiling faces lifted her sour mood. She'd practiced the translation so much she had the story memorized, but the kids liked it most when she asked them to invent their own variations.

After she finished, she herded the children to their parents, and the library's front entrance filled with the smell of their sticky-sweet sweat. She scanned the crowd for Pilar, but someone tapped her shoulder.

Rosa María gripped her daughter's hand. Though her English was near native now, she addressed Cathryn in Spanish out of habit. "When is Story Time in English?"

"Tuesdays at the same time."

Rosa María's smile was a perfect half-moon on her round face. A grade-school teacher from Mexico, she had the brightest smiles and silliest expressions. "Good. Antonio got promoted, so I don't need to work as much. I want Sofía to attend English Story Time too."

"You work with Pilar, right?"

Rosa María nodded. "One more year. Then I'll return to the classroom."

"Felicidades." Cathryn couldn't imagine a more deserving teacher than Rosa María. She'd studied relentlessly to pass her teacher's license exam in English. *If she is cutting back on hours, there might be an opening.* "Could—"

"¡Carlos, Ignacio, venid ya!" Even without the no-nonsense tone she used to call her sons, there was no mistaking Pilar's accent. The petite single mother was the only Spaniard in the neighborhood.

"I'll leave you with the witch." Rosa María winked and left.

Cathryn trotted to where Pilar collected her sons. Though Pilar had a soft side, she'd earned Rosa María's teasing. A tough-skinned pistol of a woman, the former lawyer was now learning a new language and new law code while working two jobs. Her never-surrender attitude reminded Cathryn of Minh.

"Pilar, may I ask you something?"

Pilar tightened her black stub of a ponytail. *"Solo si me tuteas, hija."*

Cathryn tried to mimic the dialect of whomever she conversed with, but usually her own Spanish came out as a mix. Pilar asked her to use the informal pronoun. That paired with her using the endearment "hija," daughter, proved she was more mentor than "witch."

"You"—Cathryn fumbled with the informal pronoun—"you work for Pemko, right?"

Pilar nodded. "Why?"

"My mom is looking for another job."

Pilar gave her a searching look before nodding. "Leave it to me."

THE LIES SHE WORE

Cathryn walked home with her shoulders a little straighter than usual. She and her mother were one step closer to freedom.

Chapter 3

Gus sulked in the back of the car. His parents were driving him to school so they could retrieve him early for their trip out of town. His classmates envied the mini vacation, but he dreaded being trapped in a vehicle with his parents. He would even prefer to spend the weekend enduring Minh's laser-eyed glares.

As much as he resented Minh's attitude, her forcing his new nickname proved an unexpected boon. He loved thinking of himself as Gus. It was a new identity, one his parents knew nothing about. Any barrier between him and them was welcome, regardless of who erected it.

They entered the parking lot, but the car lurched to a stop with a loud pop. Within seconds, smoke billowed from beneath the hood. Gus lingered near the trunk while his parents investigated, and soon Gus's mother came as close to screeching as her pedigree allowed.

"You can navigate the central nervous system, but you can't repair a simple internal combustion engine?"

"Perhaps if you ceased your wailing, I could concentrate," came his father's retort. His mother narrowed her eyes at the hint of a twang that snuck into his father's speech whenever he was angry. Gus's maternal grandparents hadn't approved their marriage at first, but the boulder-sized diamond ring his mother no longer wore bought their tolerance.

Gus leaned against the smoking sedan and calculated the probability of escaping before being associated with the raging intellectuals. Far from favorable.

"Car trouble, Gus?" Tony marched to the open hood before Gus could adequately encode a warning.

"I publish articles in journals whose names you cannot even pronounce, young man. I am perfectly capable of repairing a vehicle as simple as a car." His father's face alternated white and red like a slow strobe light, but Tony didn't appear to have understood the insult.

"There's your problem. You got a Leatherman?"

Gus's father looked like a failed chemistry project heading for an explosive finish.

"A multitool? Actually, I think I have one." Tony dug through several pockets in his hole-riddled backpack. "I always say you don't need specialty tools if you know how to use a good old-fashioned multitool. I'll have this fixed in a jiff."

The three Heins stared in stunned silence as Tony buried his head in their defunct car. Within minutes, it purred like a contented feline.

"Now, this here is just a slap job, all right? You gotta take her in to get her fixed up real good. And make sure you know how to treat her come winter."

A picture of Mrs. Hein's face would have fit with the dictionary's definition of incomprehension.

"He said his solution is temporary. You will need to take your car to a professional mechanic for a permanent repair. You will also need to adjust your driving practices in winter. Temperatures well below zero degrees are routine for Minnesota and can affect the engine's functioning."

Gus wasn't sure how long Cathryn had been standing there, but her amused smile told him long enough. He was so grateful for the rescue he almost smiled back.

* * *

Cathryn kept an arm's length of space between her and Gus as they walked to class. Her "safe" list did not include him, but she couldn't resist engaging in their quizzing game. Around Gus, her brain switched from a watch battery to a nuclear power plant.

"Schadenfreude."

"That's a German word," Cathryn said. "I told you to stick to languages I know: English, Spanish, and beginning Somali."

Gus's face retained in its usual stony stoicism, but his eyes twinkled. "I suspect you know this one anyway."

Unlike Gus, Cathryn couldn't restrain her grin. "To take pleasure in another's misfortune. From the German *schaden,* meaning 'harm,' and *fruede,* meaning 'pleasure.' There is a little-known English equivalent: epicaricacy, from the Greek *epi,* 'upon,' *chara,* 'joy,' and *kakon,* 'evil.'" She searched her mental index for an element. "Meitnerium."

"Atomic number one hundred nine. A radioactive synthetic element whose most stable isotope has a half-life of seven point six seconds."

"And named after a woman: Lisa Meitner, one of Germany's foremost nuclear scientists before the Nazis drove her out because of her Jewish heritage."

Gus snorted, the closest he ever came to laughing. "For someone with no scientific aspirations, you are awfully proud of female scientists."

Cathryn shrugged. "Just because I don't break gender stereotypes doesn't mean I can't admire people who do." She caught her reflection in one of the classroom door windows. A brownish-green smudge peeked out from beneath her makeup along her jawline, the remnants of a bruise.

"Cathryn?" Gus's eyebrows weren't as articulate as Minh's, but their raised position nonetheless communicated his question.

Cathryn drew her ponytail around her shoulder to block his view of her jaw. "You go ahead. I need to stop in the bathroom." She strode away without waiting for a response.

What are the odds he didn't notice? Not good. Yesterday, Gus noticed Mr. Bard had moved one of his posters two inches to the left. Cathryn's legs felt as if they trudged through quicksand. If Gus noticed, he'd tell.

She was so lost in her anxiety she didn't hear the giggles emanating from the bathroom until she was already inside. A group of girls with much more expertly applied makeup passed a cigarette around as they chatted.

"God, he is so handsome." A dark-haired girl drew out the word "so" such that it lasted the length of her exhaled smoke.

"Too bad he's a freak," Belinda said, apparently still smarting from Gus's rejection.

"Who cares?" a third girl said. She snatched the cigarette and took a puff. "You're just jealous because I have gym with him."

Cathryn backed away one step at a time to avoid making noise. She'd have to try another bathroom. She made to turn around, but the warning bell rang, and the girls' eyes snapped to her like a pack of hunting dogs who'd caught a scent.

"Hey, translator-girl," Belinda said. "You agree Gustaf is a freak, right?"

"Not being interested in you doesn't make him a freak." Cathryn clamped a hand over her mouth, but the gesture was too late. As much as she wanted to reel the words back into her mouth, they were out, floating to the ceiling with the smoke.

Outrage flashed on Belinda's face, but soon she pursed her lips in a pout and her eyes filled with false pity.

"You think he's interested in you? Let's look at the facts."

The three girls circled her, and Belinda pushed her toward the mirror. She spoke in a low voice next to Cathryn's ear. "You make Plain Jane look like a supermodel. You can't even keep your makeup from smudging." She pressed her finger into Cathryn's bruise and shoved her into the sink. Laughing, she turned to leave. "He's a freak, and so are you. Hope you find your happily-ever-after Freak-erella." The other girls snickered as they followed her out.

Cathryn wouldn't hear any more sighs of longing or see any more admiring gazes in Gus's direction. She'd just witnessed his fall to the bottom of the social ladder. *Well, almost the bottom.* She examined her reflection. Belinda was right. He was way out of her league.

The practical part of her brain forced her eyelids to blink back her tears. Mascara was expensive, and she already had one makeup error to fix. *It won't matter come June.*

Unbeknownst to those girls, Cathryn didn't apply makeup to enhance her beauty; she used it to conceal her father's ugliness.

* * *

Gustaf's Notes on Transitioning to Minnesota Life

I am on the opposite side of the country and the opposite end of the social hierarchy, one of Cathryn's "collection of misfits," as Minh phrases it. The label would offend me if the social elite weren't idiots. Better a misfit than a moron.

I joined the debate team, but not one of my teammates is a match for Cathryn. She is my sole source of intellectual conversation, but her timidity impedes her participation—a problem I intend to rectify. "Being shy" is no excuse for playing dumb.

Mr. Ainsworth once warned me not to treat people like test subjects, but Cathryn fascinates me. Her role as my "translator" seems to have upset the status quo. At first, I attributed her aversion to speaking to glossophobia, but I now believe she is cleithrophobic. Last Tuesday, Mr. Bard shut the door on hallway noise, and Cathryn gripped her pencil so tightly it snapped, as if she feared being trapped in chemistry class. Personally, I wouldn't mind that.

She may also be androphobic. Whenever a male classmate gets too close, she fidgets with her sleeves or hair. Cathryn doesn't sit near Tony, even though he is shorter than she is, and it's clear the only face he is interested in punching is mine.

My parents could provide a more accurate diagnosis, but I dare not ask. Their arguments have increased in frequency and duration, which can only mean one thing.

Funding is running out.

Chapter 4

B eatrice Banks fidgeted with her ponytail as her day-shift boss went over her performance review.

"You're great with the customers, and you get eight hours of work done in the six hours you're here." Mrs. Delone ran a hand through her gray hair and repositioned a chewed wooden pencil behind her ear.

"But?"

"But you're ... scatterbrained."

"Scatterbrained?"

Mrs. Delone nodded. "You skip steps in procedures, put things away in the wrong places ... Last week, you came in at the wrong time."

Beatrice forced a chuckle. "I like to say I gave my brain to my daughter when I was pregnant. She has a photographic memory." Mrs. Delone fixed her with a stare. Beatrice put her smile away with the awkwardness of a teenager who'd asked the wrong guy to prom.

"And last Tuesday when you rushed off without logging out?"

Beatrice lowered her gaze. "I have to be home by six."

Mrs. Delone rubbed the bridge of her nose as if warding off a migraine. "Look, Beatrice. You're a hard worker, and I want to keep you on, but— See, that's what I'm talking about. What are you looking at?"

Beatrice's eyes had strayed to the front entrance, where a thin woman entered. This time she wore a red headscarf. "That lady was here a couple weeks ago. She'll want a loaf pan."

"You remember what that woman wants, but you can't remember your own access code?"

Beatrice opened her mouth to respond but nodded instead. How could she explain the pain she'd seen in the woman's eyes? She may not have a head for figures, but she recalled even the subtlest emotions.

Mrs. Delone handed her a clipboard. "Checklists for what you need to complete during your shift. Don't leave until you go through them, and get more sleep. I don't need a tired *and* scatterbrained employee."

"Oh, thank you. You have no idea how much I need this job." Never mind that her other job was a night shift. *Just drink more caffeine.*

Mrs. Delone waved away her gratitude. "Go sell a loaf pan."

Beatrice zipped out of the office but slowed her pace as she approached the woman in the headscarf. "Decided to buy a loaf pan after all?"

The woman whirled to face her, blinking in confusion that faded to recognition before landing on embarrassment. She cleared her throat. "Yes."

"About the other day, I'm sor—"

"It's fine." The red streaks in the woman's eyes said otherwise, but Beatrice understood hiding behind those words. Sometimes the lie was the only thing holding you upright.

"Why don't I show you a couple brands?"

* * *

Cathryn shifted her weight on the plum-colored pillow that separated her tailbone from the hardwood floor in Minh's bedroom. The library and Minh's house were her safe havens, but if she didn't want Minh to end up like her old neighbor, Joaquín, she had to be careful. She wasn't allowed to have friends. She shuddered to think what her father would do if he discovered how much time she spent with a cop's daughter.

A rustle sounded from the closet, as if shivering from her dark thoughts. Minh, oblivious to Cathryn's ominous mood, crossed her arms in front of her chest.

"Ghost, I know you're in there."

Cathryn chuckled as the pale five-year-old, whose tendency to "disappear" earned him the nickname, popped out of Minh's closet. His flaming curls bounced as he scurried out the door.

"Your brother is so cute."

"Demarius insists he'll be a cop, but he's just trying to make Dad feel better. Pops has been complaining about being 'outnumbered by artists' since Biological Betty left for college." Of the Joneses' four children, only the eldest, Beth, was biological. She was studying prelaw on a volleyball scholarship at the University of Minnesota.

"Your mom is a singer/poet, Demarius is a musician, you draw and paint . . . what about Ghost?"

"That boy has dancer written all over him."

Ghost proved a perfect addition to a family Cathryn described as "classier than a three-ring circus but too wild for Cirque du Soleil." The Joneses had been her window into the world of loving families ever since she met Minh in kindergarten. She still couldn't think of that day without laughing.

Ms. Collins had made a classic first-year-teacher mistake: she stepped outside to speak with a parent and left a room full of five-year-olds to devolve into chaos. A gurgled giggle prompted Cathryn to peek out from behind the bookshelf where she'd hidden. Two boys took turns making faces at Minh, staying just out of her reach. Minh scowled, locked her brakes, and launched herself out of her wheelchair, but not at the boys. She landed next to a bin of recess equipment, grabbed a ball, and threw it smack into the biggest boy's nose. Tears streamed from his eyes and blood from his nose as his coconspirator dragged him away.

Minh leaned against the bin as though lounging on the beach. She looked at Cathryn and said, "You going to join me or hide like a fraidy-cat?"

Cathryn admired her friend's spunk, but judging by the look she threw Cathryn from atop her bed, she'd soon receive it.

"You seem to get along well with Mr. Heinstein."

"We have a lot of classes together." Cathryn maintained a neutral tone, but Minh's single raised eyebrow signaled she wasn't buying it.

Cathryn abandoned her futile charade with a shrug. "He's so . . . articulate." For someone as passionate about polysyllabic words as Cathryn, listening to him was feeding an addiction, but her interest went beyond that. With no internet and only one TV at home, Cathryn barely followed her classmates' pop culture references, but Gus talked about things she'd learned in books. He was a library come to life.

Minh cleared her throat, and Cathryn snapped her eyes into focus. "Besides, I'm the only one who understands him. He's like . . . a lost puppy."

"An arrogant lost puppy."

"Yes, but—"

"Look, it's great that you're finally interested in a guy, but trust me, don't fall for this one's gorgeous puppy-dog eyes. He'll walk all over you."

"Actually, I hadn't noticed his eyes. I'm attracted to . . . his brain, I guess."

"Only you would be attracted to tall, blond, and handsome for his brain." Minh used to say the phrase "you are so weird" out loud, but at this stage in their friendship, she had a designated look for it. "Be careful, okay?"

"Relax, Minh. Gus doesn't strike me as a romantic. I doubt he even registers me as a person. He probably has me classified as 'female thesaurus.'" Even better. If Gus wasn't interested in friendship, he wouldn't ask questions about her personal life.

"You two giggling about something I should know?" Warren Jones poked his head through the door. Cathryn had seen old pictures of him with a thick afro, but middle age had reduced it to a shallow layer of black fluff.

"Chill, Dad. I'll keep Cat out of trouble."

"It's not Cathryn who worries me."

Minh's mother cut off the argument. "Cathryn, honey, will you be staying for dinner?" Cathryn loved the rhythmic cadence of her voice, rich as her ebony skin. Attendance at Story Time was always good when Sylvia Jones read poetry.

"It's dinnertime already?" Cathryn leaped to her feet. "Thank you for the offer, Mrs. Jones, but I have to be home by six. See you at school, Minh."

She darted out the door before the last word left her mouth.

* * *

Minh and her parents watched Cathryn sprint out of sight.

"She all right?" Minh's dad asked.

"Don't bring work home with you," her mom said. Minh's dad never turned off his detective's instincts.

"I'm just saying, she's been coming to our place for ten years, and she's never stayed for dinner. She's never invited Minh to her house either."

"She's probably embarrassed. You've seen her clothes. Her family doesn't come from money."

"All the more reason to stay for dinner."

Minh's mom exhaled the dramatic sigh she reserved for poetry slams and marital arguments. "Minh, tell your father he's being paranoid."

A shiver ran across Minh's bare arms as she stared after her friend. Minh had appointed herself Cathryn's protector the day she spied her hiding behind that bookshelf. She could handle school bullies, could even handle the pretentious word-vomit that was Gus, but when it came to homelife, Cathryn was a closed book.

When they were young, Cathryn told her she lived at the library. By the time Minh figured out she'd lied, she was old enough to know not to ask.

Cathryn had always been twitchy about time, too. In fourth grade, they planned an unapproved sleepover at Minh's. After sneaking through the window, Cathryn spent the evening stealing glances at the clock. As six o'clock approached, she stopped responding to Minh's attempts at conversation. Minh watched her friend boil in a pressure cooker until 5:40, when Cathryn muttered something about her neighbors and raced home. At the time, Minh had been furious. Now she wasn't sure what to think of her friend's obsession with punctuality.

"Minh?"

Minh shrugged. "Her dad is strict."

* * *

Cathryn picked up her pace as she got closer to home, but she tripped over a bicycle by the dumpster. *Shoot, I'll have to patch my jeans again.*

Her keys clanked to the ground as she fumbled with the locks. She snatched them and pushed through the door. Her hands shook as she relocked them from the inside.

"You're cutting it close, Cathryn," her mother said from the stove.

"I know, I—"

Gravel rumbled, a car door shut, keys jingled, locks clicked—the symphony of her father's arrival. Cathryn steadied her breathing as she and her mother completed their dinner ritual. She'd almost recovered when she spotted blood seeping through her jeans. In an instant, the air became so dense she had to drag it into her lungs.

Cathryn waited in silence for her father to finish his meal. The wicker seat beneath her sagged, and she forced herself still to avoid wobbling on its uneven legs. *Breathe. He won't notice.*

Her father slurped his last mouthful of soup and placed a hand on her thigh, inches away from the cut. "I love you, Cathryn."

Cathryn forced her lips into a smile to keep them from trembling. "I love you too, Dad."

While her mother cleared the dishes, Cathryn dashed to the downstairs bathroom. She stood with her back against the door's withered wood and took deep breaths, but her hands still shook. She scrambled to the toilet and threw up.

"Cathryn, you okay in there?" Her father knocked. Any extended time in the bathroom made him suspicious.

Cathryn flushed, wiped her face, and opened the door with a smile stretched across her face. "Fine. I have a big test tomorrow.

Better start studying."

She rushed upstairs before he caught sight of her ripped jeans. As much as she hated her room, it was the one place in the house her father wouldn't monitor her every move.

Cathryn sat with her back against the bed, mind whirling. *Calm down.* She recited Macbeth's soliloquy, Martin Luther King Jr.'s "I Have a Dream" speech, and the first page of *Don Quixote* before her breathing normalized.

That was close. Too close. She needed a faster way home. Her bloody knee gave her an idea.

Chapter 5

Gus turned from his locker as Minh and Cathryn's laughter bubbled down the hallway. He waved at Cathryn, which sent Minh into further hysterics. *Strange.*

"Looks like the girls got the giggles this morning."

Gus tensed, but Tony made no move to displace him. He leaned against a pilar and gestured to Minh and Cathryn, who continued their conversation as they headed toward Minh's locker.

"What do you mean?" Gus had learned the burly mechanic responded best to truncated questions.

"Girls at your old school didn't giggle?"

Gus thought of his boarding-school classmates. "Ladies at the academy were more inclined to scheming, sneering, and slandering than giggling."

"Ugh, sounds like my cousin Katrina. Here, girls giggle when they're talking about guys."

"What evidence—" Gus wished Cathryn were there to translate, but he understood the inherent awkwardness in that scenario. He mentally rephrased his question several times before asking again, slowly. "How do you know?"

"Trust me. I got loads of sisters. Every time I hear the giggles, it's time to punch some guy's face in. Minh is friendly as a cactus, so I'm guessing Kitten has her eye on a guy."

"Cathryn? I haven't observed her with anyone."

Tony laughed.

* * *

Cathryn slowed her approach, assessing Tony's mood. She'd waited until the end of the day, aware that timing was everything. Gus was at science club, so he wouldn't be around to spark Tony's wrath.

Despite his frequent threats, Cathryn had seen Tony "punch someone's face in" only once. She and Minh had been heading to the bus when they heard a string of nervous babbling punctuated by the squeaks of a boy's voice transitioning to manhood.

They found the wide-eyed freshman in the center of a ring of upperclassmen who were trying to convince him to smoke something that smelled like burnt rubber mixed with cow dung. The boy insisted he didn't smoke, but the upperclassmen jeered and pushed him around the circle.

Tony's fists shut them up. He charged like a bull through a set of bowling pins, soundly beating two of them before the group scattered. His breathing was more like growling when he poked a meaty finger into the freshman's chest.

"Don't do drugs." After that, he walked away, kicking the dirt and whistling a cheery tune as though he'd just chatted about the weather instead of brawling with guys a half-foot taller than he was.

Cathryn and Minh hadn't been the only witnesses. Tony received multiple girls' phone numbers after that incident, but his relationships never lasted more than a few dates. The pattern repeated so often Minh dubbed it "The Revolving Door of Love Doctor Tony."

Tony had eaten lunch with "the misfits" every day this year, but Cathryn still wasn't sure she'd refer to the hothead as a love doctor. She classified his temper as the firecracker sort—quick to trigger, but equally quick to dissipate.

Cathryn observed as Tony shoved things from his locker into his backpack. His neck muscles were relaxed, his stance casual, and his skin its typical ruddy shade. She swallowed and closed the gap between them.

"Hey, Tony. I'd like to offer an exchange."

"A what?"

Cathryn flipped a mental switch. "I got a deal for you."

"A deal, eh? What is it?"

"You're good at fixing things, right?"

"You got it; I can fix it."

"You fix my bike, and I'll help you with your history homework."

"You sure you can handle a bike?" Tony gestured to her arm. Cathryn pulled her sleeve over the exposed bruise. Ironically, that one *had* come from tripping.

"I'm clumsy because I'm always late. If I had a faster way to get places, I wouldn't trip as often."

"What makes you think I need help?" On cue, a cascade of papers fell from Tony's locker, red ink bright against the lead smudges.

Cathryn raised an eyebrow in her best Minh impression.

"All right, Kitten, you gotta deal. Bring me the bike tomorrow and drop by the shop sometime to help with this."

"Kitten?"

"No offense, but you ain't no full-grown cat no matter what Minh calls you. My cousin Katrina, now there's a cat. With claws. Ugh."

* * *

"Giordani's Auto Care," Cathryn read. Her father believed mechanics were scam artists. If he caught her here, she'd end up with much worse than a scraped knee. She hated risking punishment for a hot-tempered guy she barely knew, but she needed that bike back.

A bell chimed as she walked through the glass door. "Hello?"

Cathryn leaned over the aged oak counter to check the hall, but no one appeared. She wandered around the lobby.

A plaque in the center of the wall read FAMILY OWNED SINCE 1936. Family photos surrounded it. She spotted Tony's face amid a myriad of grease-stained relatives. Behind him stood a man with the same round head and broad build but a larger, more rectangular nose. *Must be Tony's father.* He wore light blue scrubs instead of a mechanic's uniform. *That explains Tony's views on drugs.*

"Hey."

Cathryn yelped; her instincts brought up her left forearm to block her face.

"You okay, Kitten?"

She peeled herself off the wall as Tony walked around the desk. *Get a grip.* "For a guy your size, you're good at sneaking up on people."

Tony grinned. "You should meet my sister Lilianna. That girl could sneak up on the FBI."

Their footsteps echoed as Tony led her through a garage the size of an airplane hangar. The far wall was a mountain of stacked tires, the side wall a collage of tools. Tony weaved between cars in various states of repair hoisted on lifts or parked over pits. The scents of rubber and motor oil made their own atmosphere in the cavernous space.

"If we're lucky, we can snag some of Nonna's cannoli," Tony said.

"You better save some for me." A woman's salt-and-pepper ponytail emerged from a nearby pit. She added to the grease stains on her shirt as she wiggled her way out from under the sedan. Cathryn wasn't tall, but this woman barely reached her shoulder.

"Carlotta Giordani, Tony's mother." Her arm muscles rippled as she crushed Cathryn's hand. "I was serious about those cannoli. You think I married Big Nose for his looks? Ha. I married him for his mom's cooking."

"We'll save you one, Ma." Tony ushered Cathryn through the door to the residential portion of the complex. "She's not kidding. Around dinnertime, tourists wander in thinking this place is a restaurant."

Seeing the dining room, Cathryn understood the confusion. She imagined Paul Bunyan's dining room might look similar. *How many relatives does Tony have?* Two solid oak tables dominated the room. Grease-splattered men and women ate, played cards, and chatted around them. Kids of various ages roughhoused on the floor. One of the youngest girls squealed with delight as Tony hoisted her up and spun her around. Cathryn struggled to focus in the sensory bombardment as the smell of tomato sauce and garlic mixed with that of gasoline and sweat.

"Tony, this one's too skinny for you." A woman's beady eyes examined Cathryn through a veil of wrinkles.

"She ain't a girlfriend, Nonna. She's helping me with school. You know, school? The place you make me go to learn stuff?" Tony shouted into her ear.

"Poor Tony can't find love," jeered a teenage girl.

"Shush, Katrina." Tony turned back to his nonna. "This is Cathryn."

"How do you do?" Cathryn raised her voice above the chaos.

"How do I do? My son left the family business to be a nurse, his wife can't cook for a pig, and my grandson brought a stick home. How do I do? I'm an old wretch."

"Nice chatting with you, Nonna." Tony grabbed a plate of cannoli and dragged Cathryn to the living room. Her ears rang in the sudden silence.

"You okay, Kitten?" He plopped the plate over a water stain on the oak coffee table. "Most girls run for the exit after meeting Nonna."

"I'm overwhelmed, but fine." Tony's family definitely fit the stereotype of boisterous Italians, but Cathryn wouldn't describe Nonna as threatening. Threatening was what waited for her at home. "Do girls really run?"

"Yep. Date number three, I always take them home. They can't handle the family, I ain't interested."

"Hence 'the revolving door of Love Doctor Tony'?"

"That what they say?" Tony took a bite of a cannoli. "Too bad. If they run too soon, they miss out on the cannoli."

Cathryn tried a bite. She closed her eyes and savored the flavor for a moment before swallowing.

Tony grinned. "That's why I grabbed a whole plate."

Between mouthfuls of cannoli, Cathryn helped Tony with history and math. While she was at it, she explained the week's science lesson. Around the time they ran out of cannoli, Tony decided he'd had enough of homework and led her back to the front office.

"Wait here. I'll get your new ride."

The bike he pulled into view didn't remotely resemble the gnarled mess Cathryn handed him the week before. The frame shone with a fresh coat of indigo paint. Wires that before were twisted into a rat's nest looked factory-new. The shredded seat was re-stuffed and patched. Most important, the wheels turned smoothly.

"Tony, I had no idea you were so talented."

"I'm better with cars." Tony shrugged off her praise, but he walked with more swagger. "Here." He handed her a lock. "No use my putting in all this work to have some guy steal it. And you be safe out there, ya hear?" He knocked the breath out of her with his bear hug, but the warmth of his concern told her there was more to Tony than his burly appearance. Cathryn added Giordani's Auto Care to a mental list that contained only Minh's house and the library. She added Tony to her list labeled SAFE.

* * *

Cathryn's mother pounced as soon as she walked through the door.

"Where were you? I started to worry."

"What do you mean, Mom? I told you at dinner I was going to tutor a friend." She told her father her friend "Antonia" needed help with her home-ec homework. By some miracle, the lie worked.

"Oh. That's right."

"Where's Dad?"

"Asleep." It had been a third-helping day. *That explains why Dad let me out.*

"Cathryn, have you seen my bus pass? I don't want to be late for work."

"It's in the top-left drawer of the dresser under your blue socks, but you don't work until eleven tomorrow." Cathryn's mother had been more scatterbrained than usual the past few months. "Mom, are you okay? Are the night shifts too much?" Cathryn grabbed her mother's hand to stop her rummaging.

She rubbed her temples. "I'm fine. It's a couple nights a week, and I don't work a full day shift."

"Why don't you go to sleep, Mom? You take the bed tonight." Before her mother could object, Cathryn herded her upstairs, avoiding the weak spot as she went. She settled her mother beneath the lavender bedspread and added a pillow in front of the iron headboard.

The bed was Cathryn's first memory. Her father had been so proud he could afford to buy her a "big girl" bed that he hadn't considered the twin-sized mattress would swallow his toddler. He tucked her in and read her stories long into the night. The bed outlasted the stories.

Now, Cathryn and her mother alternated who slept in the bed and who on the floor next to it. Her father demanded a night free of snoring before work, so he only allowed his wife in his bed when "called." Even then, her mother usually joined Cathryn afterward. The smell of sweat, alcohol, and anger was not conducive to sleeping.

"We should light the candle," Cathryn said. She retrieved the thick prayer candle from its place next to her grandfather's military funeral flag. A yellowed picture of Jesus clung to the wax; one loose corner curled outward. Cathryn had never adopted her grandmother's faith as her mother had, but she recognized the candle's calming effect. Her mother's worry lines ironed smooth. As a child, Cathryn had marveled at the candle's magic. Now, she wished she had her own version.

"Goodnight, Mom."

Her mother snored in response.

Chapter 6

Mark Ostergaard reached for the car door, but Laurel pushed him away.

"I can do it myself." She'd have hurt him less stabbing her chef's knife through his chest. She took her seat and used the rearview mirror to adjust her headscarf. He caught a glimpse of a shock of grey intruding on his own chestnut locks, added to the bags beneath his brown eyes and ashen tone of his tan face.

They drove to church in silence.

Laurel left the service five minutes early. Mark found her rearranging her towers of brownies, cupcakes, and cookies until the treat table resembled the cover of *Gourmet*.

"They're perfect, honey, as always."

"See, I can do it." She kept her gaze on the table and brushed a stray crumb from the checkered tablecloth.

"It's different, Laurel, and you know it."

His wife glared at him, but the expression fled her face when she yelped. The Joneses' redheaded boy peered out from under the table.

"Ghost, sweetie, you can't be under there." Laurel reached for his hand. "Let's go find your daddy, okay?"

The congregation filtered in and flocked to the treat table. Laurel's cookies were more addictive than cigarettes. Too tired to smile through small talk, Mark drifted to the edge of the room. *What am I doing wrong?*

"Hey Mark, have you seen Ghost?" Sylvia Jones's smooth voice broke into his thoughts.

"Laurel just took him to find you."

"Oh, good. That boy will give me a heart attack one day." Her eyes filled with sympathy. "How's Laurel? Better?"

"She thinks she is."

"Mm-hmm. Like you."

"What—"

"Don't deny it. My husband wears that same face after seeing something at work he can't un-see. Life threw a lot at you two. God may have calmed the sea, but you're still swimming for shore."

Leave it to a poet to capture the situation in one sentence. "'Recovery is a long road filled with potholes,'" he quoted. "I'm worried about her. She overestimates herself."

"I know it's none of my business, but if I were you, I'd fire the maid."

"What?"

"You didn't need one before, right? Laurel just wants some control. Housework is an easy start. If she has a bad day, so what? You can live with a dirty house, and you can always hire another maid if she can't handle it."

Mark had hired the maid to take the stress off Laurel, but maybe Sylvia was right. It couldn't make things worse. "Thanks, Sylvia. I'll talk to her about it."

Mischief snuck into her smile. "You can hire a maid for *me* anytime."

* * *

Cathryn looked up from her lunch to answer Tony's question. "April 14th. Paragraph three on page thirty-four. Coincidentally, that's also the day John Booth assassinated Abraham Lincoln."

"How do you do that?"

"Cat's on the fourth of her nine lives. She spent the last three as an encyclopedia." Minh kept a straight face, but her eyes gleamed.

"Ha! I'd forgotten that one." Cathryn once gave that same answer to a kid at the library.

"As entertaining as reincarnation as a work of reference is, more likely you've developed the retention skills people mistakenly refer to as a photographic memory." Gus looked at her as though she were a specimen under a microscope. Cathryn hid her blush behind a forkful of steamed carrots, careful to take a small bite.

She'd experimented with several methods of disguising how much she ate at lunch. So far, the best was to take a little of everything and hope Gus didn't notice she ate all of it. She'd rather he think her indecisive than explain why she was afraid to eat at home. There was only enough food at home for one, and Cathryn wasn't him.

Cathryn patted the filched granola bars in her pockets— dinner/breakfast—and searched her brain for a change in subject to break Gus's focus. "Reincarnation isn't limited to cats. It has a basis in several religions."

"Unsubstantiated nonsense," Gus said.

"You don't believe in God?" Minh said, more a challenge than a question.

Gus rolled his eyes, an expression, ironically, he'd picked up from Minh. "'God' is nothing more than a superstition used to mollify the plebeian masses."

Minh leaned forward. "They killed Jesus, and he stuck it to them by coming back to life. I dare you to think of a scientist that badass."

Gus stared at her as if she had put a Monopoly piece on a chessboard and claimed it was her queen. "Wh—"

"What about you, Tony?" Cathryn cut into the impending argument.

"I'm Italian. Where do you think the Pope lives?" He kissed the crucifix that hung from his neck and returned to eating.

"That's ridiculous, not to mention a ghastly misrepresentation of many brilliant Italian scientists." Gus turned to Cathryn. "You aren't so delusional, are you?"

Cathryn sipped her water to buy herself time. If God existed, He hadn't been kind to her, but she couldn't deny her mother's candle.

"I may not believe religion is factually true, but I believe in the power of its influence."

"Religion detracts from humanity. Science advances it."

Normally, Cathryn would smile and nod until someone changed the subject, but something in Gus's superior tone grated on her. Who was he to say religion had no benefits? *Mom has every right to take comfort from her candle.*

Cathryn pushed her lunch tray aside and looked Gus straight in the eye. "Your argument implies religion and science are mutually exclusive. On the contrary, Albert Einstein said, 'Science without religion is lame, and religion without science is blind,' and Gregor Mendel, the 'father of genetics,' was an Augustinian friar."

"You assume science is infallible, but it's as biased as religion. Funding scarcity and the 'publish or perish' mentality impact the research conducted. Publishers rarely select studies without positive results, and a 'positive' result in an experimental environment may have no practical significance."

Gus's mouth hung open, but slowly one corner of it lifted into an expression that was almost a smile. He'd liked her challenge.

Cathryn lowered her gaze, but Minh put on her sassiest grin and scooped a spoonful of chocolate pudding. "Human Encyclopedia: one. Human Calculator: zero."

* * *

Cathryn penned the last sentence of her essay on the suffragettes. She'd type it in study hall tomorrow.

"History?" She jumped at her father's voice and snapped her textbook shut. "What are you learning about now?"

"Nuclear family units. School started emphasizing family values this year. They're worried we teenagers may turn rebellious."

Her father smiled. "Not my kid. Raised you better than that, didn't I?"

Cathryn nodded. *What's going on?* Changes in routine never ended well.

"I saw a commercial for a special on Elvis. Thought since your mom is sick, we could have some father-daughter time. What do you say?"

"Really?" The last time they spent quality time together was after her ninth-grade choir concert. He said she sang like an angel and took her out for ice cream. She hadn't had the heart to tell him she mouthed "watermelon" over and over because she was too nervous to sing.

"Yes, really. Go close the window. I'll find the channel."

Cathryn scrambled to the window. They'd left it open to air out the house after her father re-painted the coffee table he'd broken last week. The crank complained as she turned it; then it stuck. *Oh, please work.* She grunted and twisted it harder. The crank broke off, and the window popped open even farther. A gust of cold air swept into the room, but Cathryn chilled from the inside out.

"What did you do?" Her father's form was an outline in the lamplight. He grabbed her wrist and squeezed until her hand opened. The crank clattered to the floor. "I work all day to put a roof over your head, and you thank me by being careless?" He flung her to the floor.

"I didn't mean to. I can fix it. I promise. I—" Cathryn scrambled to her feet, but a kick to the small of her back knocked the breath out of her. Her father grabbed her shoulders and slammed her into the patched drywall. Stars swam across her vision. Her tiptoes barely touched the floor.

"I'm sorry. I'm so sorry."

His face softened. He released her right shoulder and brushed a tear off her cheek. "Oh, Cathryn. Why do you make me hit you? I don't want to, but we can't afford to break things." His right hand remained a vice on her bicep. "I love you, but it's my job as your father to teach you responsibility. You're lucky I use my hands." He tightened his grip. "My daddy used a bat."

"I'm sorry."

His jaw tensed as he pulled her off the wall. She didn't have time to gain her footing before he dragged her toward the stairs.

"No. Please. I can fix it. I can—"

He jerked her arm until she fell, but he had no difficulty dragging her full weight up the steps. The loose stair sank with a sick groan when he stepped on it. He opened her bedroom door and threw her inside.

"No. Please, no." Her cries left her throat in a whisper. They were as useless as the tears that flooded her face. Her father closed the door, quietly, and locked it from the outside.

Her mother shifted in bed but didn't wake. She barely disturbed the blankets in which Cathryn's father had tenderly wrapped her. The cool towel he brought still lay upon her hot forehead.

People said love and hate were separate emotions, opposites. Cathryn wasn't so sure.

Cathryn rubbed her arm. She'd bruise, but it wouldn't matter because she wouldn't see her classmates any time soon. She ate a granola bar from her stash and pulled out her textbooks.

Cathryn missed a lot of school, but she never fell behind. In fact, she would be two weeks ahead, because until her father unlocked that door, books were her only escape.

* * *

Cathryn's Diary

My father is ambidextrous. He uses one hand for love and the other for rage. Sometimes he uses both at once. He reminds me I love him while giving me every reason not to. Those days he is most dangerous.

Mom says it's not my fault, but I can't help wondering. If I cooked the perfect egg, got home on time, never broke a dish . . . Would he smile more? What if I were more "mainstream?" Would I please him if I spent less time reading and more time doing my hair?

I'm thinking in circles. I already tried that. A pretty face bruises just as easily.

I have a photographic memory, but some things I wish I could forget —locks, screams, the look in my father's eyes, the smell of our neighbors' house.

We are a broken family. No matter how hard I try, nothing is good enough to fix us. My mother prays to a god who must be deaf not to have heard her by now. He can't fix us either.

Our only hope is escape, but even then, I fear we may be damaged beyond repair.

Chapter 7

Minh rolled along the sidewalk after school, crunching over dry leaves and admiring trees aflame with color. Though she dreaded navigating her wheelchair through the snow, she savored every second of fall. Chilly air, hot apple cider, carved pumpkins—even the nearly bare tree by the flagpole pleased her. Its long limbs stretched into the clear blue sky, reminding her of Cathryn's skinny arms reaching for a book. Maybe she'd convince Cathryn to pose near it whenever she came back to school.

Cathryn had been AWOL the past couple days. Knowing her, she'd taken an extra day off after being sick to catch up on her homework. *Guess that's why she's an A student, and I'm a B student.*

Minh was halfway to the street when her wheel entrenched in a rut—the one she'd reported to the principal last year. *"We'll get right on it, Ms. Jones."* B.S. She'd have to find a workaround herself.

Minh lurched forward, but her wheel slipped right back into the rut. She took a deep breath and wrenched it free, but her momentum sent her careening over the sidewalk's edge, and she fell onto a large rock. Blood seeped from her scraped elbow.

Several guys laughed, no doubt amused to see the tough-girl floundering like an overturned turtle. Minh screamed enough profanity for her parents to ground her for the rest of high school. The guys laughed harder.

I'll deal with them later. She shifted her seat on the grass and set her chair upright, but the collision had bent the bearings on one of her wheels, locking it in place. *Of course.* Her skin burned, and her vision went red. She pounded her fist into her wheel, scraping her knuckles, but a shadow caught her attention before she could do more damage.

"You got something to say, Tony?"

"Looks like your wheel needs a tweak." He pulled his multitool out of his backpack.

"I didn't ask for your help."

"You shouldn't have to."

Minh scowled with all the nastiness she'd learned watching Gus. "If you're trying to impress me, don't bother. I'm not interested."

"I'm fixing a bearing, not asking you to prom." He twisted the bent metal with the pliers. "Trust me Wheels, if I ask you out, you'll know."

Minh's tone darkened. "Wheels?"

"It's that or Cactus." Tony spun the wheel, frowned, and tinkered with it more. "Face it, you're prickly. If you don't believe me, ask Kitten. Then multiply her answer by ten because you know she's too nice."

Minh didn't need to ask. Cathryn told her she pushed people away with her insistence on her own invulnerability. *They don't understand.*

"Why give us nicknames? What is this, the second grade?"

Tony paused his tinkering, lips pouting as if he *were* in second grade, and by rejecting his use of her mode of transportation as a name, she was rejecting his homemade valentine.

Minh rolled her eyes. "When did Mr. I'll-punch-your-face-in get so sensitive?"

"Hey"—he pointed at her with the pliers—"I ain't never hit a lady."

"Why not? I could take you."

"You shouldn't have to." Tony's face reddened in splotches. "A real man knows how to treat a woman, whether it's a date or a tire change. Jeez Minh, you're as clueless as Gus."

"And you're as weird."

Tony finished repairing her wheel, lower lip protruding in an expression that would be comical if his eyes weren't so sad. He set her chair before her with a similar expression as a child presenting macaroni art to an inattentive parent.

"Thanks," Minh said, dismissing him. She locked the brakes and transferred from the ground.

"Don't mention it." Tony said, tone flat.

Minh spun in a slow circle, testing the wheel. Good as new. She looked back at Tony, who shuffled away, head low. *I am not a cactus. He is oversensitive.* An oversensitive guy who fixed her wheel when everyone else laughed.

Minh's sigh was half growl. "Okay fine."

Tony faced her, eyebrows raised.

"You can give me a nickname, but could you be more creative than wheels?"

Tony cocked his head. "How about Ink?"

"Ink?"

He grinned. "You got more on your hands than I have engine grease on mine."

Minh examined the remnants of color that clung to her fingers despite her vigorous scrubbing. *Ink.* Short, tough, and predictive of a career in tattooing that her parents wouldn't approve of.

Minh returned Tony's grin. "Ink it is."

* * *

A jingle echoed through the garage as Tony's mother threw him a set of keys.

"Put these in the office, would you? I'll be out in a sec."

Tony wiped his hands on an old T-shirt rag and hung the keys on the designated peg behind the front desk. As he filed the accompanying paperwork, a luxury sedan parked in front of the glass entrance. Gus's parents boiled out as though its doors couldn't contain their argument. Without taking his eyes off his wife, Mr. Hein pulled his wallet out of his suit coat and handed it to Gus, who entered the shop alone.

"Hiya, Gus. How's it going?"

"Fine." Gus's face was a mask of stone.

"I'll get you checked out." Tony ran the credit card and searched the wall for the keys. "Hey, Ma! The Heins are here for the Lexus."

"Top left," his mom said as she entered the office. "Carlotta, Tony's mom."

"How do you do?" Gus shook her hand, and the corner of her mouth twitched. Tony's mom judged a man by his handshake.

"Cute and Clueless, eh?" She grinned as she looked from Gus to Tony. "I can see that."

The door chime cut off Gus's retort as his mother entered. The scowl that already cut into her face twisted into a sneer as she surveyed the office.

"This was your choice?" She narrowed her eyes at her son. "I will speak to the owner."

"Carlotta Giordani. I run the joint." She held out her hand. Mrs. Hein's sneer exaggerated to clown-like proportions as she took a step back.

"You're certain you aren't violating code living on the property?" Gus's mother referenced the adjoined residential complex that housed much of Tony's extended family.

Tony's mom crossed her arms over her chest. "Everything is zoned properly. We find living nearby means we can finish the work faster, but if you're unhappy—"

"I may contest—"

"Mother," Gus interjected. "They repaired the car. They deserve the compensation."

Mrs. Hein fixed her gaze on her son and held her hand out to Tony. "Keys?"

"Keys and receipt." Tony dropped them into her hand.

Gus's mother grabbed his arm and dragged him outside, where she and her husband abandoned their prior argument and united their screams against their son. Gus stood silent, spine straight, eyes locked with his father's. His expression never shifted from its chiseled scowl.

Tony's mom shook her head. "There's where he gets the clueless part."

"Yeah," Tony said, "that explains a lot."

* * *

Cathryn hesitated at her front door, not eager to return home after her first day back at school. Her friends believed she'd stayed home to care for her sick mother and spent another day catching up on homework, which wasn't a total lie. Her mom was still feeling a little off, which was why Cathryn came straight home instead of stopping by the library.

She took one more breath of crisp fall air before stepping into the stale insides of her house, but the sight that greeted her stopped her dead in the entryway. Every drawer and cupboard was open, every trash can emptied onto the floor, and every piece of furniture flipped upside down. Cathryn's mother stepped out of the wreckage, face strained and eyes panicked.

"I can't find my keys. Mr. Kadesh will be furious if I'm late to work again."

Cathryn's stomach churned as if it had been caught in the tornado that ravaged the living room. "You mean Mrs. Delone, right Mom? You don't work for her again until Wednesday, and you don't work for Mr. Sanders until Thursday night. Who is Mr. Kadesh?"

"Right. Sorry. Mr. Kadesh was my boss after high school. I just mixed up the names." Her eyebrows furrowed as though she knew she was lost but forgot her intended destination. "I need to find my keys."

"Mom, why don't you lie down? I'll clean up and get dinner ready. Then we'll look for your keys together."

Her mother's shoulders relaxed, as if Cathryn had handed her a map out of her confusion. "What would I do without my beautiful, smart, daughter?"

Cathryn sent her mother upstairs and listened for the creaking of floorboards to cease. *Good thing I came straight home.* She focused on reassembling the house to avoid thinking about what would have happened had her father discovered the mess. Why didn't her mother consult the calendar Cathryn updated with her work schedule? *One problem at a time.*

With the cupboards open, Cathryn saw they were running low on soup. There was, however, a half-loaf of bread that needed to be eaten. *I think we had some turkey left. If I toast the bread and heat the turkey on the stove, it might be good enough.* She opened the fridge to look for turkey, and there, next to the milk, sat her mother's keys. Cathryn wasn't sure what that meant, but she knew it was nothing good.

Chapter 8

As soon as the bell dismissed his last class, Tony marched to the parking lot. He found Gus with his head buried in his trunk, rearranging several boxes filled with tubes, wires, powders, and a cone-tipped tube. Kitten wasn't with him, which would make this harder.

"Hey, Gus. My buddy Patrick and I are thinking of pumpin' iron this week. You in?"

Gus straightened, spine stiff as if someone had welded it to a metal rod. He never seemed to tolerate Tony looking down at him. "In what?"

"Do you want to come? Jeez, Gus, for a know-it-all, you're real thick sometimes."

Gus's neck muscle twitched. "I resent—"

"You coming or not?" Tony picked up a glass bottle and squinted at the clear liquid inside.

Gus took it from him and gingerly nestled it back into its box. "Coming where?"

"To lift."

"Lift what?"

Tony rolled his eyes. "Bicep curls, bench press, standing dead lift?"

Gus nodded. "Strength training is an excellent supplement to sports."

"So you're coming?"

"Lift weights? With you? To what end?" Gus's brow furrowed as he assessed the powdery contents of a plastic container.

A gust of wind blew a dozen dry leaves into the trunk. Gus set down the container and frantically picked them out. Tony used the interruption to count to ten and unclench his fist.

"This ain't that complicated. It's just hanging out. Guy time? What friends do?"

"Friends?" Gus flinched, hitting his head on the tailgate.

"Yeah. Friends. You know what those are, right?"

Gus rubbed the lump forming on his scalp. "I have numerous acquaintances with whom I regularly socialize."

Tony took that as a no. "You in?"

Gus's eyes narrowed and widened as if adjusting their focus. "When?"

"How about tomorrow?"

"I have martial arts training."

"Wednesday?"

"Debate."

"Thursday?"

"Science club."

"Jeez, Gus, do you ever go home?"

"Not if I can help it." Gus delivered the words with the same matter-of-fact tone with which he'd said he had debate on Wednesdays. "I prefer boarding schools."

He moved a box to the back corner of the trunk, evidently finished with the conversation. With parents like his, it was no wonder Gus feared Tony's friendship more than his fists, but Tony wouldn't give up that easily.

"How about Sunday? We can grab pizza afterward and head to my place to watch the Vikes kick some Cowboy butt."

Gus cocked his head to the side. "You remind me of my paternal uncle. He had a brash sense of humor, loved sports, and lived on bratwursts and cherry cola."

Where's he going with this? "And?"

"He let me fire his pistol on my seventh birthday, and my mother forbade me from speaking to him again." Gus shut his trunk. "I will see you Sunday."

Tony popped a stick of gum into his mouth as Gus drove away. *What do you know? Cute and Clueless has a rebellious side.*

* * *

Mark Ostergaard sank into the worn cushions of the Joneses' tweed couch. Laurel sat as far away as she could and still qualify as next to him. The other couples in their church group didn't notice, but Mark got the message. Some people communicated anger with shouts and shoves, others with silence and space.

"Laurel," Sylvia Jones said, "I was wondering, since you're feeling better, if you'd join the church's Meal Train. We provide meals when people have a new baby, illness, death in the family, that sort of thing."

Laurel straightened, her eyes alight like a someone who'd just won the lottery. "I'd love to." She turned her gaze to Mark, daring him to object. The day they met, he'd vowed to be the bridge between her and her dreams. When had he become the wall?

"That's a great idea," Mark said. The surprise on his wife's face hurt more than her anger. "Could someone pick up the food from our place? Laurel can't drive, and I'd like to spare her the stress of bussing so much."

Sylvia nodded, and the conversation shifted to an upcoming fundraiser for the homeless shelter. Mark kept one eye on his wife. Twenty minutes into the conversation, Laurel's eyelids drooped. Five minutes later, her head nodded, and she jerked back awake. Fatigue—the ghost that continued to haunt her, the one none of the medications banished.

Before, she would have curled up against Mark's shoulder and dozed. Now she fought to stay alert with the same fervor with which she fought him. She covered a yawn. Mark bit the inside of his cheek to keep from reaching out to her. How did this happen? Since when did he hesitate before taking his wife in his arms?

Her eyelids fluttered, and Mark took the risk. He wrapped his arm around her, and to his relief, she leaned into him, almost like before. Almost. Almost was enough for now.

Laurel's breathing steadied as she fell asleep. Mark had missed most of the conversation.

Michael Bentrigaard scratched his red goatee. "We're having trouble with Jeremy. We've never fostered a teenager, and, well, Jeremy is a troubled boy."

Nichole, Michael's wife, glared at him. *At least we aren't the only ones.* Her narrowed eyes pulled at the strawberry-blond hair synched in a bun, giving her face the appearance of a drumhead.

"He hasn't responded well to the usual methods." The child psychologist sounded offended by the boy's lack of cooperation with her treatment protocol.

Temporary authority. The kid had no reason to obey them if he knew they weren't permanent. Same reason Mark hesitated before hiring contractors. Either the employees worshipped them as experts, or they ignored them as outsiders. Mark kept his thoughts from leaving his mouth. He had no authority when it came to raising children.

"You guys have four kids," Michael pleaded with the Joneses, "and they're so well behaved. How do you do it?"

A crash sounded from the hall, followed by a stream of expletives long enough to make each group member take a sudden interest in their shoes.

Sylvia Jones rose. "That was our 'well-behaved' daughter making a mess because she's too stubborn to ask for help." She left the room, and two loud voices filled the hall—one with scolding, the other with swearing.

Warren Jones turned to Michael. "You were saying?"

* * *

Cathryn looked up from her homework as the ending theme of the evening news played from the living room. Her mother finished the dishes and retreated upstairs to fold laundry. *Now or never.* Cathryn approached the couch where her father watched commercials. Today had been a two-helping day. She wouldn't get a better chance.

"Dad?"

"Yes?"

How do I word this? "Have you noticed Mom's been . . . absent-minded?"

"Not everyone has your brain, Cathryn."

"I know, it's just . . . she loses things. She's tired all the time. She talks about things that happened a long time ago as if they happened yesterday. I-I think we should take her to a doctor." Cathryn winced as the words left her mouth.

"No doctors. You're overreacting."

Every muscle in her body tensed, but she forced herself to continue. "Dad, it's getting worse. You don't notice because you're not around her as much. I—"

"What are you saying? That I'm neglecting her?" He leaped to his feet and grabbed Cathryn's arm.

"No. I didn't mean— I'm just worried."

"No doctors. If there's something wrong with your mom, we can take care of her ourselves."

"But—"

He squeezed her arm. She lowered her eyes. "Yes, Father."

Cathryn returned to the kitchen and pretended to study. *It could have gone worse.* She hadn't seen a doctor since she got the required immunizations for school. Her father claimed no one could care for them better than he could, but she knew the real reason. Doctors were mandatory reporters, and you couldn't hide bruises from them like with teachers. She'd learned the hard way not to talk to teachers.

In first grade, Cathryn entered the gifted program. She'd thrived on the extra attention. She didn't remember what she told the teacher, but it was enough to prompt a call to child services. Two police officers came to their house the next day. They looked around and asked Cathryn questions she didn't understand. Her father stepped outside with them. He returned angry.

He installed the third set of locks on the front door and another set on Cathryn's bedroom door. He said they would homeschool Cathryn to be safe; public school would tear their family apart. Her mother objected. She paid a heavy price for her defiance. After his fists tired, he broke her arm with a frying pan.

He apologized, broke into tears even. He fashioned a splint out of broken furniture and brought her ice from the store. When Cathryn's teacher called to ask where she'd been, he looked at his wife's bruised face. He told the teacher the whole family caught the flu, but Cathryn would be back Monday.

Her father made a show of complimenting her smarts, but Cathryn knew her mother's crooked forearm was the only reason she'd made it to high school.

Time that investment paid off. Cathryn vowed to read every book in the library on memory strategies.

Chapter 9

Cathryn hunted for a trickier quiz question while she and Gus walked to class, but her brain still swam with memory aids for her mom.

"Move it freak!" Joshua Friedman, star of the tennis team, shoved Gus as he passed, but Gus hadn't lied about his martial arts training. He remained standing.

"Are you okay?" Cathryn placed her hand on his arm but snatched it back when she felt the tension in it. Gus's jaw clenched the way Tony's did when angry, but unlike Tony, his eyes burned with a calculated rage too long restrained.

"I am tired of tolerating imbeciles in this cesspool you call a school."

Cathryn's thumping heart demanded she run. Her brain advised her to give Gus time, but her outrage rooted her to the vinyl floor. Tense dinners, covered bruises, her mother's crooked arm—school cost too much to be a "cesspool." *Everything I do to get here, and he views it as nothing.* Something white and hot and altogether unfamiliar blazed inside her. She shot it at Gus.

"This 'cesspool' is the only way some of us can get an education."

"Why educate witless paupers who neither appreciate nor deserve such a benefit?"

A witless pauper? That's all I am to him? "Well forgive us for supporting life, liberty, and the pursuit of happiness."

"'Pearls before swine,' as you and your tiresome quotations would express it." Gus swept his arm to gesture to the entire hallway.

Cathryn straightened until she came as close as she could to matching Gus's height. "I've had enough of your ego. You should be grateful to study here."

"For this monument to mediocrity? No thank you."

Time and space blurred. Everything ceased to exist except for Cathryn, Gus, and the volley of malignant words they launched at each other.

* * *

Minh and Tony gawked at the fight that sounded more like a spelling bee.

"I don't know what they're saying, but my money is on Kitten."

"I've never seen Cat so angry," Minh said. "Come to think of it, I've never seen her angry at all."

"... *stubborn adherence to a system that degrades intelligence rather than engenders it* ..."

"... *bombastic elite too blinded by their own reflections to recognize value beyond their antiquated paradigms* ..."

"This fight is so slow," Minh said.

Tony nodded. "It's like watching a couple snails in a boxing match."

"... *assemblage of fools that incentivizes ineptitude* ..."

"... *syndicate of megalomaniacs that demands conformity* ..."

"You know"—Tony titled his head—"with his face all red like that, Gus looks like a giant matchstick."

"... *insensate and naïve* ..."

"... *supercilious, self-aggrandizing, narcissist* ..."

"You tell him, Cat!"

"What did she say, Ink?"

Minh shrugged. "I don't know, but she used bigger words, so I figured she won that round." A small crowd gathered as the screams grew more ferocious.

"... *prefer the company of profligate simpletons* ..."

"... *perhaps I do ¡hijo de puta!*"

Minh's eyes widened. "I don't speak Spanish, but I'm guessing she didn't learn that one from the kids at Story Time."

* * *

"That's enough!"

Coach Karne's shout hit Cathryn like a splash of cold water. Her tunnel vision expanded, revealing a crowd of onlookers encircling her and Gus. Her mouth went dry.

"Let's go." The tawny-skinned wrestling coach grabbed each of them by the arm.

"No, wait." Cathryn resisted as he dragged her. *Teachers can't hit kids, can they?* Her breath came in short bursts as the worn soles of her tennis shoes slipped on the smooth floor. *Aren't their laws against this?*

"They can walk on their own, Ryan," Mrs. West said. The English teacher's ivory face communicated a subtext Cathryn didn't understand, but Coach Karne did. He grunted and shoved Cathryn and Gus forward with such force they collided. Cathryn skittered out of the way. Gus spun toward the gym teacher, muscles bulging, but Mrs. West cut off any argument.

"Office. Both of you." Her stern but calm words settled the guys, though Coach Karne insisted on escorting them. Thankfully, Mrs. West accompanied them as well.

Cathryn tried to steady her breathing as she walked. *Mrs. West won't let anything happen.* When they reached the office, she and Gus sat in the "gotcha chairs." The teachers barged through Principal Evans's door without bothering to close it after themselves, as if they wanted Gus and Cathryn to overhear of their pending punishment.

"Broke up a screaming contest outside the cafeteria," Coach Karne said.

"They're two of the junior class's brightest," Mrs. West added. "With the words they were slinging, I'm not sure whether to give them detention or extra credit."

Cathryn straightened. Could she convince Principal Evans to dismiss their fight as a vocabulary exercise? Would he believe her if she told him they were rehearsing *Medea* in the original Greek?

Lying would require Gus's cooperation. Cathryn peered at him out of the corner of her eye. He simmered in his chair as if one more click-clack of the school secretary's super-long nails would trigger an explosion. Gus was arrogant, callous, and disagreeable, but he was no liar. He'd tell Principal Evans exactly what he thought and bring even more punishment upon them.

"I have enough on my plate without the smart kids making trouble," Principal Evans muttered as the warning bell rang. "You two get to your classes. I'll handle this."

Coach Karne marched out of the office, but Mrs. West paused in front of Cathryn.

She shook her head. "I expect better from you."

Her departure left Cathryn cold. Honors English was her favorite class. In one stupid move, Cathryn had disappointed her favorite teacher, fought with her friend, and worst of all, attracted attention when she needed to stay invisible. *What was I thinking?* Now her fate rested in Principal Evans's hands.

What's taking him so long? He'd closed his door what felt like hours ago. *What if he calls Dad?*

Something bumped Cathryn's arm, and she shot to her feet. "Don't touch me."

Gus halted mid-stretch. Cathryn retreated to a seat near the exit. Gus eyed her as if unsure whether to restart their argument or psychoanalyze her outburst.

"Don't look at me either." Cathryn drew her knees into her chest. *Mom always handles school stuff. They'll call her first.* Unless her mother was working. Cathryn scanned her brain, but even her photographic memory couldn't recall whether the school had her mother's work number. She closed her eyes against a wave of nausea.

Principal Evans emerged from his office, walnut-brown hands clasped in front of him in controlled professionalism. "I have high expectations of students of your caliber. This behavior is unacceptable. I've called both your parents, and—"

"You called my father?" Cathryn's voice barely carried across the room.

"I left a message. Because I couldn't reach your mother either, you will spend the rest of the day in detention. Gustaf, your parents will pick you up."

Cathryn heard little beyond the word detention. *What will Dad think?* Her father had never cared about her school performance, but he might use this incident as an excuse to "homeschool" Cathryn to "keep her safe from bullies." From there, it wouldn't be a stretch to ban her from the library, and then she'd have no escape.

Cathryn closed her eyes and rested her forehead against her knees. *What have I done?*

* * *

Detention was nothing like study hall. A teacher still supervised students who flicked paper footballs at each other instead of doing their homework, but the similarities ended there. Cathryn was invisible in study hall, but detention meant attention, and attention meant trouble. Though neither the teacher nor her fellow delinquents looked her way, she felt the weight of a thousand malevolent eyes. She tried to read the next chapter for chemistry, but her insides shook too much to focus. Had she any food in her stomach, she'd have thrown up. As it was, she struggled to stay upright.

Cathryn jumped when the bell rang, darting out the door before the teacher dismissed them. She wove through a crowd of students whose smiles were too big and whose eyes focused too intently on her. Not bothering to stop at her locker, she went straight to the bike racks. A car honked as she pedaled into the street without looking both ways. She pushed her legs harder.

Principal Evans said he'd left a message. *Does Dad check the messages?* Maybe her mom got to it first. Unless the principal called her dad at work. Did her father have a work phone, or would his boss relay the news? Cathryn hoped they'd had a busy day.

She screeched to a halt at the border of the woods. She'd taken that deer trail thousands of times, but it had never appeared so menacing. Dead leaves littered the earth like fallen dreams, while empty branches clawed at each other in the chill breeze. A scraggly robin crowed as if blaming her for the coming winter.

I can't do this. Cathryn ditched her bike and headed into the library's back entrance, hands shaking as she handled her key. As if expecting her, *The Fantastic Flying Books of Mr. Morris Lessmore* sat atop the pile of books in need of shelving. Cathryn clutched it to her chest and sank to the floor. Her pent-up anxiety gushed out her eyes.

Dad's going to kill me. Her mind's gears spun too fast to generate an alternative, but before she dissolved into panic, Mr. Zabinski gingerly lowered himself beside her. He patted her knee, and she closed her eyes and inhaled the smell of old books and ink.

Cathryn swallowed through the tightness in her throat. "I f-fought with a boy at school, and I got detention."

Mr. Zabinski nodded slowly, taking his time to process what must have sounded like foreign words coming from Cathryn. After a moment's contemplation, he said, "Stay here; we'll wait out the tears."

Cathryn scooted closer to him, and he draped a skinny arm around her shoulders. She'd never allowed herself to cry with anyone but her mother, but she couldn't pretend right now, and Mr. Zabinski was safe. He'd offered to wait out the tears, but as her cheek rested against the shirt softened by hundreds of washes, her eyes dried. The gears in her mind slowed, and her nerves quieted as if obeying the library's noise protocol.

When the sunlight slanted through the window shades, Mr. Zabinski squeezed her shoulders and leaned away. "I know how you are about being home for supper, and I suspect tonight will be extra important."

Cathryn nodded. She dreaded what waited for her at home, but if she didn't return, her mother would endure her punishment.

She helped Mr. Zabinski to his feet, and he gestured to the book she still grasped in her free hand.

"Why don't you keep that?"

Cathryn brushed her fingers over the cover, and an inexplicable calm descended, much like what happened to her mother when they lit the prayer candle. She offered Mr. Zabinski a hesitant smile. "Thank you."

Cathryn walked her bike through the woods, the book's hard cover giving her an emotional armor. She opened her door to find what appeared to be another tornado incident—except this time, her mother was bleeding. *I'm too late.*

"Dad came home early," her mother said around a swollen lip. Jedidiah Banks followed a more rigid schedule than any army officer. He returned home every day at six as if reeled in by an invisible angler. Not 5:59. Six. Only one thing explained his early arrival.

"It's my fault. I got in trouble at school, and the principal called Dad." Cathryn's short-lived bravery fled her as she fell into her mother's arms.

"Shh. It's okay, my sweet girl." Her mother stroked her hair.

"He'll never let me out of my room again." The words left Cathryn's mouth a jumbled mess, but like all mothers, hers had a way of understanding tear-mangled speech.

"Yes, he will." Her mother squeezed her shoulders one more time before she started setting the kitchen chairs upright. "He had several beers before he came home, and he just left for the bars. He may not even remember anything by tomorrow." She frowned at the missing leg on one of the chairs. "If he does, we'll tell him the principal is making you tutor kids in detention as a punishment. It'll look suspicious if you don't show."

Cathryn brushed her eyes dry with the edge of her sleeve. "He hit you because of me."

Her mother pointed at her with the chair leg. "This is not your fault. It started long before either of us."

Cathryn did the verbal equivalent of walking on tiptoe as her mother retrieved a bottle of wood glue from the cupboard. The only explanation she'd ever received for her father's behavior was, "Sometimes the angry monster takes control of Daddy."

"What do you mean?"

"When your father was eleven, his mother took half their savings and ran off with a guy from work. His father . . . well, like father, like son." She glued the leg back in place and fastened it with a vice. "Your father started drinking heavily after his mother showed up at your grandfather's funeral with her new family."

"That's why he's never let you work? He's afraid you won't come back?"

"That's why he's so tight with money." She leaned against the now upright table. "We met after my parents died in a car accident. I was lonely, and he made me feel treasured and protected with his talk of family togetherness. My only worry was decorating the baby room, until *he* became my only worry." She shook her head. "We're getting out of this, Cathryn. With God's help, we'll escape."

How can you be so sure? Cathryn retrieved the first aid kit from the bathroom and tended a cut on her mother's cheek. The wounded woman didn't even flinch when Cathryn swabbed it with disinfectant.

"You go to bed early, Mom. I'll finish cleaning up." Cathryn shushed her mother's protests and ushered her upstairs. While her mother undressed, Cathryn shifted her grandmother's prayer candle and her grandfather's military funeral flag to make room for Mr. Zabinski's gift. *At least I can always escape into books.*

Once her mother rested quietly, Cathryn grabbed a broom and set to work erasing aftermath of her father's rampage, but she froze mid-sweep when she spotted the calendar. Thursday. *I could have sworn* . . . She tiptoed as quickly as she could to the panel in the back of her closet. Her mother's color-coded work schedule stared back at her.

Cathryn blinked to be sure her eyes weren't fooled by an illusion. They weren't. Her mother should never have been home to receive her father's beating. She was scheduled to work.

Chapter 10

Cathryn was one of many students at Brooks High who qualified for free lunch. When her father had a rough day, it was the only meal she ate, but Cathryn hadn't eaten lunch yesterday. She'd fought with Gus.

Forty-eight hours had passed since Cathryn had eaten more than granola bars. Gym class had been torture. She didn't remember what excuse she'd muttered when Tony asked if she was okay. Now in her last class before lunch, invisible blacksmiths battered her head with sledgehammers.

Time distorted. The clock's ticking became a thunderous boom, the hands fixed in place. Mr. Mosen's speech became a low murmur. Cathryn crossed her arms in front of her abdomen to muffle her stomach's growl as it writhed inside her.

The buzzing din that surrounded her paused as the class waited for her to clarify something Gus said. Cathryn hadn't heard what Gus said. Her head felt too heavy for her neck to support.

"He can speak for himself."

Mr. Mosen shrugged, and the drone continued.

After he'd drawled on long enough to read all thirty-two books of Encyclopedia Britannica, the bell rang for lunch. Cathryn waited for her legs to stop wobbling before she entered the hallway. The walls of lockers distorted like the hall of crooked mirrors she'd seen at the state fair when she was five. Students wavered like mirages. Cathryn tried to steady herself, but the world tipped upside down and went black.

* * *

Adrenaline surged through Gus after Cathryn dropped to the floor. "It's probably low blood glucose. She—".

"Back off you overstuffed peacock!" Minh looked like a panther prepared to pounce. Illogical as it was, Gus felt certain she would leap out of her chair and strangle him if he took even one step closer to Cathryn.

"She'll be all right, Ink. She just needs some sugar water."

Sugar water—precisely what Gus surmised. He'd long suspected Cathryn had a metabolic disorder. How else could she consume so many calories at lunch and maintain her frail figure?

To Gus's surprise, Tony's reiteration of his diagnosis was not what irked him. What made his jaw clench was that *Tony* offered Cathryn his bottle of Gatorade, and *Tony* helped her to her feet.

Tony. Not him.

* * *

A cafeteria worker shouted at a group of sophomores to quiet down. Cathryn's eyes wandered.

"Don't look at him."

"He's so miserable sitting alone," Cathryn said, ignoring both her watery green beans and Minh's demand.

"No. Cat, look at me. You do not feel sorry for that jerk. He deserves to be miserable."

Cathryn lacked the energy to argue, so she focused on eating the lunch Tony had brought her. After the school nurse gave her a cursory once-over, Tony convinced her to let Cathryn eat while he explained what happened, sparing her a dangerous interrogation. Nurses were human lie detectors with x-ray vision for spotting bruises under clothing.

Cathryn shuddered, which Minh mistook for further regret about Gus. She stabbed her steamed carrots as though skewering him.

"He went too far. You stood up for yourself. Don't back down now."

Cathryn thought back to their argument. Never had she been more aware of her father's blood running through her veins.

"I shouldn't have fought with him."

Minh smacked the table. "*He* started it, and he's not even sorry." Minh gestured to where Gus sat stiff as a statue with his characteristic scowl chiseled onto his face.

"He's not exactly easy to read."

Minh held up her milk as if giving a toast. "I say good riddance to the walking circuit board." She downed her drink and slammed the empty carton on the table, officially terminating their friendship with Gus.

Cathryn ruminated as she finished her green beans. What was the difference between Minh's anger and her father's? How could she stop herself from crossing the line? *What if there's an angry monster in me too?* What if *she'd* started the fight?

Cathryn peeled back the layers of emotion in search of what triggered her outburst, but she didn't find an angry monster.

Not anger. Hurt. *"No one can make you feel inferior without your consent."* Eleanor Roosevelt never met Gustaf Hein. He made it clear Cathryn was worth less than the snot he blew out his nose. His scorn, not her anger, sparked their fight, and now it produced a sharp, twisting pain under her rib cage.

Minh warned her this would happen. *How could I have been so stupid?* Minh was right. She should forget Gus.

Cathryn changed the subject as she and Minh finished lunch, but she stole another glance at Gus on the way out of the cafeteria.

* * *

Gus rose from the lunch table, but a heavy hand atop his shoulder pushed him back into his seat.

"You don't deserve to lick the mud off Kitten's boots." Tony thrust his finger in Gus's face. "I ought to—"

"Punch my face in. I know. You ought to consider varying your threats."

Tony's face went from ripe tomato to cherry red. More than his face. The red tint spread down his chest and gave his white T-shirt a pinkish hue. Tony took a breath and released it, and his coloring returned to normal. He sat in front of Gus.

"The key to fighting with women is this: The woman is always right."

"That's absurd."

"The woman is always right."

"But what if—"

"You want to sit by yourself for the rest of the year?"

Gus didn't mind sitting alone. It spared him the aggravation of engaging in inane small talk. His classmates rarely discussed anything interesting. Except Cathryn. She made being alone seem . . . lonely.

He scanned the cafeteria and spotted Cathryn's ponytail just before she rounded the corner. "I suppose not."

"It ain't that hard," Tony said. "'I was wrong. I'm sorry. Will you forgive me?'"

Gus shook his head. "Why do women require arbitrary rituals to reestablish rapport?"

"This is why we need to get you back on Kitten's good side. I didn't get a word of that." Tony gestured as though explaining something to a small child. "You hurt her feelings. She's scared you'll hurt her again. She needs to know you're sorry before she can trust you. Girls are like that."

Gus frowned. His parents lanced barbs at each other every day. His mother never appeared frightened. She merely awoke the next morning with a fiercer argument. Then again, his mother was at the opposite end of the emotional spectrum as Cathryn.

"You're saying women are averse to relational risk taking?"

Tony looked heavenward and pulled at his hair. "This ain't that complicated. You hurt a girl. The girl puts up walls. The more you hurt the girl, the higher the walls get. You want to get back inside the walls? Apologize."

The cafeteria emptied, leaving tables scattered with dirty napkins and candy bar wrappers. Teachers at the academy would have punished such sloppiness with ten rounds of stairclimbing the bleachers, but laziness infected this entire school. The pitifully low standards frustrated Gus to no end, but the other day, he'd been frustrated in Cathryn's direction.

He didn't remember everything he'd said, but he did recall how Cathryn looked at him. Her face turned red; her voice, venomous, but her eyes—whose color he still couldn't categorize—held no anger. She looked at him with the eyes of a wounded animal before a hunter fired the killing shot.

Gus's lunch soured in his stomach. *He* caused that look in Cathryn's eyes. He remembered the first time he saw her smile.

"Very well, reiterate the method for a proper apology."

"All right, but Gus, you hurt that girl again, and—"

"I won't."

* * *

Cathryn leaned against the tree. "Like this?"

"No," Minh called. "Stand up straight and put your arms out from your sides a little."

Cathryn had more time than she needed to bike to the library today, so she'd agreed to pose in front of the scraggly tree near the flagpole. As much as she supported her friend's art, the attention Minh paid her when sketching unsettled her. She glanced at her arms to ensure her sleeves covered her bruises. *I should have double-checked my makeup.*

"This isn't for a contest, is it?" Knowing her luck, her father would see it somewhere.

"Relax," Minh said as she drew a few more lines. "I'll make you an undead fairy. No one will recognize you."

"Halloween was last week."

Minh waved away her observation. "Inspiration never strikes on schedule. Now, get back in position."

Minh pursed her lips as she sketched, but her expression shifted into a scowl as Gus approached.

"Cathryn, may I speak with you?"

"No," Minh answered.

Gus held out a candy bar to Cathryn. "I heard chocolate has a mitigating effect on a woman's ire."

Cathryn's stomach took control of her body. She reached for the chocolate.

"Hold still, Cat."

Right. I'm still mad at him. Cathryn shifted back into position. *I will not let his extensive vocabulary and gorgeous blue eyes fool me.* A breeze tickled her nose with the scent of chocolate. She stiffened to keep from breaking her pose.

Gus swallowed. "I would like to apologize for my behavior. Upon further reflection, some of my—"

"Some?" Minh said as she changed pens.

"Most—"

Minh cleared her throat.

Gus clenched his fists for a moment before unfurling his fingers. "*All* my arguments were inconsiderate. You were the unintended recipient of my frustration. I realize my error, and I hope our relationship can return to an amicable status."

"Relationship?" Minh scrambled to retrieve the pen she fumbled before it hit the ground.

"He means friendship, Minh." Cathryn shifted. "Are you finished? I can't pose and translate and assess his sincerity at the same time." She hadn't prepared herself to resist an apology.

"You doubt my sincerity?"

Stay strong. Cathryn clenched her fist to keep from reaching for the chocolate. "I think you want someone to translate for you."

"Atta girl, Cat." Minh smirked at Gus's glare.

Gus exhaled slowly and fidgeted with the candy bar. "On that subject, I wanted to ask if you would tutor me in more . . . colloquial speech."

Cathryn looked everywhere but his puppy-dog eyes. She missed talking to someone who enjoyed learning as much as she did, and the hallways felt lonely without their quizzing game.

"The idea has potential."

"No it doesn't," Minh said, wheeling closer. "First, he treats you like dirt, then he has the gall to ask you for help?"

Cathryn spread her hands. "He apologized. It's only fair to give him a second chance, right?"

"*Fair* would be throwing him off the Stone Arch Bridge."

Gus ignored the threat. "Then we have an agreement?"

Cathryn wavered. He seemed sincere, but could she risk giving him a second chance?

"Cathryn, I won't hurt you again," Gus said.

Cathryn rubbed her arm. Her father said those words often. How many times had her mother forgiven him?

"Gus, I . . . I don't . . ."

"Of course." He cleared his throat. "I understand." He wore the same expression she'd glimpsed the day they met, the look of a misfit struggling to adapt to a hostile new environment. She of all people understood being quirky outside while hurting inside, but she'd still denied his request for help. She'd rejected her friend.

"Wait." Cathryn launched into her next sentence before she could second-guess herself. "As Alexander Pope said, 'To err is human, to forgive divine.' I'll forgive you on one condition."

"What?"

Cathryn snatched the chocolate bar out of his hand. "I get to keep this."

* * *

Minh glared at Gus as he followed Cathryn, wondering whether the school had a policy on pushing classmates in front of the light rail. Behind his back, she referred to him as "Cathryn's pet genius." Everything from his perfect posture to his expensive cell phone grated on her nerves like a crying baby on an airplane.

"Looks like they made up," Tony said from behind her. Evidently, he'd witnessed the entire exchange.

Minh shook her head. "If that blue-eyed cyborg breaks her heart, I will break his neck."

"You'll have to get in line, Ink." Tony said.

"...n't have to begin now," Tony said.

Chapter 11

As they approached the parking lot, Cathryn reconsidered holding their first colloquial speech lesson at Gus's house, despite his claim that his computer was faster than the library's. He lived across town, and though she'd memorized the bus route, the extra distance left room for errors. After her mom nearly forgot to hide her work uniform, they couldn't afford more mistakes.

Gus misinterpreted her hesitation. "I assure you, you will be more secure with me driving than you would with either of my parents."

Far from reassured, Cathryn slipped onto leather seats so soft she worried her jeans would scratch them. As if to prove himself a safe driver, Gus waited for her to buckle her seatbelt before he started the engine.

They drove past Lake Calhoun/*Bde Maka Ska* to a neighborhood Cathryn had only seen on bus route maps.

"Aren't you out of district?"

"My parents have methods for ensuring the rules do not apply to them."

Cathryn knew his scowls well enough to drop the subject.

The farther they went from school, the grander the houses became. From the well-manicured lawns to the decorative water fountains, the homes whispered, "We're better than you." Cathryn never imagined an inanimate object could have a superiority complex, but Gus's house exuded an air of disdain that made her stomach clench.

The tightness spread through the rest of her abdomen when she stepped through the front door. Though not ostentatious, even one of the living room chairs cost more than her father's car. The hardwood floors and ebony cabinets shone as if smiling for a camera, not a speck of dust upon them.

"Gustaf." Gus's mother had the most perfect posture Cathryn had ever seen.

"Mother, this is Cathryn Banks. Cathryn, my mother."

"I remember," Cathryn said, but Gus's mother must have forgotten their meeting the day their car broke down outside of school. The slim woman's eyes took aim as if each patch on Cathryn's jeans had a flashing target attached to it.

"Son, I admire your charitable instincts, but I hope this"— Cathryn resisted the urge to squirm as the reproving eyes scanned her—"girl is not distracting you. I do not want your academics to follow the trajectory of your debate performance."

"Precisely why I recruited Cathryn. She is a gifted linguist and an expert in several areas of concern." Gus spoke with the even tone of one accustomed to placating disciplinarians.

"Very well." His mother's face said she didn't believe him any more than she believed Earth was flat.

Gus led Cathryn up an ornate staircase that was far more structurally sound than the one in her home. He ushered her into a room he referred to as "his study," where a multi-monitored computer dominated a mahogany desk, and a telescope pointed out the window.

"Don't," he said upon closing the door.

"I'm sorry?"

"I often contemplated my mother's ability to look down her nose at people who exceed her in height. After testing multiple hypotheses, I concluded she supersedes the laws of physics."

Cathryn chuckled. "Good to know."

She shifted her backpack to her other shoulder. At Minh's place, she'd plop down on the floor, but she didn't know Gus's norms. She glanced at the door and risked a request.

"Do you mind cracking that open?"

Gus's expression implied he was filing her question in a mental folder labeled STRANGE THINGS CATHRYN SAYS. Cathryn searched the room for a change in subject.

"Did you make all these?" She would sound like Dr. Seuss if she tried to describe the variations on a cylinder that lay organized with military precision across a wide table, each with a thick set of notes attached to it.

Gus shrugged. "I've yet to optimize the design."

And his mom is disappointed in him? "Didn't the debate team take second last weekend?" Cathryn peered at a shelf full of plastic containers filled with white and gray powders.

"If my parents were content with second place, they would never have enrolled me in Wilcott's Academy."

"Sounds . . . prestigious." *Ammonium nitrate. Isn't that used in fertilizer?*

"They only admit students with superior intellectual *and* physical skills. Only a fraction maintain enrollment through graduation." His tone implied he'd planned to be one of them.

"Did everyone there speak like you?"

Gus moved one of the containers so that the labels were organized alphabetically. "Yes, but I suppose a boarding school filled with prodigies creates a linguistic microcosm."

Cathryn squinted at the other jars. *Aluminum powder, ammonium nitrate, ammonium perchlorate, magnesium powder . . .* She did some mental chemistry. *Oh my god.* Her mouth dropped open as she faced Gus, but she spotted the winged cylinders and exhaled with relief. "You're making *rockets.*"

Gus wrinkled his forehead. "Of course. Why else would I need a composite propellant?"

"To build a bomb?"

Gus snorted as he unloaded his backpack onto his desk. "Cathryn, I have better things to do than bomb a school that's weeks away from being condemned anyway."

Cathryn wasn't sure whether to take offense on the school's behalf or be concerned that his rationale derived from time management more than morality. She filed both feelings in a mental folder labeled STRANGE THINGS GUS SAYS and pulled up a chair.

"The academy sounds like a lot of pressure."

"Actually, I enjoyed the competition. For me, school is—"

"An escape."

Gus locked eyes with her. "Exactly."

Cathryn averted her gaze. *Careful.* She added her folders, which were covered with scribbled Somali verb conjugations, to his clean ones. "My parents are happy I do my best."

"But you don't."

Cathryn stiffened. "What?"

Gus counted on his fingers. "You never speak in class. You never contradict our classmates, and you rely on Minh to make all your decisions."

"That's not . . ." Cathryn fumbled for words.

"You should join the debate team." Gus reached for a pencil, as if he planned to enlist Cathryn himself.

"Didn't you just say I'm too timid?"

"Exactly. Debate would allow you to practice speaking your mind."

Cathryn opened her folders, hoping he'd take the hint. "I don't like arguing, and the tournaments are on the weekends."

"So?"

Shoot. Cathryn fidgeted with her ponytail. "Some of us have family obligations on the weekends."

Gus snorted. "All weekend, every weekend? Admit it. You're afraid."

"I am not afraid." Cathryn scooted back. Of course she feared sharing her opinions. At home, she wasn't allowed to have them. *Change the subject. Now.*

Gus reclined in his chair like a principal who'd caught a student smoking. "Name one risk you've taken without Minh's encouragement."

"I befriended you." Cathryn launched to her feet. "Talk about being afraid. You won't even admit you want friends."

"I—"

"You 'only want a scholarship to whatever university is farthest from here.' Liar. You want to lift weights with Tony without needing a translator."

Gus stood and leaned over his desk. "I do not need friends."

"Then why am I still here?" She gathered her folders and turned to leave, tempted to knock over his rocket shells on the way out.

"Wait." Gus rubbed the back of his neck. "It's just . . . I don't understand you. You research word etymologies for fun, and you can list every US senator from the Civil War era. You even translated Macbeth's soliloquy into Somali, despite being 'a beginner.' Cathryn, you are not smart. You're brilliant, but you hide your intellect." He gestured as though she were Exhibit A in The Museum of Contradictions. "You are my sole source of intelligent conversation, but to hear your opinion, I must provoke an argument."

Cathryn dropped her chin to her chest. "You could try asking nicely."

Gus adjusted his shirt and straightened the line of pencils on his desk.

Cathryn looked toward the open door. She should leave. If she did, she'd be guaranteed to get home on time. Gus would stop prying, and she could focus on creating a better calendar system for her mother.

"Please." For the first time, Gus's voice lacked its imperious tone. "Please, will you stay and tutor me in the local vernacular?" He needed her help. Moreover, he wanted it.

Cathryn set her backpack beside his desk. "Why don't we start with Words and Phrases Frequently Used by Tony."

* * *

Cathryn expounded upon the history of anthropomorphizing modes of transportation to explain why Tony referred to cars as "she," but they soon digressed to other topics. Once Cathryn's words flowed freely, she couldn't stop them. Minh rolled her eyes at Cathryn's nerdy discourse, but Gus challenged her to delve deeper. Like a child calling "faster, faster," Cathryn's brain couldn't get enough.

She liked sharing her opinions.

Liked it so much, she lost track of time.

Cathryn snatched Gus's wrist: 5:25. "*¡Mierda!*" She shoved her things into her backpack.

"I beg your pardon?"

"It's Spanish for shit which in this context means I lost track of time, and I'll be in colossal trouble for getting home late."

"I could drive—"

"It'll be faster to take the bus to the library and cut through the woods." No way she would let Gus anywhere near her house. "See you tomorrow."

Cathryn took the imperious stairs two at a time and burst through front door. She sprinted to the waiting bus and hopped aboard just as it pulled away. *What was I thinking?* For over an hour, she'd forgotten her father, but Cathryn couldn't afford to relax with friends like a normal teen. Life had rules, and mistakes had consequences.

Cathryn's efforts to catch her breath were fruitless. *I'm not going to make it.* She wheezed as a knot of panic tightened around her throat. *Calm down. You'll be fine. Inhale. Exhale.*

The bus ambled like an elephant on its way to sunbathe. Cathryn's legs twitched as the wheelchair lift beeped, but a pang of guilt forced them still. Her best friend used a wheelchair. How could she be so prejudiced? It wasn't that man's fault she'd mismanaged her time.

The guilt grounded her. Three more stops until the library.

When the bus reached her stop, Cathryn leaped out the door. She managed a quick, "sorry" to the woman she toppled as she raced toward the woods. She knew every rock and tree root like she knew the Dewey Decimal System. She gathered speed. Her gym teacher would be shocked to see her running so fast. Apparently, she just needed the proper motivation.

At the sight of her house she wrenched to a halt. The door stood open, a gaping wound in a building that was always armored shut.

"Dad?" Her sweat turned to ice water as she stepped into the entryway. The kitchen table lay on its side on a battlefield of broken-dish shrapnel and soup entrails.

"Mom?"

A rough pair of hands shoved her against the wall.

"Where were you?" Her father's voice ground into her.

"I'm sorry. I-I'm sorry. I'm sorry." Cathryn's prodigious vocabulary reduced to two words. Her father flung her from the wall. The corner of the coffee table bit into her back.

"You find a better family out there?" His eyes burned.

"No, please, Dad—"

His backhand sent her tumbling. The hardwood floor creaked as she crawled away. He yanked her hair and threw her into the card table. She lay dazed in a tangle of bent metal poles. Had she been quicker, she might have avoided the kick to her abdomen. He repeated the kick two more times before she scrambled to her feet and ran.

The wicker-seat chair made impact in the center of her back, and she fell her to her knees. Her father grabbed her shoulders and forced her against the wall. Their dingy lamp fell to the ground and shattered.

He punched her in the ribs. Cathryn knew better than to scream. He hit her again. She dropped to the ground and drew herself into a ball. She did her best to block the blows with her forearms as he got into a rhythm: punch, punch, kick; punch, punch, kick. The pattern repeated until Cathryn lost sense of time.

Satisfied, he clenched her bicep, yanked her to her feet, and dragged her to her room. The loose stair groaned as he stomped their weight into it. She hit the floor with a thud. The door slammed, and the lock clicked from the outside.

Her mother lay unconscious next to the bed, the first victim of Cathryn's tardiness. No apology could wash away the blood that dripped from her mother's nose.

Cathryn sat at her mother's feet and stared at the popsicle-stick cross hanging on the wall. She'd been five, six maybe? She remembered how proud she'd been, hiding it behind her back and surprising her mother after Sunday school. Her mother oohed and aahed before hanging it with the same reverence she might a Van Gogh. She refused to take it down no matter how much Cathryn insisted she was old enough not to care.

Cathryn no longer shared her mother's belief in God, but she definitely believed in the devil.

* * *

Cathryn's Diary

Feminism gives the worst of gifts—false hope. We can provide girls with the right to vote, an education, and equal pay, but it's all for naught. Elizabeth Cady Stanton said, "All men and all women are created equal." She lied. There is one fact no amount of feminist idealism can change: he is bigger than I am; therefore, I am his.

Chapter 12

Laurel Ostergaard cleaned the kitchen for the third time in the last two hours. Her footsteps echoed through the house as she put away the sponge and walked to the living room sofa. The channels got worse with every click of the remote. She frowned as a famous Food Channel star appeared. *I can cook better than that heartless phony.* She turned off the TV and contemplated the pile of magazines she'd already read.

Beautiful people smiled at her from beneath the titles. Laurel looked to the wall where a framed copy of *Twin Cities Entrepreneurs* hung. She and Mark graced the cover, their smiles blinding. The journalists hailed them as entrepreneurial juggernauts—movie-star looks and rock-star success. Laurel returned her gaze to the other cover features and wondered if their smiles hid pain too.

She threw the magazines in the trash and returned to the kitchen.

Laurel plucked *Mastering the Art of French Cooking* from its place of honor, and its worn pages warmed her as she flipped through recipes she'd memorized years ago. The warmth abandoned her when she reached the end.

She'd planned their meals for the next month; Mrs. Nelson was handling treats at church this weekend, and group was at the Bentrigaards' house. She could experiment, but she had no one to test her recipes except herself. *Thank God I got my sense of taste back. I don't think I could've handled living the rest of my life tasting iron.*

She searched her surroundings for something to replace that thought but found only empty rooms, closed cupboards, and carpets that still showed vacuum tracks.

"God, why did you spare me?" The vacant house swallowed the prayer. *I need to get out of here.*

The outside air hit her with a blast of autumn air. She considered returning for a warmer jacket, but she liked the way the goosebumps made her feel alive. The bus stopped a few blocks away. *I'm not that desperate.* Not being able to drive was one of the most irritating parts of her new reality. Shopping bags and busses didn't mix. *I need fresh air anyway.*

Mark had surprised her with the deed to their house, which sat across from Lake of the Isles. He knew how much she loved to walk and people-watch. *Just what I need.*

With every step, her lungs cleared, and her mood lightened. She walked around the finger-shaped projection that was the bane of runners and paused at a street sign at the south end of the lake.

The parkway led to Lake Calhoun/*Bde Maka Ska*. Following the trail around the controversially named lake would mean another three miles of walking. She hadn't walked around both lakes since before her life fell apart, but the thought of returning to her silent house decided her.

The walk energized her more than a mocha latte. *I can do it.* A mother with a stroller approached from the opposite direction, her toddler bundled inside. *Don't stare.* The woman swiveled to avoid a pothole and put herself briefly in Laurel's way. Laurel forced her lips into a salon-perfect smile and nodded as she passed. *Don't let it ruin your day. Keep walking.*

The incident leached energy from her legs. She looked for a cross street to check her progress. Sheridan Avenue. She was only halfway around. *You can do this.* The steps that previously took her mood from grouchy to energized now brought her to fatigue. Her head wobbled on her neck, and her vision blurred. *One little break.* She sat at the roots of an ash tree and leaned her head against its trunk.

"Laurel? Laurel!"

She opened her eyes at the familiar voice. "Did I fall asleep? Where am I?"

"Laurel, are you all right?"

She squinted at the man who knelt in front of her and waited for her vision to clear. Waking was like this sometimes, like being born into a new world. The fog cleared from her eyes, and she saw close-cropped fuzz atop the man's head.

"Warren? Warren Jones?"

"I spotted you on my way back to the office. Your hands are freezing. Here, put on my jacket. I'll drive you home." He helped her to her feet and led her to his car. A chuckle escaped her lips.

"The last time a police officer drove me home was for much less virtuous reasons."

Warren's smile didn't reach his eyes. "Don't worry. I'm not that kind of officer."

The seatbelt's click struck the humor from her. "Thank you, Warren. This could have ended differently had you not spotted me."

"You can always call Sylvia or me if you need anything."

Laurel nodded as Warren started the engine.

"Warren?"

"Yes?"

"Don't tell Mark."

* * *

Cathryn squinted at the mirror and added another layer of foundation. Her father had let her out of her room the day after his "lesson," but the bruises took another two days to heal enough to cover with makeup. Even today was pushing it. *Good thing I caught my reflection before anyone saw me. I need more light at home.* She assessed her handiwork once more before leaving the bathroom.

"There you are." Minh rolled to her and frowned. "Makeup day, huh? You want to talk about it?"

"What?"

"You only wear that much makeup when you had a sucky day. I get it. When I have a crappy day, I either paint my nails or buy

86

myself a new set of pens."

I should have known she'd notice by now. "I'm fine, Minh. I'm still a little sick, and I didn't want to come to school looking like a ghost."

"Okay, but if you need someone to paint your nails, I'm always available."

Cathryn faked a grin. "Why wait for a bad day?"

Minh winked, and they parted ways. Cathryn proceeded to her locker. "Good morning, Gus. I want to apologize for my abrupt departure the other day." Another student bumped her as he passed. She winced and inhaled sharply.

"You okay, Kitten?" Tony witnessed the incident from where he stood behind Gus.

"I'm fine. I'm not the most graceful person to begin with, and I've been sick the past couple days. Yesterday morning I ran to the bathroom to throw up, and I fell down the stairs. I have an impressive set of bruises from the wipeout." The I-fell-while-sick excuse never failed. *Good thing none of them knows my bathroom adjoins my room.*

"You ought to be more careful."

Cathryn blushed at the concern in Gus's voice. "I'm more embarrassed than hurt. Next time I'll keep a bucket by my bed."

The warning bell rang, and Cathryn's smile faded. Lying came with disturbing ease.

* * *

"The end."

Gus watched the group of Story-Time children wiggle out of their seats like a frozen hive of ants come to life again. Some laughed; others pouted. One girl tugged Cathryn's pant leg and begged for another story. *If patience could be measured objectively, Cathryn's would be twice the average.*

She had a remarkable effect on people Gus would find fascinating if he weren't its principal victim. Though she never drew attention to herself, her presence calmed the wiggly children and diffused her friends' volatile tempers.

The simplest things brought her joy—a cardinal's song, a child's silly expression, a polysyllabic word with an interesting etymology. Gus found that last one particularly effective in eliciting a smile.

Focus. Gus tore his eyes off Cathryn and fastened them to his history assignment. Cathryn had invited her friends to study at the library, and since she rarely initiated get-togethers, Gus and Minh took her up on it. Tony declined, saying he had to cover his uncle's shift. He and libraries didn't get along well anyway.

"You two are awfully quiet." Cathryn dropped a stack of cognitive therapy textbooks on the table next to them, no doubt a collection for a patron. Her face held the touch of concern it acquired whenever she left Minh and Gus alone, as if she feared one of them might not be breathing when she returned.

"We are mature enough to abide by the library's regulations, Cathryn."

Minh looked up from her sketchpad and shook her head. "Can't you just say everything's peachy like a normal human?"

"How does fruit relate to human interaction?"

Cathryn pinched the bridge of her nose. "Go easy on him, Minh. I spent two hours yesterday trying to convince him to say 'scar' instead of 'hypertrophic cicatrix.'"

"'Scar' is imprecise. It could refer to a fibrous collagen that protrudes from the skin or depressed blemishes." Gus made a mental note to return to the figurative use of peach later. He'd learned the hard way Cathryn tolerated only one argument at a time. Once, he'd needed multiple chocolate bars and, per Tony's suggestion, a bouquet of lilies to reenter her good graces.

"You sacrifice precision for clarity," Cathryn said, again. "'Scar' is the colloquial term for hypertrophic cicatrix. To refer to atrophic, say, 'acne scar.'"

"Not all atrophic cicatrices arise from ac—"

"As much as I love when you two forget I exist," Minh said, "I could use your opinion on this nose."

Cathryn squinted at Minh's sketchpad. "The nose is fine, but you're missing the single freckle below his left eye."

Gus's hand shot to his eye. "Did you—"

Minh turned her sketchpad around. "You should let me sculpt you. You have a good face for it. Strong bones and facial muscles."

"You depicted me angry."

"I could count the number of times I've seen you smile on a fingerless hand."

Gus appealed to Cathryn. She glanced at the front desk as if hoping a patron needed her assistance. Seeing no one, she wrapped the end of her ponytail around her finger. "Your expression does tend to alternate between a disgruntled scowl and a derisive sneer."

"You need to loosen up." Minh added more lines to her sketch.

Gus took a breath to stay his irritation. "Even if there were an internationally accepted quota for daily smiles, Cathryn smiles enough for at least three people." As if proving his point, Cathryn smiled.

"I don't think you *can* smile." Minh smirked and leaned back.

"I am fully capable of forming a variety of expressions."

"Prove it."

He took the bait. It felt awkward, like writing left-handed. The girls winced.

"Um, that's more of a grimace." Cathryn's voice resounded with a pained variant of sympathy.

"Picture something happy, like baby bunnies," Minh said.

"I have never understood the appeal of infant lagomorphs."

Minh rolled her eyes. "Then visualize test tubes or something."

Ridiculous. Better to emulate someone adept at smiling, which of course meant Cathryn. If there was anything distinctive amidst Cathryn's otherwise generic features, it was her smile. Cathryn's smile was kindness with the addictive potency of a narcotic. He felt its impact deep in his chest, and it reverberated through his entire skeleton. For a moment, time stopped, the air stilled, and background noise harmonized. He had no explanation for the phenomenon. Her smile was . . . magical, as the children might describe it.

"There. Right there. That's perfect," Cathryn said.

"He can be taught." Minh's loud voice earned her a shush from Cathryn, but she stuck out her tongue and continued sketching.

Gus had the disturbing sense that something significant transpired, but he couldn't identify what.

* * *

Cathryn jotted the number on a scrap of paper, grateful her stint in detention hadn't revoked her computer privileges. After scouring the library for weeks, she admitted she needed help. She just hoped that help wouldn't come at too high a price.

The bell signaled the end of study hall, and Cathryn ducked into the office. "Excuse me, may I borrow the phone? I forgot something, and I want to see if my mother can bring it."

"Sure. Dial nine first." The school secretary gestured with her long fake nails and walked toward the bathroom.

Cathryn checked for eavesdroppers, picked up the receiver, and consulted her scrap-paper note. *Here's hoping.* "Hello? Yes, I'm calling to schedule an appointment with a neurologist. Beatrice Banks. For concerns about memory loss. Short term. That's the soonest opening? No, that's okay. We'll be there. Thank you."

Cathryn returned the phone to its cradle. *Guess my color-coding system will have a last a while longer.*

Chapter 13

Gus tuned out Minh and Cathryn's chitchat as he tinkered with the wiring in his watch. His parents' arguing had woken him up early, and he'd come to school hoping the seat outside the office would serve as a quiet workspace. Unfortunately, the girls found him, but they seemed content to converse with each other, though why they remained in his vicinity baffled him.

Heavy footsteps interrupted the girls' chatter. Gus pulled his watch closer to himself as Tony barreled toward them.

"Hey, guys." Tony launched into his next sentence before they could return his greeting. "I was going to catch a movie tomorrow night, but my date flaked. Rivershore Theater is playing oldies for three bucks. You in?"

"Bucks means dollars," Cathryn clarified.

Movies didn't interest Gus any more than TV did. He returned his attention to his watch, grateful Minh's glare wasn't directed at him.

"If you think I'm stupid enough to fall for that, you're dumber than you look," she said.

Tony rolled his eyes. "I told you. If I ask you out, you'll know. You're not dumb enough to turn down a free movie, are you? Besides"—he lowered his voice—"don't you think these two need a chaperone?"

Gus's hand slipped, tearing out a wire. He clenched his fist over the tiny screwdriver, unsure what irked him more: the broken watch or Tony's assertion that he needed a chaperone.

"It sounds fun," Cathryn said, stalling Gus's protests with a hand, "but I'd better pass. I already spent my allowance."

"You don't have to pay; that's Gus's job," Tony said, thumping Gus on the shoulder and knocking the screwdriver to the floor. Gus ground his teeth and retrieved the tool, not trusting himself to speak without sparking a fight.

"Why would Gus pay for me?" Cathryn asked.

"Because the man pays. What, you never been on a date, Kitten?"

Minh chuckled. "That's so old-fashioned, Tony. What about going Dutch?"

Tony's round head reddened until it resembled a ripe tomato. "The Du- the Dutch! When have they done anything worth rubbing two pennies together? Pansies. A real man *pays for the girl.*"

Gus failed to see the connection between the Netherlands and a movie. Fortunately, Cathryn read his expression.

"'Going Dutch' refers to both parties paying for their share of an outing. It stems from the seventeenth century when the British used 'Dutch' as a synonym for 'false,' as in 'Dutch courage,' for 'alcohol-assisted bravado.'"

Tony spread his arms. "I rest my case."

Gus pondered the phrase as he bagged the pieces of his now thoroughly broken watch. "My prior social engagements have been more . . . structured." If "structured" meant torturous evenings dodging questions regarding exactly which organizations benefited from his parents' "charity balls." "Going Dutch seems sensible."

"No, no, no. Don't listen to them. Come here." Tony grabbed the bag, handed it to Cathryn, and dragged Gus away from the group. Had he been taller, he might have put his arm around Gus's shoulders, like a father giving advice to his son. Not that Gus's own father ever did that.

"You're smart, Gus, but when it comes to women, you're a dunce." Tony continued before Gus could argue. "Look over there. You like the girl, right? You think she's cute?"

Gus took a steadying breath before glancing at Cathryn. "I would judge her average in appearance."

Tony groaned. "You like being around her, right? You think she's *smart?* You like her *smile?*"

Gus shifted his weight from foot to foot. Cathryn was the first person he'd met whose company he enjoyed, and her smile did possess an undefinable magnetism. "I suppose I consider her attractive in that sense."

"Then you *pay for the date. Insist* on paying. You hear? Buck up and ask her to the movies. Buy the ticket, get her popcorn, a drink, whatever she wants. You make the girl happy, and she'll make you happy. You got it?"

"I think you've made a mistaken assumpti—"

"Trust me."

They rejoined the group. For the first time, Gus understood Cathryn's habit of fidgeting with her ponytail. He'd barely grown accustomed to having friends. This seemed like a step beyond that, one much more complicated than watch wiring. *Stop being a coward.*

Gus straightened his shoulders. "Cathryn, I would greatly appreciate it if you would accompany me to the movie"—Tony gestured for him to continue—"and I insist on paying."

Cathryn looked as uncomfortable as he felt. She peered around Gus to the organizer.

"When did you say it was?"

"Tomorrow night. They're showing *Grease*."

Cathryn grinned. "You would choose *Grease.*"

"Will you come, Cathryn?" Gus said.

Her smile faded. "Um." She glanced at Minh, whose expression Gus couldn't read. Perhaps they'd had their own heart-to-heart. She turned back to Gus. "I . . . I think I can make it work."

"Great," Tony said, putting his arms around them both. "It's a date."

* * *

If Cathryn's father caught her sneaking off to the movies with a boy, he'd install iron bars on her windows, but she had to risk it. Minh was tiring of her usual excuses, and Cathryn couldn't afford to let her friend get suspicious. To pass as a normal teen, she'd have to behave like one.

Cathryn laid her clothes on her bed, wishing she had a normal teen's wardrobe. She owned seven long-sleeved shirts and four pairs of jeans, one of which she should replace, but she lacked the nerve to ask her father for the money. *It's not a real date. Tony is just having a little fun with us. Gus has seen all these shirts. Stop fretting and pick one.*

Her internal tongue-lashing did little to aid her decision. Before this year, she'd considered boys boring barbarians—sweat, sports, and smut. Conversations with Gus, however, shot an electric current through her. He not only understood her verbosity, he encouraged it. She learned more walking beside him in the halls than sitting in class.

Her body couldn't decide what temperature to be in his presence. When he brushed against her, goosebumps shivered onto her skin. When his blue eyes shone with interest, her face flushed with fever. *Is this how love feels?*

Cathryn's stomach plummeted. *Is this how Mom felt when she met Dad?* She'd witnessed the train wreck of her parents' marriage. Was she another car on the tracks, doomed to collide with the already smashed engine?

Cathryn bit the inside of her lip as she fingered her shirts. *I should have told Tony I wasn't interested.* Tony had no difficulty launching into potentially disastrous relationships, but Tony could afford to be brave. He didn't face the same consequences for choosing wrong.

Forget the outfit. Start with makeup. Bottles, brushes, and powders formed an arsenal on her desk. A few brushstrokes and a layer of lip gloss completed her look. She rubbed her lips together and examined her reflection. A mask of normality returned her gaze. What if Gus saw beneath it?

The garbage disposal broke her thoughts.

"Cathryn?" her mother called from the kitchen.

"Up here."

The stairs creaked as her mother ascended. "What are you up to?"

"Nothing."

Amusement bounced from her mother's eyes to her smile as she spied Cathryn's clothes. "Deciding what to wear?"

"You're sure you can cover for me?" *You're sure you won't forget?* Part of Cathryn hoped she'd say no, but her mother pointed to the closed panel in the back of the closet.

"Tomorrow is a blue day—night-shift only. I have all night tonight and all day tomorrow to keep your father busy, which means *you* need to pick an outfit."

Cathryn frowned at her clothes. "I know it doesn't matter, but I'm stuck anyway."

Her mother took her hands in her own. "This Gus, is he a nice guy?"

Cathryn heard the deeper question, the same one she'd asked herself. "He's honest, and he expresses himself well, with *words*. He's very . . . smart. I'm not sure he knows how to be nice yet, but we're making progress. The other day, Minh and I taught him to smile."

Her mother chuckled. "Well, no one knows smiling better than you. You look fabulous in any outfit. Even if you didn't, the Bible says beauty should come from a gentle and quiet spirit. If that's not good enough for Mr. Smarty-pants, then he doesn't deserve you."

"Thanks, Mom." Cathryn's nerves loosened their grip.

"That being said"—a mischievous gleam weaseled into her mother's eyes—"even though it's a fake date, you can still make yourself gorgeous. Let's see if any of my old things fit you."

Cathryn spent the next hour trying on her mother's clothes, most of which mostly fit. Her mother oohed and aahed, or they both burst out laughing. If the movie were a complete disaster, it would still be the most fun Cathryn had had since she and Minh broke into the Joneses' freezer and ate the entire box of chocolate ice cream bars.

They settled on a green dress with a fitted waist and a skirt that fell to Cathryn's shins. Light for November, but Cathryn was Minnesotan. She could handle chilly weather. The half-length sleeves worried her more. Though her arms were currently free of bruises, she felt vulnerable with them exposed.

Her mom hugged her. "I'll make sure your father is occupied, but be careful going down the drainpipe. We can't take any chances."

"Bet you never imagined you'd *help* your teenage daughter sneak out. Are you sure you can cover for me?"

Her mother nodded. "I wish I could give you a normal childhood, but you'll have to settle for this." She turned in the doorway. "Cathryn?"

"Yes?"

"Don't hold back on living your life for fear of reliving mine."

* * *

Minh scanned the parking lot as her sister drove. Tony had insisted on picking her up at her house, but Minh talked him out of it by describing her dad's badge-and-gun routine. She could have met the others at the theater, but she wanted to be there in case Cathryn's first date started badly, so she'd grudgingly agreed to let Tony drive her halfway.

"There they are." She pointed. Cathryn had suggested they meet at the library. Minh suspected she didn't want Gus to see where she lived. Cathryn never invited friends over, never spent money, and never went out after 6 p.m.—all points Minh made yesterday when she insisted Cathryn break the rules for once.

"*That's* your date?" Beth said. Her eyebrows rose to almost touch the thick headband she always wore to keep back her corkscrew curls.

"He wishes."

"If it's not a date, why did you ask me to drive you instead of Dad?"

"Dad ended up working late; Mom's at a poetry slam, and even if Demarius could drive, he's babysitting Ghost. Sorry, Sis. You're the one without a life."

Beth looked heavenward. "Side effect of law school."

Even if another family member had been available, Beth's car was Minh's favorite. It was the perfect height for an easy transfer into her wheelchair.

"Later, Betty." She rolled to where Gus and Tony waited by their respective cars.

"Let's review the rules," Tony was saying.

"Both my short- and long-term memory are fully functional. I do not need to 'review the rules,' though I still don't understand your theory that women are incapable of opening doors."

"Just humor me. Kitten gets here. You make small talk, and you .."

"I open the car door, accompanying the gesture with a compliment regarding her choice of apparel."

"Good. Then you drive ..."

"Below the speed limit. I have been driving for over a year without incident, Tony."

Tony grinned. "You haven't driven with a girl in the passenger seat." He waved away Gus's next protest. "When you get there you .."

"I purchase tickets, popcorn, a beverage, and anything else she may desire."

"Because ..."

"Because 'the woman is always right.'" Gus's hands tensed as though preparing to strangle his unwanted mentor.

Cathryn's emergence from the woods rescued Minh from her struggle to contain her laughter.

"Looking good, Cat. I didn't know you owned short sleeves."

"It's my mom's. We had our own vintage fashion show tonight, and I couldn't resist."

Minh couldn't remember the last time she'd seen her friend so happy. *Lover-boy-in-training better not mess this up.*

Cathryn and Gus exchanged small talk until Gus, as directed, opened the door. Minh chuckled and wheeled toward Tony's burnt orange truck, but Tony moved in front of her.

"You think I don't follow my own rules?"

"I can get in myself, Tony." She'd need to use the grab handle hoist herself into the behemoth, but she but was confident she could manage.

"I'm sure Kitten can too."

"This isn't a date, Tony." Minh pinched the bridge of her nose to ward off the on-coming headache. Tony meant well, but sometimes "helping" was better classified as "annoying."

"I don't date my nonna, but I still open the door for her."

"I'm not a seventy-four-year-old invalid."

Tony groaned. "Look, Minh. Sometimes you gotta let a guy be a knight in shining armor, for *his* sake, not yours. Now, I got this friend. He's an eight-foot mountain of a guy, but he's a real softie. I'm not setting him up with a human cactus."

Minh's jaw dropped. "Where do I even begin? I don't know what's worse: setting me up without asking, or thinking I need help getting a date. What makes you think I'd even be interested in your eight-foot mountain of mush?"

Tony matched her volume. "He's a good guy, a *great* guy. He spends his weekends helping old ladies with their groceries. Besides, he likes art, and he has a tattoo. But if you're scared like all the other girls, I'll tell him you're not interested."

Minh chewed the inside of her cheek. "What's his tattoo?"

"You'll have to see for yourself." Tony smirked. "Now Miss. I-Can-Do-Anything, can you let a guy do something nice for you?"

Minh's breath hissed through her clenched teeth. She refused to surrender a lifetime of fighting for her independence just to appease Tony's ego. Part of her wanted to show him just how "prickly" she could be, but the part of her that was transitioning to adulthood acknowledged he had a point. He was trying to show he cared, but accepting kindness wasn't her forte.

Maybe she just needed to set some ground rules.

"Okay," Minh said. "You can open the door for me. You can stand by in case I fall, and you can load my wheelchair into the back once I'm finished, but I transfer myself. Deal?"

"You the boss." Tony gave her a sharp nod and flung open the passenger door.

Minh wheeled as close as she could to the seat and locked her brakes. Her left leg spasmed briefly before she lifted it into the vehicle. She scooted as far forward as she could and took a steadying breath. The large gap and huge height difference made this a risky transfer. As much as she hated to admit it, Tony's presence reassured her.

Minh punched her left fist into the seat, grabbed the roof handle, and hoisted herself into the truck in one smooth motion. Her muscles complained, but the look on Tony's face made the exertion worth it.

Tony stowed her wheelchair and followed Gus's car out of the parking lot. He pursed his lips as he drove. "Patrick's a big guy."

"The mountain of mush?"

Tony nodded. "He'll want to lift you." He wiggled his jaw from side to side. "Just ask him to hold your purse or something, okay? He gets to help, and you get to show off your monster biceps."

Minh gifted Tony with a genuine smile. "I think I can manage that."

* * *

Gustaf's Transition Notes

If there is any benefit to my forced relocation, it is freedom from Nadia Moore. Nadia did not open doors; she burst through them like a conquistador. As usual, my parents secured funding from her father by implying I might one day become his son-in-law. I only agreed to the charade after they threatened to remove me from the academy and enroll me in a school closer to home.

Nadia frequently asked my opinion, which meant I was to praise her own. I expressed my honest opinion once and found her reaction immensely amusing. My parents did not.

Cathryn, however, exudes a calm humility in discussions, using her intelligence to encourage rather than belittle. Not that Cathryn is without foibles. She has the most aggravating habit of avoiding eye contact, as if meeting a person's eyes would incite them to strike her. She fidgets with her hair whenever anyone asks her a direct question, and her reluctance to displease others makes her true opinion difficult to ascertain.

For example, at the movie theater, she spotted a sign advertising kettle corn. She was appalled to learn I had never tasted it. She said it was "regular popcorn's more delectable cousin." However, she diminished her enthusiasm by stating I shouldn't feel obligated to purchase any "just because Tony decided to play matchmaker." I then realized the merit of Tony's rules. Having already committed to purchasing anything Cathryn desired, her contradictory statements did not hinder my decision. To her credit, she was correct. Kettle corn is far superior to traditional popcorn.

The movie was tiresome drivel, and I told Cathryn as much afterward. She laughed and said, "Yes, but . . ." She analyzed the film's portrayals of masculinity and femininity, explained the themes of friendship and compromise, and related the development of the car as a symbol of socioeconomic status. That she attained so much from a single movie was astonishing. Far more incredible was the metamorphosis she underwent when speaking.

Cathryn typically collapses in on herself as though attempting to avoid offending people with her physical presence. The longer she spoke, however, the more animated she became. She became . . . luminescent. That is an inadequate description, but I can't think of one more fitting. Regardless, the phenomenon made it difficult for me to focus on driving, just as Tony predicted.

Back at the library, I assembled my telescope, which I had packed in the trunk. I directed her attention to the planet Mars and several landmarks on the surface of the moon, but she was more interested in the stars. I reminded her stars were nothing more than burning spheres of gas. Her response was one I have come to know as quintessential Cathryn:

"Beautiful burning spheres of gas." The impish gleam in her eyes she'd clearly acquired from Minh, but the radiant smile was her own. "It's no wonder stars have inspired people for thousands of years. Think of it, the light we see began its journey over four years ago. Stars are inspiration for the artist, divinity for the worshiper, navigation for the pragmatist, and burning spheres of gas for the scientist. What else transcends so many perspectives?"

Seeing her glow in the moonlight like a celestial being herself, I had difficulty determining whether I was going into cardiac arrest, having a stroke, asphyxiating, or all three at once. My heart rate accelerated, my throat constricted, and my brain lost its capacity for intelligent thought.

Cathryn finished with the telescope. Her smile unraveled the last of my solidity.

"*I know tonight was the result of Tony's benevolent machinations, but I had a nice time. Thank you.*" *She gave me the most innocent peck on the cheek, her lips a flicker of warmth in the chill night air.*

As she faded into the woods, I was seized by a compulsion to spend my every penny on movie tickets and kettle corn.

Chapter 14

Minh stifled a yawn as a group of student council girls strutted past her. After a remarkably successful blind date, she'd spent almost every night texting the "eight-foot mountain of mush." She pounded her locker, but the lock must have jammed.

"Hey, Ink. How'd it go with Patrick the other night?" Tony smacked her locker higher up, and it opened. He took out his multitool and started fixing the busted latch.

"He has potential." More than potential, but she wasn't about to admit that to Tony.

"That's Minh's way of saying he's fabulous. I'll bet he even won over her dad." Cathryn gave Minh a taste of her own teasing as she approached from the girls' bathroom. *Another makeup day. I hope she's just trying to impress Gus.*

"You coming over today?" *Maybe she'll talk to me if we're alone.*

Cathryn shook her head. "I have a doctor's appointment."

"You sick again, Kitten?" Tony said, looking up from the lock. *He noticed too.*

"It's for my mom actually. She hates doctors, so I offered to go with her."

Tony nodded. "Nonna's the same way." He reached into his backpack. "Now that you're both here, I got something for you." Tony pulled out two chocolate bars.

"What's wrong, Tony?" Cathryn and Minh asked in unison.

"What? A guy can't spoil his favorite bookworm and his favorite doodle factory?"

Minh snatched the candy bar. "The chocolate buys my forgiveness for referring to my art as 'doodling,' but it doesn't get you out of answering the question."

Tony held up his hands. "All right, all right. You caught me. It's about my girl." He returned to tinkering with the latch as if he preferred mechanical problems to relational ones.

Minh and Cathryn exchanged a look.

"*You*, having problems with a girl?" Minh said.

"I should document this. It's a historical event."

"Ain't no problems with the girl." Tony emphasized every word with a hit to the locker. "She's cute. She's funny. She comes from a big family, wants loads of kids, *and* she can cook." He blew the dust out of the lock and frowned. "I like her. The folks like her. Nonna would like her too, except . . ."

"Spill it, Tony," Minh said.

He twisted his pliers a final time. "There's one little issue I'm hoping you two can help me, er, navigate."

"What is it, Tony?" Cathryn asked.

Tony shut Minh's locker and ran a hand through his hair. "She's Greek."

* * *

Beatrice paused as a white woman in a headscarf pushed past her and out of the doctor's office. The woman walked with the determined stride of one who wasn't sure whether to punch something or collapse onto the nearest soft surface and sob.

"Mom, you okay?" Cathryn asked.

"I remember that woman, but I can't place her. I just remember the sadness in her eyes." Beatrice shook her head. "Doesn't look like much has changed."

"Don't worry about that now." Cathryn took her arm, and they followed the nurse to the neurologist's office.

Beatrice sat next to her daughter in the least sterile doctor's room she'd ever entered. Apparently, the head of the Minnesota Neurology Association got to personalize his office. A Newton's cradle sat on the desk, but instead of a row of balls clicking together, Viking's helmets did. Vikings pens protruded from a Vikings cupholder. A signed game ball perched on the shelf, and a squadron of Vikings players stared at them from a poster on the far wall. The doctor was a fan. So was Beatrice's husband.

"We shouldn't have come. If your father finds out—"

"He won't." Cathryn squeezed her hand. "He didn't notice we came for testing. He won't find out we're getting the results."

Two different doctors had seen them before referring them to the head neurologist. With every follow-up appointment, the risk of discovery increased. Beatrice fidgeted with her hair, but the doctor's entrance cut off further argument.

"Mrs. Banks. Miss Banks. Good to see you again." Dr. Kuznetsov stroked his salt-and-pepper goatee as he pulled up Beatrice's file on his computer. "Do you have a family history of memory problems, Mrs. Banks?"

"I-I don't know. I wasn't close to my grandparents, and my parents died in a car crash when I was eighteen."

He nodded as if he'd expected that. "Dr. Hernández suggested your symptoms fit with chronic traumatic encephalopathy, or boxer's dementia, which would imply you've received frequent blows to the head."

He pulled his glasses down his nose and peered at her over the thin frames, piercing eyes bright against his pale skin. Beatrice stopped breathing. *I knew this was a bad idea.* Cathryn squeezed her hand.

The doctor pushed his glasses back into place. "I suspect he is on the right track, but I doubt CTE is the only issue. You're far too young to be symptomatic, and your memory loss is progressing at a much faster rate than typical. Another factor must be accelerating the decline."

Beatrice swallowed. "What do you mean?"

Dr. Kuznetsov launched into an explanation, but Beatrice couldn't follow him. What she did catch, she didn't understand. Words like corpus callosum and prefrontal cortex sounded like a foreign language.

"Cathryn, what did he say?"

"He says parts of your brain aren't working."

The doctor continued, this time addressing Cathryn. He seemed accustomed to bypassing patients. Offended, Beatrice tried to focus, but the words zipped by in a jumbled rush. She caught the phrases "neurofibrillary tangles" and "progressive cognitive decline," but couldn't put meaning to them.

"You mean like Alzheimer's?" Cathryn asked.

"CTE and Alzheimer's are similar, yes, but this is a unique presentation, and we cannot be sure of a diagnosis until autopsy."

Beatrice's stomach dropped at the word "autopsy," but the doctor spoke even faster now that Cathryn demonstrated she understood. Cathryn's face drained of blood until she resembled a white-marble statue, her eyes glassy and expressionless.

The doctor prattled on. He pointed to images on a diagram and handed Cathryn several thick pamphlets. Cathryn jotted something on the back of one. Knowing her, it was a list of book recommendations for researching on her own.

"Take however long you need," the doctor said in lieu of goodbye.

"What did he say?"

Cathryn squeezed her hands. "He said your brain is ... dying."

"Dying?"

"Mom, it's already gotten worse. You don't notice because I compensate for you. I've gone through a dozen systems to help you remember your schedule."

Beatrice tightened her grip on her daughter's hand as the words sank in. When Cathryn continued, her voice was steady.

"They can't reverse it. There are experimental medications that might slow the process, but the results haven't been promising. Even if you wanted to try, Medicaid won't cover an experimental treatment, assuming we could even get Dad to agree to it."

Beatrice leaned back in her chair. *My brain is dying.* What would she forget next? What had she already forgotten?

She looked at her daughter's eyes, whose color defied genetics. Cathryn had always been special. Beatrice remembered the first time she held her. She couldn't believe the nurses let her just walk out the door with her. Didn't caring for something so precious require advanced training?

In the end, the training came from Cathryn—one word at a time. Determination: Cathryn taking her first wobbly steps across the kitchen floor. Creativity: Cathryn building a cast of snow-people to play in her stories. Joy: Cathryn's face the first time she saw the library.

All those nights combing Cathryn's hair, drying her tears, encouraging her dreams—would Beatrice forget them? Would she forget the best thing to happen to her?

Beatrice straightened. *Never.* If she was to die, then she'd spend the last of her present ensuring her daughter had a future.

"How long?"

Cathryn opened her mouth, but no words left her trembling lips. Tears filled her eyes, and she swallowed.

"Three to five months."

* * *

Had Cathryn's classmates paid attention to her, they might have thought she was lost, but she knew exactly where she was going. She drifted through the crooked hallways of the over-renovated school, heading for the oldest wing. It most recently housed home ec, before the program fell prey to budget cuts, but the wing must have served a dozen functions over the years. Now the rooms stored broken equipment and spare parts, but rumors claimed the stoves still worked.

Even from the end of the hall, Cathryn could smell the weed.

The first and only time she'd sought drugs was after she'd gotten her first period. The flood of hormones coincided with a string of beatings, and the combination left her chasing oblivion. Her mother caught her investigating their neighbor's "recreational" plants. After a long lecture, they brainstormed escape plans.

No matter how difficult their lives became, Cathryn's mother never succumbed to despair. She'd stayed home with Cathryn the day after the doctor's appointment, but as soon as her father left for the evening, she put on her night uniform as if nothing had changed. When Cathryn objected, she'd grasped Cathryn's shoulders and said, "My life is ending, but yours isn't. I'll earn as much money as I can, and then you run. Find someplace safe, finish school, and make something of yourself." She hugged Cathryn tightly. "I love you."

Cathryn passed that evening weeping, but as she stepped into the school's old wing, she couldn't shed a tear. Her mother was dying, and something inside Cathryn was too.

Doing drugs was wrong. Even if her best friend's dad weren't a cop, Cathryn had seen enough people destroy their lives to know better, but she didn't care. She needed an escape from the pain ripping apart her heart, and there were stronger drugs than pot down that hallway.

"Cathryn?"

Cathryn jumped. "Gus? I-I thought you had science club today."

"You must have your days confused after missing yesterday. We were supposed to study together today."

Cathryn reached for her ponytail. *Shit.* "Sorry. I-I'm not feeling well."

"We noticed."

"We?"

"Tony, Minh, and me." Gus tilted his head as though debating saying his next words. "Cathryn, you are sick more than anyone I've ever met. Don't you think you should see a physician?"

"I'm fine, Gus. I . . . I . . ." Her stormy emotions threw her thoughts into turmoil, so she blurted the first excuse to pop into her head. "I have a migraine." She pinched the bridge of her nose. "It hurts worse than any headache I've ever had."

At least that last part wasn't a lie.

Gus peered down the hallway and wrinkled his nose. "If aspirin is insufficient, my parents have networked with every neurologist from here to New York. I'm sure they could refer you to a qualified practitioner."

Cathryn leaned her head against the brick behind her. She'd had enough of neurologists for a lifetime. "I'm fine. I just need to rest." She started toward the exit, but Gus followed her.

"I could drive—"

"No!"

They both halted. Gus blinked, as if unsure how to respond to her outburst.

Pull yourself together. Cathryn forced a chuckle. "I biked."

"Didn't it snow this morning?"

"It's melted by now, and the bike lanes have anti-skid paint." Cathryn knew her answers wouldn't satisfy him. The coming interrogation was written across his face, but she couldn't fake a smile and spin lies when she wanted to burst into tears and scream profanity.

She left. Let him interrogate the wall. It would give him more answers than she could.

Gus pursued her. She quickened her pace, but his long legs easily matched it.

"You answered a question wrong in English. You didn't even speak to Minh at lunch, and now you're wandering the halls near the old wing. This is hardly typical behavior."

Why can't he leave me alone? Cathryn wove around a pillar, but Gus reconnected with her on the other side.

"You're overreacting. It's just a migraine." Cathryn cut sharply around the corner.

Gud overtook her. "Cathryn, I must insist. You are clearly unwell. At least allow me to drive you home."

Cathryn took a deep breath. If she wanted to escape her life, she first had to escape her friend. "I can take care of myself."

She marched into the girls' bathroom, forced the rusty window open, and climbed out of the building. By the time she reached the bike racks, the cold had leached the dexterity from her fingers. After warming them with her breath, she tried to spin the combination, but the melted snow had dripped into the hinges, freezing the metal lock shut. She let it clang against the wheel. *I don't want to go home anyway.*

She didn't want to get high either. Five minutes ago, she would've smoked, snorted, or swallowed any drug offered to her, but her encounter with had Gus shifted her perspective. Her friends cared about her.

Cathryn closed her eyes and tried to calm her brain enough to think straight. She needed someplace—a safe place—to dump all this pain and pull herself together. Someplace quiet, and calm, and free of distractions. She flicked her eyes open. She knew exactly where to go.

Cathryn rose from her crouch and strode back to the school's entrance, but as she rounded the corner, she collided into Gus. Melted snow soaked the bottom of her jeans as she plopped onto the pavement.

"I'm sorry," they said simultaneously.

Gus cleared his throat. "I apologize for being a— What is it Minh calls me? An overbearing nitpicker?"

Cathryn almost smiled. "I'm sorry too. I'm not myself today." She let him help her to her feet. "Could you drive me to the library?"

Gus furrowed his brow. "The library?"

"Mr. Zabinski keeps some peppermint tea in his desk. He swears it's the best cure for headaches." Another true statement. *How messed up is your life when you count your truths but lose track of your lies?*

Gus retrieved a box of fireplace matches from his glove compartment—no doubt leftover from rocket-launching. He managed to melt her combination lock, and together they loaded her bike into his trunk. They drove to the library in silence, and Cathryn's nerves settled.

Mr. Zabinski raised his eyebrows when he saw her. "I thought you had a study date."

"He, uh, cancelled." Cathryn gestured to the back room. "You said we might get a new shipment of books today?"

Mr. Zabinski grinned. "We did. I was planning to unpack the boxes myself, but now that you're here, I think I shall let a younger pair of arms handle the heavy lifting."

Cathryn proceeded to the back room, opened the case of new books, and filled her lungs with the scent that was infinitely better than marijuana. She stuck her entire face inside the box, not caring that she looked ridiculous. She needed this.

As she unpacked the books, she also unloaded her stress. After a few minutes, Mr. Zabinski brought her some tea, which helped her further unwind. They worked in a comfortable silence, with Mr.

Zabinski applying the catalogue labels and Cathryn shelving. She lost herself in the methodical task.

After she settled the last book in its new home, Cathryn dismantled the boxes.

"Thank you for the extra help, my dear."

"No problem. I needed the distraction."

"Oh?"

Cathryn paused for a half-second before flattening the last box. "I've had a lot of tests this month. It's nice to do something mindless."

She glanced at the clock. 5:45. She didn't want to go home, but her mother needed her. Now more than ever.

"I have to get going. See you tomorrow." Cathryn grabbed her coat from the hook and headed toward the door.

"Cathryn?"

She turned around.

Mr. Zabinski lowered his chin and lifted his eyebrows. "If you need help yourself, all you need do is ask."

A thousand words caught in Cathryn's throat, but she shook her head. "Thank you, but I'm fine." She gave him a peck on the cheek and returned home to face her life head on.

* * *

Cathryn's Diary

If there is an entity in this world who answers prayers, it is Mr. Zabinski. Without his mentorship, I would never have learned the power of books. I'd spend my afternoons in the old wing with the stoners instead of in the story circle with the children.

He by himself has done more to promote literacy among the impoverished than all the state politicians combined. In the summer, he will often buy me lunch under the guise of a "summer bonus." He must believe me too proud to ask for help, but too poor to refuse it.

In truth, it isn't pride that prevents me from approaching him. The library is my sanctuary, my home. Defiling it with the taint of the rest of my life is unthinkable. I know Mr. Zabinski wants to help. He doesn't realize that he already has.

Chapter 15

G us dug his heels into the living room carpet.

"No." He savored the word.

"Excuse me?" His mother's thin lips tightened like a rubber band about to snap.

"I will not pander to some neurologist's daughter so you can swindle funds out of him."

His mother snapped at the maid to signal her to move a vase of flowers to the end table. "He is not 'some' neurologist. He is the head of the Minnesota Neurology Association, and I will remind you our research pays for your education."

"I will remind *you* I attend public school now, or have you forgotten the reason we're here?"

"Those accusations were false." Her voice rose to a screech. *They weren't false; this is proof.*

"This is ridiculous. What do you expect, that we'll marry and provide you with genius descendants?"

"That would be an acceptable outcome." His father stood from his chair, the first sign of his own rising temper. "Gustaf, any girl we arrange for you to meet would make an adequate partner. What is your objection?"

"I'm sixteen; I prefer to make my own choices, and I find their company intolerable."

"What do you expect, to fall in love?" His mother's dry sarcasm leached the emotion out of the word. She moved the vase back to its original location. "Love is fiction invented by people who don't understand neuropsychology."

"What does that make arranged marriages? The favorite pastime of antiquated charlatans?"

"Mind your tone, Gustaf." His father's scowl hardened into white granite.

"Stop being so dramatic," his mother said as she straightened a painting. "This is hardly an arranged marriage. It's just networking. To get anywhere in life, you must protect your interests. We are *very* interested in the doctor, so you must be *very* interested in his daughter."

Shortly after Gus hit puberty, his parents discovered that—if he kept his mouth shut—girls found him attractive. Eager to capitalize on parental overindulgence, they dangled Gus in front of every spoiled snob with a trust fund before asking her parents for donations. Only after the money stopped flowing was Gus permitted to speak freely. Girls often claimed they were "moving in different directions" when breaking up with him. They didn't know the half of it.

The doorbell rang, cutting through the room's tension. His mother's heels clicked on the hallway's hardwood floor. His father squeezed his shoulder.

"You will behave, or you will have no car and no contact with your friends."

Gus gritted his teeth. *Two more years.* Less than two years until graduation, and then he could escape this twisted game and say goodbye to his parents forever.

Voices in the hallway grew clearer as his mother led their guests to the living room.

"Thank you for the invitation, Mrs. Hein. It's hard to find people who appreciate good tea."

"We're delighted to host you, Dr. Kuznetsov. Doctor, Lydia—our son, Gustaf."

False pleasantries exchanged, they took their seats while the maid/cook served tea. Gus's mother sent a scorching glare toward his father's mug of coffee. Apart from espresso, she believed coffee was an uncivilized form of caffeine, especially the black sludge Gus's father took strong enough to stand a knife up in.

Gus tried and failed to return the maid's smile as he accepted a cup of herbal tea. She'd lasted several weeks, longer than any before her. He ought to learn her name now. *Cathryn would've known her whole life story after day one.*

"It's lovely to finally meet you, Lydia," Gus's father said. "How is your senior year progressing?"

Lydia opened her mouth, but her father answered for her.

"Straight A's, as always. She'll be studying microbiology at MIT next fall." Lydia's smile stiffened. She clenched a pleat of her earth-green skirt.

Gus's mother beamed. "How wonderful. Too many young girls fall into"—she lowered her voice—"the liberal arts."

As the conversation continued, Gus felt his face twist into the scowl he avoided making around Cathryn. His parents laughed too loudly at the doctor's jokes and agreed with each of his opinions. *Is there no limit?* Gus choked when they declared themselves Vikings fans. His parents always spent Super Bowl Sunday sailing near their favorite resort.

His mother glared at him out of the corner of her eye, and he forced a smile toward Lydia. She returned a more graceful smile and batted her eyelashes. *Naïve fool.* She shifted in her chair and placed a delicate hand on her father's forearm.

"Father, I hate to interrupt, but I don't have your tolerance for sitting. May I stretch my legs?" Her tone dripped with sweetness.

Gus's father answered, "Gustaf, show the young lady to the garden."

Gus resisted the urge to roll his eyes and led Lydia to the backyard, where frosted plants competed with garden gnomes for the title of most depressing. Gus couldn't recall which of the unsightly statues had been his mother's excuse for firing the gardener. He knew the real reason, of course. Same reason he was now socializing with a neurologist's daughter.

As soon as the door closed behind them, Lydia slouched against it. "Thank God. I thought they'd never let us out. Hey, you got a light?"

"I beg your pardon?"

"Oh great, you're as stiff as they are. Don't tell me you believe we're soul mates?" She picked up a gnome and squinted at its scratched face.

Gus snorted. "My parents hope to con your father out of grant money."

"Well, he'll happily dole out as much as they want if it means you'll straighten me out. He's never accepted that I'm an actress, not a biologist." She dropped the statue, and the black waves of her hair rippled as she shook her head. "Let's get out of here."

"How do you propose we do that?"

She brushed the dirt off her fingers and gave him a sly smile. "Amateur."

He followed her back to the living room where she again donned the guise of a debutante.

"Father, Gustaf has never seen St. Anthony Falls. May we take a walk over the Stone Arch Bridge while you finish your tea?"

"The falls are across town. Another time."

"The weather won't hold out much longer. Please." Gus had never seen more pathetic eyes.

"We'd be happy to host you as long as you like, Dr. Kuznetsov, and I'm sure Gustaf would appreciate touring the town with such a charming local." His mother's voice was as sickening as Lydia's.

"Very well. Return in time to leave for supper."

After a barely controlled exit, Lydia checked her reflection in Gus's rearview mirror. She grimaced and put a nose ring through her left nostril. "That'll have to do. Drop me off at Hard Luck Café. I told my boyfriend I'd meet him there."

"You planned this?"

She laughed. "Rebellion doesn't come easy to you, does it. Isn't there anywhere you'd rather be?"

"I prefer almost anything to tea with my parents."

"Great. Drop me off, do whatever good-looking stiffs like you do in their spare time, and pick me up in an hour and a half."

May as well. Gus started the engine. Lydia's jaw unhinged. "Classical music? Really?"

"Beethoven was a mathematical genius, but if you insist." He switched the track to Raketenwerfer. It fit his mood better anyway.

A smile slithered onto Lydia's face as the car filled with heavy metal. "Now this is more like it."

Gus followed her directions to the café and grimaced at the sight of its graffiti-like exterior. He'd barely finished parking before Lydia was out the door.

"Later gator."

Gus shook his head at her retreating back. *Now what?* Everything he wanted was in his study, but he couldn't return home without Lydia. He drove without thinking, his only desire to distance himself from the grungy café. He let his frustration seep into the music; its beat drove his pulse. Before he realized it, he'd parked in front of the Lewis Library. He shut off the engine, and his heart beat louder in the sudden silence. *What are the odds she's here?*

He found her behind the front desk. Her face was drawn, but her hair was neatly tied in her ponytail, and her posture straighter than he'd seen in days. *At least her migraines are fading.*

Cathryn squinted at a picture book with such intensity that she didn't notice his approach.

"*Galab ah ay*—" She looked up when his shadow covered her page. "*Galab wanaagsan,* um"—she shook her head—"Hi. Sorry. They moved me up a level in Somali, so I'm practicing." She rubbed her eyes, which were still underlined with bags but no longer sank into dark circles. "Well, trying to practice." She cleared her throat. "You didn't come to hear about my trouble focusing. What can I do for you?"

Gus opened his mouth. *I have no idea.* "I thought I'd go for a walk by St. Anthony Falls—"

Cathryn's tired eyes sparked with interest. "By the old mill ruins?"

"Yes." *I hope.* "I thought perhaps you'd like to accompany me."

"Um . . . I don't—"

"Fresh air will be good for you, my dear," Mr. Zabinski called from across the room, "You've been as gloomy as the weather lately."

Cathryn tightened her ponytail. "I need to be home by six."

"I need to be home by five."

She bit her lip and examined the picture book. *Brilliant, Gus. Way to be a complete fool.*

"Forget I asked."

"Wait"—Cathryn's smile drove the clouds from her expression —"let me grab my coat."

A minute later, she looked at him expectantly from the passenger seat.

He swallowed his nerves. "I'm afraid I'm turned around. Do you know the way from here?"

"Minh and I usually take the bus, but I think there's a parking lot past the Guthrie."

That would help if I knew what a Guthrie was. "I'll follow your lead," he said as he started the car.

Cathryn jumped as heavy metal blared from the speakers.

"Sorry." He fumbled with the controls.

"It's okay. It just startled me. If you like being screamed at in German, I'm not one to judge. I've spent so much time around Mr. Zabinski I've developed a taste for classical."

Gus stifled a chuckle. "Beethoven it is."

He followed Cathryn's directions to the Guthrie, which turned out to be a blue-walled theater perched above the Mississippi River. Gus parked in the lot beyond it, and Cathryn pointed out the mill ruins.

"There's a museum if you're interested, but I suppose that takes the fresh air out of a walk."

"The benefit of inviting a human encyclopedia is having a built-in tour guide."

Cathryn's smile stole his breath for three heartbeats. *How does she do that?* Lydia was far prettier, yet her smile made his stomach curdle. Cathryn's was unlike any he'd ever seen. No duplicity, no snobbery, no selfishness—it was a gift.

Cathryn chatted about the explosion that destroyed the mill, but her voice became a bell choir. She gestured toward the ruins, but Gus's eyes refused to leave her smile, as though the chilly air had frozen them. He watched her breath puff between unpainted lips, and the sway of her ponytail hypnotized him.

"Gus?"

Focus. "Fascinating."

"You're a terrible liar. I'm sorry. I get excited, and I can't stop."

"No, that's not it." *I'd better research this mill.* "I was thinking about the Guthrie. Would you like to see a play sometime?"

"I'd love to, but Minh's mom says they're playing *Macbeth.* I distinctly remember declaring you a traitor to the English language for your dislike of Shakespeare."

True. He thought back to *Grease.* "Well, I've never experienced Shakespeare with you. You have a way of making the banal intriguing. I like that."

Cathryn's smile spread into her rosy cheeks. "Okay, but only if we also do something that interests you. What do you actually enjoy?"

"Aside from debate and martial arts? Propulsion, thermodynamics, pyrotechnics—"

Cathryn laughed.

"You find that amusing?"

"You basically told me you like to blow things up. Proof no matter how high your IQ, you're still a boy playing with matches."

"What does that make you?"

Cathryn grinned. "A girl who can make insipid chatter about lip gloss in three languages."

Laughter burst out of him. Brief, but genuine.

"I've never heard you laugh. I like it."

Gus cleared his throat, grateful his cheeks were already flushed from the cold. "Shall we walk?"

Cathryn nodded. "You can see the falls from the Stone Arch Bridge. Both have an interesting history, but I'll spare you another lecture."

Gus's hand twitched to take hers as they walked. He put his fists in his pockets, telling himself he did it to warm them. These temperatures at the academy would have had all activities moved indoors, but Minnesotans seized the season's last opportunities for "fresh air." A biker passed a bundled dog walker on the path below. A pair of children raced to the bridge, the look on their parents' faces testifying to their need to run off some energy. There was even a man jogging in shorts. *Either he's a lunatic, or Tony wasn't exaggerating about winter.*

They approached the bridge, but the sound of the falls didn't travel well in the chill air. Gus's sense of smell was likewise blocked in his not-yet-runny nose. As they descended the stairs, Cathryn stumbled. Gus caught her by her upper arm, and she cried out.

"I'm sorry. Did I hurt you?"

"No." Cathryn pulled her arm away, which further destabilized her. Gus wrapped an arm around her to prevent her from tumbling down the stairs.

She steadied herself and gestured to her arm. "It's just a bruise. My bike skidded on the ice the other day."

"You should forego biking in winter. Anti-skid bike lanes or not, you have a penchant for hurting yourself." They stood so close their breath merged into one cloud between them. Gus wondered whether the rosy skin of her cheek would feel warm or cold, how soft it was.

She met his gaze. "Thank you for catching me." The world blurred until Gus saw only Cathryn's eyes. He'd never noticed the elegance in their odd coloring. *How could I miss that?* He pulled her a half step closer.

His watch alarm broke them apart.

"I have to get going." He fumbled with the alarm. *I shouldn't have fixed it.* "The falls will have to wait." Cathryn fiddled with her ponytail. They maintained six inches between them during the walk back.

When they reached the car, Gus opened the door for Cathryn, realizing after he did that he hadn't given a thought to Tony's rules.

"Thank you," Cathryn said as she took her seat. "You have no idea how much I needed the fresh air."

Her smile made his head spin. *Not as much as I do now.*

* * *

Cathryn put her clean clothes in her closet.

"Will you bring me my night uniform, please?" Her mother called from downstairs.

Cathryn retrieved the night uniform from the secret compartment and descended the stairs to find her mother on the floor. At first, Cathryn thought she'd fallen, but her lips moved silently, and her hands rested neatly in her lap. She was praying.

The past few weeks, she'd told Cathryn, "The Good Lord will give me the strength to see you free, and He'll send someone to care for you after I'm gone." Cathryn thought "The Good Lord" had made their lives miserable enough, but she wasn't about to contradict a dying woman's faith.

The dingy lamplight cast shadows on her mother's thin body, seeking out the crevices in the bags below her eyes. Even her whispered prayer sounded weak. *She can't keep doing this.* For Cathryn's entire life, her mother had arranged clandestine playdates, fought for Cathryn's education, and gone hungry so Cathryn could eat. Her crooked arm testified to all the times she'd used her own body to shield Cathryn from her father's blows. *Time for a role reversal.* She'd sacrificed to give Cathryn a better life. Cathryn would sacrifice to give her a better death.

Cathryn knelt in front of her mother. "Mom, you quit your night job, remember? Your other boss gave you a raise, and we decided you didn't need it."

"I did? Oh." Her mother's acceptance of the lie disturbed Cathryn, but she had to get used to serving as an external memory.

"Why don't you head to bed early?"

"Okay, sweetheart. I'm so blessed to have a daughter like you."

Cathryn waited until her mother fell asleep before she put on the night uniform. Her father always told her she was the spitting image of her mother. Tonight, she'd find out if he was right.

* * *

Cathryn's Diary

Not only did Mr. Sanders fail to notice that the Beatrice Banks who came to work last night was twenty years younger than the one he'd hired, he didn't realize I wasn't one of the Hispanic women who comprised a portion of his staff. His eyes never left his cracked clipboard as he yelled at me in broken Spanish. I took a chance and replied, "Sí, señor." He waved me onward.

The other employees noticed within seconds. When I told them my mother was sick, but we still needed her income, they nodded with sympathy, but no pity. I knew Rosa María and Pilar from Story Time. Thankfully, my mother was assigned to their group.

My mother's night job is for a cleaning company that dispatches small teams to restaurants and movie theaters after hours. Once I got into the rhythm of scrubbing and rinsing, I chatted in Spanish with the others. They told me of their kids' latest exploits and described new developments on a TV drama that had them hooked.

In a strange way, I felt more at home with them than with my classmates. They cherished the small joys in their lives: walking around Lake Nokomis, joking with their friends, watching their children learn to love books in Story Time. My classmates are more concerned with who has the latest cell phone.

Those women laughed at each other's stories, encouraged each other's dreams, and prayed for each other's worries. They all suffered from exhaustion, but not one shied away from hard work. They reminded me of a quote from Theodore Roosevelt: "Courage is not having the strength to go on; it is going on when you don't have the strength."

If I possessed half their courage, I could accomplish anything.

* * *

Mark jumped back as his wife slammed the bedroom door in his face. Again.

"Honey—"

"We have a huge house. Find somewhere else to sleep."

Mark rested his forehead against the door frame. Lately, no matter what he said, he was wrong. He shouldn't have reminded her the new meds might help. Help wasn't enough. Laurel didn't want to *improve*, she wanted to return to *normal*, but the doctor advised they adjust to a new normal.

His feet sank into the plush carpet as he passed the rooms that once held their dreams for a family. They now stood vacant and mournful, like mausoleums for people who'd long since decayed into dust.

The cherry-wood grandfather clock chimed as he neared the kitchen. It hadn't worked when he'd inherited it, but after a little research online, he'd repaired it himself. Now, all it needed was weekly winding.

Mark opened the glass face, inserted the crank into the winding point, and turned. The weight rose smoothly in front of the pendulum. He repeated the process with the other two weights, wishing he had a magic crank to lift his wife's spirits. If only his marriage were as easily maintained as the clock.

Mark smiled as he rubbed the spot he'd deliberately left unstained. The clock had earned that particular nick during a rolling pin sword fight when Mark was ten, and he would never paint over it. The intricate design and beautiful chime added to the clock's value, but that penny-sized notch was priceless.

At some point, he and his wife started viewing each other's scratches and dents as flaws instead of treasures. Laurel used to accept his quirks with a chuckle, but now she chafed at the slightest irritation. Mark used to admire his wife's ambition. Now, he wished she'd take joy in the life they had. She saw herself as broken, but to Mark, she would always be beautiful.

Mark settled himself on the couch. Laurel had rightly pointed out they had plenty of guest rooms, but he didn't need this mansion to be happy. He'd spend the rest of his days in a one-room shack as long as Laurel lived there with him.

*　*　*

Cathryn smiled at the children as they dropped their cards in the box and filed out to their parents.

"See you next week." In English Story time, she'd read *Boxes for Katje* by Candace Fleming. The book was set in Holland after World War II and related the tale of a girl who became pen pals with an

American. The American girl sent food and winter clothes, and, in the end, the Dutch girl sent her a box of tulip bulbs.

To help the children connect with the story, Cathryn had them make cards for people in the hospital. Since many of the children were less fortunate themselves, Mr. Zabinski paid for the supplies. "There is power in giving, especially when you have little yourself," he'd said. Cathryn wondered whether he spoke from experience.

After the children departed, Cathryn set the box behind the front desk. She checked the clock. *Half an hour until dinner, check on Mom, an hour for homework, then night shift.* Her energy drained more with every task she listed.

"Miss Cat?" A girl—who Cathryn guessed was five, but most people would estimate was only three—tugged on her pant leg. Had her hair been clean, it would have been white enough to glow in the dark. "Can you read one more story?"

"Story Time is over for today. Who is picking you up?" Cathryn learned long ago that in this neighborhood you didn't ask about mom and dad, because many kids lived with their grandparents or aunts and uncles.

The girl bent to reapply the duct tape that held her left shoe together. "Mom's asleep."

She gestured to a chair in the corner where a woman snored. Cathryn guessed the woman was in her late twenties, though she looked in her mid-forties. She wore sunglasses, and scabs pocked the inside of her arm.

"Please?" begged the girl. Tears welled in her blue eyes, but what decided Cathryn were the bruises that showed beneath her oversized T-shirt.

"All right, one more." Cathryn sat in a beanbag chair and settled the girl into her lap. She brushed the girl's matted hair behind her ears, just as her father used to do with her. The girl snuggled into Cathryn, who had to blink away tears to see the text.

"*The Fantastic Flying Books of Mr. Morris Lessmore,* by William Joyce . . ."

* * *

Cathryn's Diary

I wish I could have told her it gets better, taught her how to survive. I wish I could have given her hope, but I know better. I can't teach what I don't know, and I can't give what I don't have.

I offered her the only thing I could—something most people count as nothing, but for people like us, it's everything. I gave her fifteen minutes of feeling safe.

Mr. Zabinski was right. There is power in giving.

Chapter 16

Cathryn squinted at the board, but the letters merged into one another. She blinked to clear her vision, and an apple-shaped bruise on her left wrist caught her eye. She pulled her sleeve to cover it, but the fabric slipped through her fingers and sprang farther up her forearm. When she grasped it again, it liquefied in her hands. A purple puddle of what had once been her sleeve pooled beneath her desk. Inch by inch her sleeve melted. It didn't stop when it reached her shoulder.

Cathryn hugged herself to salvage what was left of her shirt, but it dribbled over her arms. She splashed what she could reach back onto herself, but it slipped off as though she were waterproof. Left with only her bra for covering, she resembled a snow leopard—pale skin splotched with bruises. Her classmates turned as one to stare. Her teacher's glare demanded an explanation.

"Cathryn Banks!"

Cathryn jolted awake to the snickering of her classmates. Mr. Bard, her chemistry teacher, resembled a baking soda volcano mid-eruption.

"If my lesson bores you, you're welcome to teach it yourself."

"I'm sorry, Mr. Bard. I didn't sleep well last night. It won't happen again." Night shifts took their toll. *Mom managed. I can too.*

Gus assessed her with a worried scowl, as if he didn't believe her excuse but hadn't collected enough evidence to disprove it. Cathryn tried to give him a reassuring smile but yawned instead. She made a mental note to buy caffeine.

* * *

Tony finished his last lap and dropped to a walk.

"Good time, Giordani," Coach Karne said. The gym teacher had tried to recruit Tony for the wrestling team but had to settle for P.E. Tony did enough wrestling with his cousins.

Tony stopped near a basketball hoop to stretch while Cathryn stumbled near the end of the line of runners. She rounded a corner, and her uncoordinated jog devolved into a gymnast's nightmare. She collided with the heavyset girl in front of her. The other girl continued with a huff, but Cathryn collapsed in a heap of knees and elbows. She untangled her limbs and leaned her head against the chipped tile on the wall.

Coach Karne's whistle cut through the sneaker squeaks. "Banks, if Matheson can run a mile, so can you."

Cathryn struggled to her feet but tripped again and hit the floor. Tony weaved through his red-faced classmates to reach her.

"You okay, Kitten?"

"I was up all last night studying for our chemistry test. I guess I overdid it."

"Studying, eh?" Tony helped her to her feet.

Her weak smile did nothing to brighten the dark circles under her eyes. "I'm fine, really."

Tony kept her on track as she finished the run, but his mind replayed their conversation. Yesterday afternoon, he'd lifted weights with Gus. Cute and Clueless spent fifteen minutes jabbering about the chemistry test they'd taken the day before.

Tony shrugged. Maybe honors students had more than one test each week.

* * *

Minh doodled on her bedpost while Cathryn stared at her textbook. Lately, the only way to spend time with Cat was during "study dates," but this afternoon, not even history homework held

Cathryn's interest. She sat in the same position—eyes glazed over and fingers in her ponytail—long enough for Minh to ink a portrait.

"Cat, what's up with you?"

Cathryn twirled her hair.

"Cat?" Minh rolled her eyes. "You know, I think *Don Quixote* is the dumbest book ever written." Insulting "one of the most important works of Spanish literature" should have earned Minh a twenty-minute lecture, but Cathryn's expression appeared carved in stone. Her glass-eyed gaze remained fixed on the textbook whose pages she never turned.

Minh threw her pen at her friend. "Cat."

Cathryn jumped. "Jeez Minh, you don't have to yell."

"I've been trying to get your attention for the last fifteen minutes. What is with you?"

Cathryn shifted in her seat. "Nothing. I'm just swamped. My classes are a lot harder this year."

"B.S. You memorized the first three sections of the dictionary—for fun. No way your classes are too hard." Minh's bed creaked as she leaned forward. "I may not have a photographic memory, but I'm not stupid. What's going on?"

"Nothing."

"It's Gus, isn't it." Minh clenched her fist. "I never thought you'd be one of those girls who ditches her friend for a boy."

"What? No. It's not Gus. I'm just tired. Lay off."

"Tired. We've been friends for almost twelve years, and you expect me to believe you're tired?" She put all the heat she could muster into her glare. Cathryn looked at her backpack, the closet, the dresser—anything but Minh's face. Her eyes landed on the clock. 5:20.

"Let me guess," Minh said. "You need to get home for dinner."

"My mom is sick. I need to leave." Cathryn packed her things and closed the door behind her with too much force.

Minh wasn't sure what worried her more: Cathryn's lie, or the possibility it wasn't a lie. *What did she mean by "sick?"*

* * *

Cathryn's Diary

Mom forgot Dad, or rather, she forgot the monster inside him.

The smell of something burnt greeted me when I came home from Minh's house. One glance told me there was no salvaging the pot. Mom emerged from the bathroom with a smile lighting her face.

"Go wash up. Your father will be home soon."

The door opened, and my mother threw herself into my father's arms. Her eyes shown with the blissful naïveté of a newlywed as she kissed him. My legs stiffened into planks. A warning caught in my throat. I waited for the nightmare to begin.

He kissed her. Not the ferocious kiss of a man demanding more, but the tender kiss of a lover. His eyes held the same adoration that filled hers as he stroked her hair. I felt faint. Too much time had passed since I'd taken a breath. My father's smile lacked any trace of its usual tension.

Then he saw the stove.

His smile mutated into a snarl; his face rippled as if his blood were a raging river beneath his skin. The light vanished from his eyes. My mother never saw the blow coming.

She pulled her hand away from her nose and stared at the blood dripping from her fingertips. Her expression shifted from shock to horror to recognition, as if she'd stored her memories of his abuse on a shelf, and his blow knocked them loose. She wasn't prepared for his punch to her ribs.

My mother's cry released my legs from their invisible shackles, and I rushed between them. From there, I only remember the emotions, the disorienting mixture of fear, desperation, and anger that took control of me.

I woke to the taste of blood in my mouth, the stab of pain behind my eyes, and the sound of my mother reciting the Lord's Prayer. I didn't have the heart to tell her God stopped listening years ago.

My mother believes my father's rage is driven by his fear of failure and abandonment. Perhaps it began that way, but now I think he seeks control. When he isn't drunk on alcohol, my father is drunk on power.

I wish I could go to school, but even if Dad unlocks the door, no amount of makeup will disguise my eye being swollen shut. At school, my biggest worries are keeping Minh from strangling Gus and preventing Gus from hurting Tony's feelings.

I wish I were there. I could use a friend right now.

* * *

Cathryn stared at her desk as Mrs. West approached, hand outstretched for her paper.

"I didn't finish it." Cathryn delivered the news in a whisper, as if saying it quieter would make it less true. "As George Washington said, 'Better to offer no excuse than a bad one.'"

When the bell signaled the end of class, Mrs. West called her to her desk.

"Cathryn, this isn't the quality of work I expect from you. You have several overdue assignments. You've been absent at least once a week, and when you are in class, you're distracted. I heard you fell asleep in science."

Cathryn bit the inside of her lip to keep from crying. *Mom wants me to finish school.*

"You're the only one I haven't seen counting down to winter break." Mrs. West leaned over the orderly stacks of papers on her desk. "Cathryn, is everything all right at home? You can tell me. This is a safe space."

Cathryn wanted to tell her winter break meant a tense week of "family time" spent trapped between her father's love and his rage. She pinched a bruise on her forearm. *Dad will find out.*

"Everything's fine. My mom's been sick with a nasty flu, so I've been helping around the house." *"Half a truth is often a great lie." I hope Benjamine Franklin was right about that.* "She's okay now. I just need to catch up on sleep."

Mrs. West didn't look as though she believed her, but she didn't press. Cathryn gathered her books and joined Gus in the hallway.

"Something wrong?" Gus asked.

"It's nothing." Cathryn blew by him, but he overtook her. He blocked her path, eyes questioning.

"Cathryn, what—"

"I'm fine."

"You're—"

"I said I'm fine." She mimicked his stony expression, dared him to contradict her even though her heart was pounding so hard he could probably see it through her shirt.

The warning bell saved her. She pushed past him, wondering how long before she got tangled in her own web of lies.

* * *

Cathryn's Diary

I am my father's daughter. There is a monster inside me too, and it's destroying my friendships. They just want to help, but when they get too close to the truth, the monster lashes out, pushes them away.

Every day I take one step closer to freedom, one step farther away from the people who care about me. The lies weigh so heavily upon my lips that I struggle to fake a smile. When I escape, will I still be me, or will I have liberated a monster?

I long for normalcy like the trees long for spring. I want to eat kettle corn at the movies, bike race Tony around the lake, gossip with Minh while we paint each other's nails. I want to let Gus hold my hand.

I can't afford such selfishness. They want to help, but they don't know the fire that burns in my father's eyes. My only hope is stealth. As soon as I have enough money, I'll slip away with Mom. No one will get hurt, unlike last time.

Is this the price of freedom? Must I forsake everyone I love to escape the one I fear?

Chapter 17

Cathryn closed her textbook, unable to focus on school. Jesus watched her from the photo pasted to her mother's prayer candle, his left hand covered by melting wax. Would he melt away? How much longer before Cathryn melted too?

"Why are you sad?" Cathryn's mother observed her from the bed. Every day she lost more of her memory, but she maintained her uncanny ability to read Cathryn's emotions.

"I'm not sad, Mom. Just tired."

"Well, come lie down. I need to get ready for work anyway."

Cathryn sat on the edge of the bed. "You don't work anymore, remember? You get disability benefits now."

Almost the truth. Cathryn filed the paperwork, but her father answered the return call. He accused her of hiding money and trying to leave him—exactly what she'd been doing. He beat her so badly she didn't wake until the next day. He apologized, but he didn't let her out of her room until Mrs. West, Mr. Bard, and Principal Evans each called to check on her. The extra money would have been worth the beating, but now it funneled straight to her father's drinking tab.

He'd been drinking more. Cathryn suspected deep down he knew his wife was ill. When Cathryn served him dinner, the truth sat in her mother's empty chair. She knew if her own chair were ever empty, her mother would pay the price, so she had dinner on the table by six. Each night she sat in her place and stared at the wall of silence that grew between them.

Outside of the dinner hour, Cathryn avoided her father, which was easier now that he spent more time at the bars. Once, Cathryn returned from the night shift at the same time he stumbled home drunk. The roof was too snowy to use her bedroom window, so she'd frozen outside the living room until he collapsed into bed. Thankfully, he hadn't thought to put locks on the windows yet. As long as he didn't lock her in her room on a night she had to work, she'd be okay.

"Why are you sad? Did you have a nightmare, Sweetie Kitty?"

Cathryn smiled at her childhood nickname. "No, Mom. I'm just tired."

"Well, come snuggle with Mama. You'll feel better."

When Cathryn was little, she'd often slept with her mother after waking from a nightmare. *Why not?* Cathryn lay in bed, and her mother wrapped the blanket over both of them. Cathryn breathed in her mother's scent, feeling every bit a little girl, safe in her mother's arms.

It was the best night's sleep she'd had in months.

* * *

Cathryn breezed by Mr. Sanders. After several weeks of working her mother's nightshifts, she no longer feared discovery. When she reached the locker room, Pilar and Rosa María were already deep in conversation, speaking Spanish in low voices.

"I completed the training, but it still makes me uncomfortable," Rosa María said as she zipped her uniform.

"So leave it at home."

Rosa María shook her head. "You know Antonio. He worries about me, but I'm a teacher for God's sake."

Rosa María often complained that her husband, a National Guard Sergeant, was overprotective, but Pilar looked like she sided with him this time.

"You also work nights. To me, it makes sense to carry a gun, especially with that man loose in the neighborhood."

"What man?" Cathryn dared to interrupt. Their neighborhood lay just across the woods from her own.

"Yesterday, one of Hennepin County's most wanted, Sergio Ortiz, was spotted near Spruce Lane," Pilar said as she pulled her hair into a stubby ponytail. "He has a reputation for everything: robbery, sexual assault, drug trafficking . . . We should all be careful."

They finished their preparations in silence, but on the way to that night's assignment, Pilar insisted on buying pepper spray for Cathryn. Cathryn knew she ought to appreciate the gesture, but in truth, she couldn't worry about a new danger lurking in the streets. She was preoccupied enough with the one waiting for her at home.

* * *

Gus grabbed an extra notebook from his locker. Cathryn was absent. Again. He planned to copy his notes for her.

"Psst, Gus." Minh jerked her head in summons. Aside from Cathryn, the irascible artist understood him best. At times, he suspected she feigned ignorance to mock him. There was no sign of subterfuge in her features now.

"I'm worried about Cat." Minh always came straight to the point, which Gus admitted he appreciated.

"She has been exhibiting unusual behavior. I thought I was the only one to notice."

"She's been acting weird." Their dialogue often followed this parallel pattern, as if they were having conversations with themselves that happened to overlap.

"Let's compare observations. I have noticed absent-mindedness, lethargy, and somnambulism."

"It's like she can't think straight. She's tired all the time. Wait, repeat that last one in *plebeian*." Minh had asked Cathryn the meaning of the word Gus so often used as an insult. Instead of lashing out as he'd predicted, she usurped the term and used it to signal Gus to "talk like a normal person."

"Sleepwalking, though her case is more akin to sleep-studying. She turns pages with her eyes closed. I've even witnessed her write that way, gibberish about locks and flying books."

The bell rang, but Gus stayed where he was. This conversation was more important than a tardy.

Minh lowered her voice as a cluster of sophomores passed. "I heard she fell asleep in class."

Gus nodded. "She also has several overdue assignments."

"That girl has been two weeks ahead since kindergarten." Minh shook her head. "Something's wrong."

"We could ask Cathryn."

Minh drummed her fingers on her thigh. "We could ask Cathryn, but she'd never admit anything was wrong. She's too Minnesota Nice to 'make trouble.'"

"We lack sufficient evidence to confront her. We should observe her further to collect more data."

"We don't have enough to pin her down. We should keep a closer eye on her."

"Agreed."

Chapter 18

Cathryn added the receipt to her father's budget folder. She'd finally bought a new pair of jeans and had to balance the account lest he accuse her of stealing again. She shuddered as she placed the folder on the shelf next to a broken Christmas ornament. Christmas had been a dark twelve days.

Her father was getting worse. Cathryn kept her mother away from him, which didn't help his moods. Without warning, he swung between the extremes of love and violence. He burst through the door and wrapped his arms around her, squeezing until she couldn't breathe. He kissed her head and rambled about how families love and forgive each other, but the slightest mistake sent him raging. Once he hit her for putting down the silverware crooked when she set the table. Every time he beat her, she wondered if he would lock the door for good.

They needed to escape. Now.

Cathryn went to her closet and reviewed the toolbox funds. They were far behind schedule. She'd paid for the doctor appointments out of pocket to avoid rousing her father's suspicion. *All that money to tell us there's nothing we can do.*

She closed and stowed the toolbox. *There must be another way.* She scoured her brain, but she'd been over the numbers a hundred times. *I don't want to do this. Mom doesn't want this.*

Cathryn scanned her bedroom, searching for dollars amidst the dust bunnies. Her eyes landed on *The Fantastic Flying Books of Mr. Morris Lessmore.* She picked it up and pressed her fingers into the cover as though she could push through the illustration and escape into the story. The cover held firm.

Cathryn hugged the book to her chest and sat beside her mother's sleeping form. Her breathing sent ripples through the faded lilacs on the bedspread, like a breeze through a garden. At the rate she was declining, she would pass on before they saved enough money to escape. Only one way her mother died a free woman: more income.

Cathryn pulled out the applications she'd collected in the hopes of never needing them and filled in Beatrice's name and social security number. *May as well be consistent.*

She kissed her mother's pale forehead. "I won't let you die here."

Cathryn's hand shook as she reached for the phone, as if it understood the finality of this sacrifice. Once she made this call, her dreams for the future were over, but she'd committed to freeing her mother no matter the cost. She forced her hand steady.

Cathryn dialed the number from memory and lowered her voice. "Hello, this is Beatrice Banks. No, Cathryn isn't sick again. I was calling to let you know my husband accepted a job in Denver. Cathryn won't be back at school. We don't know where we'll be living yet, but we'll have Cathryn's new school request her records once we're settled. Will do. Thank you."

Cathryn hung up, dropped to the floor, and sobbed.

* * *

The doorbell rang as Minh added a few more strokes to the night sky she was painting for Cathryn's birthday.

"Beth, can you get it?" She added another star, happy she'd decided on paints instead of pens for this. The texture added extra magic. *Van Gogh isn't the only one who can paint a starry night.*

A moment later, Ghost appeared at her elbow.

"Is it for me?"

He nodded. In his two and a half years with the family, the six-year-old had spoken only when prompted, a quirk none of them minded. Minh set her brush in the water cup and followed him.

Cathryn waited at the door wearing the smile she used when telling library patrons they couldn't check out more books until they paid their late fees. Her red eyes were a morbid splash of color above dark circles.

"Thought you were home sick."

Cathryn shook her head. *I knew something was wrong.* Minh bit her tongue. Cathryn was like a rabbit—sweet, but prone to flee at the slightest threat. *Trust me, Cat.*

"M-My dad got a job offer." Cathryn's eyes darted back and forth between Minh and the ground as if eye contact hurt.

Minh pushed Ghost behind her. "That's good, right?"

"Yeah. It's just, um, it's in Denver."

"You're moving to Denver? When?"

"Tomorrow. That's why I wasn't at school. We were packing."

Cathryn's words fell like a hammer to an anvil. Minh wanted to spout enough obscenities to make her mother faint, but a noose around her throat squeezed them silent. Cathryn's face resembled the pictures of suffering children charities used to sucker people into donating.

Minh kept her voice steady. "You're too smart not to succeed wherever you land. I'll miss you like mad though."

"I'll miss you too." Cathryn burst into tears and gave her a fierce hug. Minh's eyes watered.

When she regained her composure, Cathryn pulled a single envelope from her bag.

"Would you give this to Gus? And say goodbye to Tony? I wanted to tell them myself, but . . ."

Minh nodded. They'd been friends long enough to make words unnecessary.

Minh rolled back to her room and punched her fist through the painting. Wet paint slid around her knuckles like picture guts. She threw her unfinished work into the hall and slammed the door. She didn't come out until the next morning.

* * *

Cathryn's Diary

"Oh, what a tangled web we weave
when we first practice to deceive!"
Sir Walter Scott

I didn't set out to be a liar. I just kept adding lie after lie, link after link in a chain that now binds me like the ghost in Charles Dickens's A Christmas Carol.

My mother sleeps so peacefully, as if she need not know where the raft is going; she is content to drift with the current. She isn't afraid like me—afraid of the rapids, of tumbling over the falls, of drowning in a flood of her own tears. She trusts.

I wish I could be like her. I wish I were free.

* * *

Minh braced herself as she delivered the news.

"What do you mean she's gone?" Tony said.

"Her father got a job offer. We can't blame them." She sounded false even to her own ears. The first bell rang. A freshman wobbled around her, carrying a stack of books that reached above his chin. A junior linked arms with her latest boyfriend. For them, it was a normal day.

"This makes no sense." Gus's ever-present scowl deepened.

"Look, I don't like this any more than you do, but moping around won't change anything."

"Why didn't she say goodbye?" Tony asked, his hurt face a punch to Minh's gut. She tried to say her next words as gently as Cathryn would have said them.

"She said they had to decide quickly, or the job would go to someone else."

"That is precisely what makes this suspicious." Gus's fingers flared as though one step away from clenching into fists. "Cathryn behaved erratically for weeks. If it stemmed from a pending relocation, she would have had ample time for farewells. If the offer was as sudden as she claimed, the root cause of her behavior remains unknown."

Minh ground her teeth. Gus with a problem was like a Rottweiler with a bone; he refused to let go. Minh didn't have the patience for puppies today.

"She's gone, so it doesn't fucking matter." She forced Gus against his locker as she huffed away.

* * *

Gus's car muffled the chatter, laughter, and honks that ricocheted around the parking lot after school, but he wouldn't have heard them anyway. He fingered the envelope with his name on it.

During his first weeks in Minnesota, he felt as though he'd been forced into a parallel universe. He would have gone insane if not for Cathryn—a girl he never would have noticed at the academy.

The ordinary-looking girl was a thesaurus, dictionary, and encyclopedia rolled into one. She was a moral compass that always pointed north and a telescope through which he could see beauty in the stars.

Cathryn was more than his "translator." She was his collaborator, his supporter, his confidant . . . his friend. With little more than kindness and smiles, she'd shattered his worldview, dismantled his ego, and smashed through the armor around his heart. She understood him; not merely his words, but him, and she never expected him to be anything else. He loved it most when she forgot other people were in the room and discussed her passions freely. In those moments, she smiled without looking away.

Now she was gone.

Gus opened the letter written in Cathryn's minuscule script. She said she hated wasting paper. Several teachers told her they would no longer accept handwritten assignments they needed a magnifying glass to read. He almost smiled at the memory.

Dear Gus,

I hold our friendship close to my heart, and it hurts beyond measure to say goodbye. I admire you more than I can say. You challenged my assumptions, but you also taught me to have faith in myself. Thank you.

Though the thought of new beginnings terrifies me, I embark on this journey well prepared. A new city, a new school, a new set of strangers to turn into friends—I will be more than capable of meeting these challenges. I know this because I learned it from you. You are so much more than Gustaf, the ornery erudite. You are Gus, my friend, who showed me the stars.

I will always hold you in the highest esteem.

Yours,
Cathryn

Gus re-read the letter until the words blurred. Then he folded it neatly, placed it in his backpack, and drove away.

Chapter 19

Cathryn stowed her purse in her locker and threw her lime green cleaner's jumpsuit on over her undershirt. Pilar narrowed her eyes at Cathryn's heavy eye makeup but led the group to their assignment without comment.

Tonight, they had a one-time job at a manufacturing plant where a malfunctioning machine had spilled stinking black goo everywhere. *Good thing I don't have homework anymore.* They were in for a long night.

Cathryn cleaned by Rosa María, who chatted excitedly in Spanish about her sister's new baby.

"His name is Joaquin, and he's darling."

Cathryn lowered her eyes and scrubbed harder.

"You don't like the name?"

Cathryn paused; her scrub brush sank in the putrid pond. "It's just, I had a neighbor named Joaquin." She resumed scrubbing. "He moved."

Rosa María cocked her head to one side, and Pilar stopped scrubbing. Cathryn abandoned her brush and got up to mix more cleaning solution. She could feel Pilar's eyes following her to the jug. She poured the mixture, but her mind traveled to the day her old neighbors met the monster inside her father.

Cathryn lost her grip on the jug and yelped as caustic liquid burned through her soaked sleeve. She sprinted to the bathroom, tore off her shirt, and ran her arm under cool water. After a minute, the burn eased. She grabbed a stack of paper towels and froze.

Pilar stood in the doorway, eyes hopscotching over the bruises that covered her arms like paint splatters.

"Who did that to you?"

"I fell."

Pilar crossed her arms in front of her chest. "I'm not stupid." She took a step forward. "I don't have to know American laws to know the person who hit you is a criminal."

"I fell." Cathryn dried her arms and threw the paper towels away.

Pilar shook her head. "Cathryn, hija—"

"You aren't my mother. Quit meddling in my life."

Cathryn rinsed out her shirt and put it back on. "I fell." She pushed passed Pilar and returned to cleaning.

Pilar followed her, and the two of them scrubbed in a silence so intense that Rosa María moved to another section of the warehouse.

Part of Cathryn was relieved someone knew the truth. Pilar wouldn't say anything. Even if she tried, her beginners' English was no match for Cathryn's fluent lies.

Pilar didn't speak to Cathryn for the rest of that shift, but she watched her like a prison warden from then on.

* * *

Cathryn tried to ignore the creaking stair as she hauled the laundry basket to her closet. Balancing the basket on her hip, she pulled open the door, but the sight of her backpack pinned her still. They would be studying World War II by now, one of her favorite subjects. She stroked her backpack's frayed strap. Then she buried it beneath her shoes and put the clothes away.

She'd left her friends, but she couldn't banish them from her mind. She saw them everywhere: in the smell of gasoline, the splash of color on a billboard, the light of the stars. There was no escape. Cathryn wasn't sure she wanted one.

"We should light the candle tonight." Her mother couldn't remember five minutes ago, but she could smell melancholy like a bloodhound.

Cathryn lit the candle and put the makeshift gate over the stairs. She trusted the staircase even less than she trusted her mother's failing coordination.

"Let's make ourselves gorgeous." Cathryn loved brushing her mother's hair. It reminded her of when her mother used to brush hers. That memory formed part of her definition of love.

Her mother smiled at her reflection in the hand mirror. No matter what else this strange condition took from her, that smile was invincible.

Cathryn ensured her mother changed position as she settled her back into bed. She'd read enough about bedsores to commit to preventing them.

"Will you read to me?" Her mother's voice was as soft as the down pillow Cathryn had splurged on.

"Of course." Cathryn read *The Fantastic Flying Books of Mr. Morris Lessmore*, parting from the script now and then to add her own embellishments. When she finished, her mother took her hand.

"Thank you. You're a nice girl."

The doctor warned Cathryn they would enter a time when her mother no longer recognized her, but that didn't stop the moment from punching her in the ribs. She had prepared for this, practiced in front of the mirror while her mother slept. Those well-rehearsed words dissolved in her mouth. She shook herself. Too long a delay might frighten her.

Cathryn kissed her mother's forehead. "Thanks. I learned from the best."

* * *

Minh restrained a stream of curse words that would have burned the ears off her parents. She had reached for her new art pens, but they clattered to the floor. *They better not have broken.*

She positioned herself beside a pen and leaned sideways, holding the opposite wheel to keep herself from falling. Her fingertips flicked it away. She repositioned herself and snatched it. *One down.*

She scanned the hallway for her other pens, only to discover she had an audience—gawkers wondering how she reached the floor. With as many pens as she'd dropped, she'd give them quite a show.

Minh unleashed the curses.

"That is anatomically impossible."

When did Gus get here? "Do I look like I'm in the mood for an anatomy lesson?"

"Do I look like I am in the mood to hold your pens all day?" He held out his hand.

Minh accepted her pens with narrowed eyes. "When did his majesty, the king of chemistry, start caring about someone other than himself?"

"Approximately the same time her majesty, the queen of sarcasm, attempted to instruct him in the art of smiling." Minh saw her own sass reflected in Gus's grin. "Fortunately Cathryn was present, or you'd be forced to endure my derisive sneer for all eternity."

Minh laughed and shoved him. "All right, Heinstein. Get lost before you make a habit of rescuing damsels in distress."

Gus snorted. "No one with half-functioning eyes would describe *you* as a damsel in distress, Minh." He turned to leave, his posture perfect as always.

"Gus," Minh called.

He looked over his shoulder.

Minh swallowed. "I miss her too."

* * *

Cathryn's Diary

"He who permits himself to tell a lie once, finds it much easier to do it a second and third time..." Thomas Jefferson is wrong. Lying is anything but easy.

I feel like a victim of the Dancing Plague of 1518. I spin from work to home to work, concealing my intent to flee while soothing my father's temper. No matter how exhausted I become, I cannot rest. I will dance myself to death in this waltz of lies.

I can imagine my friends' pain when they realize I'm not sending a forwarding address. It is the same pain I feel now. What I would give to see Tony's crooked-toothed smile, to hear Minh's biting wit, to feel Gus's warmth next to me.

"The worst solitude is to be destitute of sincere friendship." Sir Francis Bacon is right. I am so alone.

* * *

Gus parked the car. "We will get caught."

"We got a good thing going, Gus. Don't ruin it with a bad attitude." Lydia bounded off to the theater to meet her boyfriend.

Gus shook his head and cranked the music. Today was definitely a Raketenwerfer day.

His parents arranged an entire afternoon with Lydia. Gus planned to use the time to help the Giordanis fix a glitch in their computer system. He drove toward the shop and tried not to think about St. Anthony Falls.

A day with Tony wouldn't be bad. Through their half-year acquaintance, Gus had learned one only needed a half-day to get to know Tony. Tony's answers to life's problems consisted of hit it with a wrench, punch its face in, or buy it chocolate, depending upon whether it was inanimate, male, or female. He was simplistic, belligerent, incorrigible . . . and the best friend anyone could ask for.

A day with the soft-hearted mechanic wouldn't be bad, so why did Gus need to white-knuckle grip the steering wheel to prevent the car from driving itself to the library?

Traffic slowed as a bus merged back into the flow, its passengers deposited on the street corner. Gus pumped the break to avoid rear-ending it. Tony hadn't exaggerated about winter. The cold and snow turned the roads into skating rinks.

He eased past the corner where the bus's passengers dispersed. *Cathryn?* Her odd-colored eyes peered out from among the others. *It can't be.* He turned to get a better look.

Mid-glance, an SUV slammed into his front bumper and sent him swerving through the slush. He wrenched the wheel around and controlled his skid to the shoulder. *Shit.* He checked the sidewalk. No sign of Cathryn.

Gus exchanged insurance information with the impatient SUV driver and described the accident to the even less patient policewoman. He ignored their muttering "stupid tourist" and surveyed the damage. The driver's-side headlight resembled a can crushed in a vacuum chamber. *My parents will kill me.*

He climbed into the driver's seat and rested his head against the wheel. *What was I thinking?* He knew the answer. He didn't believe Cathryn had moved. Her explanation had more holes than a sieve. She'd hidden something.

Or I'm an emotional fool. He couldn't deny the emptiness that had plagued him since she left. Was he inventing conspiracies to give himself hope? He started the engine. *One problem at a time.*

Minutes later, Mrs. Giordani greeted him in the lobby. "Hey, Cute and Clueless. What are you up to?"

"Chauffeuring a neurologist's rebellious daughter."

Her expression shifted into something he couldn't read. "Tony, get in here." She kept her gaze fixed on Gus until her son arrived. "Help Gus. Then take the rest of the day off. You two could use some guy time."

There must have been something dreadful in Gus's expression because as soon as Mrs. Giordani left, Tony's face acquired the same combination of sympathy and intrigue.

"You here about the computers?"

"I was hoping we could make it an exchange."

"Car trouble, eh? Pull her in."

Gus parked his car in the main garage, where a blue frame leaned against the back wall.

"You repair bicycles as well?"

Tony's smile melted into a frown. "Not anymore." He led Gus to a boxy computer at the end of the garage. A few keystrokes granted Gus entry into the system.

"Tony, this is a mess—an ancient mess. Have you considered upgrading?"

"No way. We need this thing so dumb even Katrina can use it. Just make it talk to the one in the lobby. Tunes while you work?"

"What's your opinion of Raketenwerfer?"

Tony laughed. "Metal, huh? You always struck me as a classical kind of guy." Gus rolled his eyes. "Here"—Tony held up a CD —"best of both worlds." He loaded it into the stereo, and soon Italian symphonic metal reverberated through the garage, earning smiles from the other mechanics.

Gus weaved through webs of code. His focus on the task numbed his emotions better than the frigid air outside. *I could build them something more efficient than this.* Another project would keep him from thinking about Cathryn.

Just as he was finishing, Tony tapped him on the shoulder.

"I got the light working again, but we'll have to order the housing."

Damn. "Thank you."

Tony stared at him.

"What?"

Tony cleaned his hands on an old T-shirt rag. "The car I can handle, but I don't got a wrench to fix what you got broken."

Gus tensed. "I'd rather 'Love Doctor Tony' punch my face in than waste time *mis*diagnosing broken hearts."

Tony grinned. "I'm always up for a good brawl."

Gus shook his head.

"Then what?"

Gus surveyed the shop. "Heart-repairing wrenches may be in short supply, but you have gasoline, a blow torch, and a vacant lot out back. In my trunk, I have excess ammonium nitrate and magnesium powder from my last rocket."

"Where are you going with this, Gus?"

Gus mined his brain for a simple explanation. *How would Cathryn put it?* His heart lurched as he remembered.

"Let's blow stuff up."

* * *

Cathryn's Diary

I wasn't raped tonight. What has my life become that I evaluate it in those terms?

I paused my walk home from night shift to stargaze, a guilty pleasure I rarely indulge. Clear skies made for a good view, but an icy wind kept me from lingering. Perhaps it was trying to warn me.

I had just started walking again when a man whistled. How anyone could find me attractive in my lime green cleaners' jumpsuit, reeking of disinfectant, is a mystery. Usually ignoring catcallers made them go away. Not tonight. On my bike I could have outrun him, but the roads were still too narrowed by snowbanks to share with cars.

As the catcalls got closer, I increased my pace and diverted my course to a gas station, hoping the light would dissuade him. Before I could reach it, I slipped on a patch of black ice.

"Hola, rubia."

I tried to regain my footing, but I slipped again, adding another bruise to my right hip. The man entered the dingy light. He was short but muscular, exactly as Pilar had described the fugitive. With no chance of outrunning or outfighting him, I imagined what Minh would do.

"¡Vete al carajo!" I shouted, too frightened to blush at my profanity.

The man's expression turned from amused to menacing. I fumbled for my pepper spray, but it was buried in my purse. I should have heeded Pilar's advice and kept it accessible.

The man stepped toward me, but a gunshot broke into the space between us. When I braved an upward glance, Rosa María and Pilar stood beside me. Both held guns. Both guns pointed at the man.

"Oye, señori—"

Pilar fired. The bullet flew within inches of the man's left foot. He got the message.

I broke into sobs. Too distraught to separate my languages, I alternated "thank you" and "gracias."

"From now on, we leave together," Rosa María said.

Pilar helped me to my feet. I apologized with my eyes. She forgave me with a nod and taught me to shoot: feet set, line up the sights, pull the trigger. She made me fire practice shots into the dumpster, one with each hand since I'm ambidextrous. After the second shot, I threw up. I moved my pepper spray to a keychain outside my purse.

Too much adrenaline ran through me to nap when I got home, so here I sit, writing by the light of my mother's Jesus candle. I don't know about Jesus, but I now believe in angels.

Chapter 20

Cathryn held the phone between her shoulder and her ear so she could take notes.

"That includes the first month's rent and the security deposit?"

"Yep. You can knock off fifty bucks if I don't have to get it cleaned before you move in." The woman's nasal tone warbled through the staticky connection.

"That will be fine." If Cathryn had learned anything working her mother's night job, it was how to clean. "When will it be available?"

"It's free now."

"I won't have the money for"—Cathryn did the mental math —"another three weeks."

"First come, first serve, Miss Beatrice." Cathryn's heart sank. The landlady must have sensed her distress because her tone softened. "Look, I got an older gal leaving about three weeks from now. Family's putting her in one of them old folks' homes. Basement apartment, so twenty-five bucks a month less than what I just told you."

"Perfect. I'll pick up the paperwork tomorrow." Cathryn arranged to meet the landlady and ran upstairs to hide her notes in the toolbox. She recounted the money. Not as much as she'd planned, but with the new job Rosa María helped her get—scrubbing dishes for a restaurant owner who paid in cash—she needn't worry about social security numbers.

Cathryn taped the phone number to her notes page. Pilar had slipped it into her hand after their last shift, saying, "At least let me help you." Cathryn didn't ask where she'd gotten the number for a landlady with such low standards. She didn't care. For the first time in months, she had hope.

Cathryn's mother rolled over in bed. Cathryn readjusted her blankets and frowned at the barely nibbled piece of toast by her bedside. She kissed her mother's forehead.

"Try to eat more, Mom. You need your strength." She smiled, though her mother didn't open her eyes to see the expression. "We're getting out of here."

She gave her mother one more kiss before hopping downstairs to prepare soup for her father. *Three more weeks.*

Gravel churning outside announced her father's arrival. Keys jingled to the ground. He cursed twice, and the locks clicked open.

"Honey, I'm home," he bellowed.

"Hi, Dad. Soup is ready." Cathryn wriggled her nose as she took his coat. This wasn't the first time she'd smelled alcohol on his breath *before* dinner. *Hasn't his boss noticed yet?* Even Mr. Sanders would notice if she showed up drunk.

"I don't want soup. Eggs and bacon for me."

"But I thought you didn't like bac—"

"Bea," he called up the stairs.

Cathryn darted in front of him. "She's sick."

"She's been 'sick' long enough." He pushed past her.

Cathryn grabbed his arm. "She needs to rest."

"A man has a right to see his wife."

Cathryn's vision darkened. *You have no right to her, you monster.* Her mother had endured enough abuse. She deserved to sleep in peace.

Cathryn squeezed past her father, taking the high ground in the stairwell. "She needs to rest."

He backhanded her, but for the first time in her life, she hit him back. She rammed his chest and pushed him to the base of the stairs. He staggered to his feet drunkenly. His red-rimmed eyes blazed as he came after her.

The staircase groaned and shrieked, but neither Cathryn nor her father did more than grunt. Cathryn couldn't escape the narrow confines of the stairwell, so she made herself small, shrinking his target zone. Even so, his blows knocked the breath out of her.

After covering her back and arm with welts, he lifted her over his shoulder, hauled her upstairs, and threw her into her room. Only after the locks clicked did Cathryn scream.

"No." She pounded on the door, but her father's car rumbling to life signaled his departure. "No, no, no, no, no." She worked tonight.

What was I thinking? Ever since the snow had blocked her bedroom window, she'd acted submissive enough on worknights for her father to unlock her room before he went to the bars. She'd been late once when the living room window froze shut, but she'd never missed a shift. Tonight, her new-found hope made her bold, and her heroics ruined everything.

One no-call-no-show was enough for Mr. Sanders to fire her. No job, no money. No money, no apartment. No apartment, no escape. *We were so close.*

Pain stabbed her left side as she sobbed, but it wasn't enough to stop the tears. With only three weeks between her and freedom, she'd failed.

"I'm sorry, Mom. I tried."

Her mother groaned from the bed.

Cathryn rushed to her side. "Mom? It's okay. I'm here."

Ashen gray skin stretched over her mother's gaunt face. *She needs to get out of here. There must be another way.* Cathryn looked at the window. *That's suicide.* The first weeks of March alternated freezing and thawing. A layer of ice would coat the roof beneath the two inches of fresh snow.

She squeezed her mother's hand. Staying here would be suicide. The way her father's alcoholism was progressing, he'd leave her with worse than bruised ribs next time.

Cathryn changed into her work undershirt, gingerly pulling it over her sore body. The window creaked as she forced it open, and it struggled against her as she pushed it closed behind her. Frigid air burned her lungs. *Slow and steady.*

Her new bruises made her movements awkward as she inched along the roof toward the drainpipe. Her foot slipped, but she caught herself and froze, both literally and figuratively. The cold air stiffened her muscles. *Keep moving.*

An icicle hung from the second story like a frozen waterfall. The full moon glowed through it. Cathryn inched past in the night's silence.

Almost there. The drainpipe hung less than four feet away. Her foot crunched through a layer of snow but found no grip. It slipped out from under her, and she crashed through the icicle and over the roof's edge.

She grabbed the gutter, but it cracked and tore free of the roof. The maneuver bought her enough time to grab an exposed plank. Bits of icicle tumbled to the ground. She dangled, her fingers weak in the cold.

"You overestimate the drop." Gus's voice sounded in her mind. *"Your eyes are higher than your feet."* Cathryn tightened her grip.

"You can do it, Kitten." She could see Tony smiling in his gym clothes. *"Bend your knees to soften the landing."*

Cathryn risked a glance below, yelped, and tried to pull herself up to the roof, but her movements destabilized her grip. *I can't do this.*

"Stop being such a 'fraidy cat." Minh's voice was that of her five-year-old self.

"You're always getting me into trouble, Minh," Cathryn said to her hallucination. She tasted salt as a tear ran into her mouth.

Cathryn closed her eyes, took a breath, and let go.

Her feet hit the snow and plunged through it. She bent her knees as they reached the frozen earth, and she fell backward. When she opened her eyes, she lay in a small snow drift, unharmed.

Cathryn wiggled to her feet, brushed herself off, and looked back to her window.

"We can do this, Mom." Three more weeks.

*   *   *

Laurel Ostergaard limped into the kitchen with the grocery bags. She'd overestimated her coordination yesterday. *So I have to give up heels. I can still get the rest of my life back.* She glanced at the clock:

1:00 p.m. The bus had taken longer than she expected. Now she had only five hours to make four dozen mini-croissants and sixty caramel tarts. Five hours to show Mark she was ready to return to work.

She reached into the fridge for the croissant dough she'd painstakingly mixed and folded in the wee hours of the morning. Sleep often eluded her in her new reality. *Too much to do anyway.* The leftovers she'd set aside for lunch lay in front of the dough, but Laurel wasn't hungry. Her appetite came and went according to its own whims.

One more set of folds for luck, then rolling, cutting, and shaping. The first batch of croissants went into the oven. Adrenaline rushed through her as she set one of the six timers that stood like a line of soldiers by the stove. *Now for the tarts.*

A simple shortcrust pastry. Laurel could make that in her sleep. She popped it into the fridge to chill and reset the timer for the second batch of croissants. Time to boil sugar for the caramel. She clipped the candy thermometer to the edge of her pot and dug through the pantry for chocolate. *What's a caramel tart without a chocolate glaze?* The timer rang as her hand grasped the bag. *What was that one for?* A headache nudged her temples.

She dashed to the stove and found her sugar boiling darkly. *That was close.* Caramel went from golden to burned in seconds. Another timer rang. *Now what?* The timer's beeps beat into her head like drums into a hangover. She shut it off and tried to think of what she'd been doing.

The bag of chocolate weighed heavy in her hand. *Right. Tarts. I should roll out the crusts before I make the chocolate sauce.* Tossing the chocolate aside, she walked to the fridge, but it swayed in her vision. She grabbed the door handles to keep herself upright. *I can do this. I just need to add little breaks.*

She sat on a kitchen stool, and her head sank to the cold marble.

The smell woke her. Smell—another sense she could have lost but didn't. This smell she wouldn't mind living without: burned pastry. She peeled her face off the kitchen table and raced to the oven. A blast of heat and smoke sent her sputtering backward. She crawled to the cupboard beneath the sink, snatched the fire extinguisher, and doused the oven. The croissants had burned to ash. Her hope burned with them.

The front door opened an hour before schedule. Mark stepped into the kitchen.

"Laurel? Honey—"

"Don't." Tears poured from the faucet of her eyes. "Just don't."

* * *

Gus ground his teeth. *I am a straight-A student. I can decipher a bus schedule.* His parents had been remarkably lenient about his car accident—until Lydia's father discovered their scheme. Now Gus relied on the bus to get home after lacrosse.

The bus lumbered to the stop. Gus double-checked the route number as a handful of passengers disembarked. Once boarded, he dropped his quarters into the farebox, grateful the low number of other riders allowed him to sit by himself. Yesterday, he'd sat next to an old woman who reeked of floral perfume.

He cursed under his breath as the bus pulled away. He'd waited on the wrong side of the street, meaning the bus he'd boarded traveled in the wrong direction. *Why can't I get this right?*

Across the aisle, two men chatted in Somali. Had Cathryn been with him, she'd have insisted on eavesdropping to learn new vocabulary. He once asked her why she enrolled in Somali instead of French or Latin like the academy required. She'd smiled and asked, "Why not?"

Knowing that answer wouldn't satisfy him, she continued. "My old neighbors taught me Spanish, and now I can help more people at the library. Minneapolis has a lot of Somali speakers, so that was the logical next step."

Typical Cathryn. Learning languages so she could be nice to people in their native tongues. To Gus, her kindness was a foreign language, one that bore no resemblance to his parents' squabbles. At first glance, she was all clumsy gait and patched jeans, but the more he saw of her heart, the more beautiful she became.

Languages, books, stars—Cathryn was always looking to escape to another world. They had that in common, but he'd never asked what drove her. He wished he had. He wished he knew everything about Cathryn—her passions, her pet peeves, her dreams, her fears—but she was gone, a book with its last chapter torn out.

Icy pinpricks stung Gus's cheek. He jerked his head off the bus window. How many stops had he missed? *Don't think about her. Get off this stupid bus and get home.* Not that home was better.

Gus rose to exit and froze, still half-seated. In a window seat toward the front of the bus was a familiar ponytail. He missed his chance to disembark. He didn't care.

Over the next few stops, he tried to convince himself he was hallucinating again, seeing Cathryn because he missed her. The hair was hardly distinctive. Most people wouldn't notice.

Gus was not most people. He knew Cathryn's profile like he knew the quadratic equation. The mystery woman disembarked at the next stop. Gus peered through the window. The Lewis Library. *I must be insane.* He dashed after her.

The woman headed into the woods, exactly as Cathryn had the night he took her to the movie. *I've yet to see her face.* His mind shouted logic, but his legs refused to obey. *People get arrested for stalking.* He followed her into the trees.

Half-melted snow clung to the shadows, making the already unfamiliar terrain treacherous. His impatience propelled him faster, and he stumbled. The woman paused. Gus held his breath until she continued.

They emerged from the trees to the sight of a dilapidated two-story house across a gravel road. The woman unlocked a set of three locks as though performing the ritual entrance to a spy's hideout. She seemed to sense his gaze and turned. Gus ducked behind a tree and dared a glance. Her face was drawn with exhaustion, but there could be no mistake. Cathryn hadn't moved to Denver. She'd lied.

Gus wasn't sure whether to feel outraged at her deception or overjoyed to discover her. She disappeared into the house, but his cell phone's vibrating stole his opportunity to follow her.

"Yes, Mother?"

"Do not dawdle after practice."

Gus struggled to keep his tone diplomatic. "May I ask why?"

"The chairman of the McKnight Foundation is dining with us tonight. He has a daughter your age, Alycia. Lovely girl, wants to study immunology. No interest in acting. I expect you home in time to wash and dress. You are to behave exceptionally. Understood? I am in no mood for histrionics." His mother's pitch rose two octaves during her last sentence.

Gus held his phone away from his ear. "Did someone introduce you as Mrs. Hein again?"

"It's Doctor and *Doctor* Hein! Imbeciles. I have just as many letters trailing my surname as your father." She spoke the words "father" and "imbeciles" with equal vitriol.

Gus took one, then another breath. The United Nations couldn't negotiate with his mother in this state. He couldn't risk losing more of his freedom.

"I'll be home soon."

The truth would have to wait.

* * *

Cathryn's Diary

Who am I? Every day I am less certain. Or is it every night? Days and nights blur together. Today is my seventeenth birthday, but I respond to my mother's name more readily than my own. It is as though the more my mother loses herself, the more I become her. This leads me to wonder: if I am transforming into Beatrice Banks, what is happening to Cathryn?

Chapter 21

Cathryn paused to enjoy the spring sunshine before heading inside. She was glad to be home earlier today. Yesterday, she'd sensed someone watching her. *I need more sleep. I'm becoming paranoid.*

Cathryn approached the oversized kitchen sink where the family washed dishes and, as of four days ago, themselves. The bruises she'd received after the shower broke still made her wince. She suspected her father refrained from fixing it to punish her, but she'd already given sponge baths to her mother, so cleaning herself that way didn't require much adjusting.

Cathryn reached under the sink, retrieved a black plastic tub, and filled it with warm water and body wash. As had become the norm, her mother lay curled around her Jesus candle. *It must be terrifying to wake up alone and not recognize your surroundings.*

"Let's get you clean, Mom."

Cathryn rubbed her mother's shoulder, but she gasped once and fell back asleep. She rarely woke and hadn't eaten in two days. Cathryn unbuttoned her mother's nightdress and wiped her frail body. She reached her knees and stopped. They were a mottled purple. Her hands and feet showed the same discoloring. Cathryn checked the incontinence pads. Clean. She gripped her mother's wrist and counted. Her pulse was slow and irregular.

"No, Mom, not yet." She swallowed a sob. "Please, I can't do this without you." She sank to her knees and struggled to breathe as the truth set in.

Her mother was dying. Cathryn would be alone.

Tears poured from her eyes, one for every bedtime story, every hug, every night spent laughing at nothing. Through watery eyes Cathryn saw her mother covered in sand as they made castles by Lake Nokomis, checkered with shadows as she read beneath the maple tree, dusted with white powder as she made a snow angel. *"Look, Sweetie Kitty, God sent someone to look after you."*

Her mother would never see her walk across a stage to collect a diploma, wouldn't welcome her to adulthood with a cake crowned with eighteen candles, wouldn't hold back tears when she left for college. Those dreams died with her.

Cathryn's tears strung together like the words in a prayer. When she'd wrung herself dry, she covered her mother in blankets and took her hand.

"I'm here, Mom. I'll wait with you."

* * *

"Banks. My office. Now."

Jedidiah Banks winced as the shout penetrated his hangover. He followed his boss to the closet-turned-office and stood in the only square foot of space that wasn't covered in paperwork.

Mr. Fifer slammed the door. "What the hell happened?"

Jedidiah gritted his teeth. "I had the warning light on."

"You totaled the forklift. Boada is in the hospital." He leaned into his desk, knuckles white. "You been drinking again?"

"No."

Mr. Fifer pounded his fist on his desk. Jedidiah winced.

"You're fired."

* * *

The jingle of keys followed uneven footsteps in the gravel. *Dad. How do I tell him?* Best handle dinner first. Cathryn kissed her mother's cheek. "I'll be back."

She hopped over the loose stair and hurried to the kitchen. After lighting the stove, she reached for the pot, but it clattered to the floor when the door exploded open.

Her father held an empty bottle of whiskey. Blood dripped from a tear in his shirt.

"Dad?"

His backhand knocked her to the floor.

"Please, I—"

He cut her pleas short with a feral howl. Spit dribbled over his swollen lip. Glass shattered, and everything went dark.

* * *

Gus fidgeted in his seat. *Confounded public transportation.* Walking might have been faster, but at the moment, speed was irrelevant. He still hadn't the faintest idea what to say when he confronted Cathryn.

"Looks like someone's having a bonfire," the man next to him slurred as he pointed to a plume of smoke out the window. He reeked of urine.

"Fascinating." Gus scooted farther away.

* * *

Cathryn awoke in hell. Flames dominated her vision. Her last memory was the whiskey bottle crashing over her head. She pulled herself onto her elbow, and the circuits in her brain reconnected.

Mom.

She forced herself to her feet and sprinted out of the kitchen. Smoke obscured her vision as she rushed up the stairs two at a time. She hit the weak step. Her foot fell through, and the impact of her fall took the rest of the staircase with her.

Cathryn plunged into blackness.

* * *

Gus forced himself to slow when he reached the woods, but his frantic thinking drove his pace quicker. How should he approach her? *Where is Tony when you need him?* He cursed and tried to focus. She looked dreadful yesterday. He should be gentle, but he wasn't sure how. Cathryn was gentle. He was direct.

The smell of smoke infiltrated his thinking, and his mind flashed to the repulsive man on the bus. *Cathryn.* He raced through the woods, tripping over roots as he ran. He emerged to the sight of the house engulfed in flames.

Gus sprinted through the open door. "Cathryn!" His face flushed in the heat. "Cathryn!" He scanned the interior, but the contrast between the bright flames and the smoky darkness blinded him. "Cathryn!" He choked on the smoke and dropped to his knees. Wheezing, he crawled onward.

She lay under a heap of rubble, her head bleeding.

Gus smelled his own flesh burning as he gripped piece after piece of charred debris and tossed it aside. A large beam pressed Cathryn's left ankle to the floor. He gripped it, but it refused to budge. The room spun, and the exertion forced Gus to his knees. He looked at Cathryn's unconscious form, clenched his teeth, and tried again. The beam resisted, but he shoved once more, and it lurched to the side. Gus crumpled to the floor, but one task remained.

A twisted metal rod stabbed through Cathryn's left forearm, pinning it to the floorboards through a pool of blood. Before his instincts of self-preservation could protest, Gus grabbed the rod and yanked. A scream roared from his charred throat as the metal seared his hands. His vision blurred. He dropped the rod and leaned against the rubble, but the smoke prevented him from catching his breath. He looped his arms beneath Cathryn's armpits and dragged her as far from the inferno as he could.

The early spring breeze was an arctic blast.

"Cathryn?" He couldn't tell whether she was breathing. Bright lights and sirens hovered at the edge of his awareness. "Cathryn!"

A pair of strong arms tore him away from her, and uniformed men loaded her into an ambulance. Someone shook him. A fireman materialized at his side.

"Is anyone else inside?"

"I-I don't know. She lives with her parents." His last words drowned in the thunder of the house's collapse, and a wave of heat and dust knocked him to the ground. The fireman pushed him into the ambulance, where he glimpsed Cathryn between the paramedics who hovered around her like a swarm of hornets.

Sirens wailed like mourners.

Chapter 22

Gus stared at the dark stitches that zigzagged across Cathryn's forehead like drunk railroad tracks. He tried to tune out the monitor's beep, but her shallow breathing was still lost beneath the hissing oxygen tube and ticking clock. Her hair splayed out on the pillow, tangled and singed. No ponytails in this nightmare. No smiles either.

He had no photographs of her smile, no evidence of how her eyes gleamed when she talked about her favorite books, how her lips pursed as she puzzled through a problem, how her cheeks reddened when she caught him looking at her. He had no recording of the patient sighs she breathed when her friends fought, the staccato of her fingers drumming on her desk, the bell choir of her laughter.

How could he be so stupid? How could he not have something, anything, to mark their friendship? Now the smell of smoke, burnt flesh, and ointment smothered the scent of old books and ink that usually surrounded Cathryn.

Gus grasped her fingertips, the only part of her left arm not covered in bandages.

"Cathryn, I—" He didn't know what to say, only that he needed to say something. "Cathryn, I-I would greatly appreciate it if you would accompany me to the movies"—his voice broke—"and I insist on paying." Tears mixed with the soot on his cheeks. "We can fill the whole car with kettle corn, and . . . and spend all night gazing at those beautiful, burning spheres of gas." His breath came in ragged gasps. "I'll listen to insipid chatter about lip gloss as long as you like, but you have to wake up ... Cathryn?"

Tears surged until he was an empty husk. Still grasping Cathryn's fingers, he fell into an exhausted sleep.

* * *

Cathryn's Medical Chart

Patient Demographics

Name: Cathryn Joy Banks
Age: 17 yrs.
Sex: Female
Race: White, Non-Hispanic
Primary Care: Unknown
Emergency Contact: Unknown
Next of Kin: Unknown

Diagnosis

Multiple trauma; Second- and third-degree burns; Concussion with loss of consciousness

Estimated Length of Stay

Greater than three nights

History of Current Illness

Patient was pulled from a house fire by a Good Samaritan and arrived at the hospital via ambulance. Cause of the fire is under investigation, but preliminary evidence suggests the kitchen stove.

Patient presents with lacerations on the forehead and left arm near the wrist, fractures in left rib number two and the left fibula near the ankle, and multiple second- and third-degree burns across the left side of her body.

Additional Notes

RN noted multiple contusions across the abdomen and back that appear to predate the current trauma. MD concurs with RN's conclusions. Child services notified.

* * *

Gus preferred the oblivion of sleep, but the stinging smell of hand sanitizer dragged him into consciousness. He checked his watch, but his wrist was bare, and his hands bandaged. The wall clock read 5:30 a.m.

"Hey, kid." A tiny nurse with spiky hair addressed him. "That was a brave thing you did. You saved her life." Tattoos extended from her wrist into the sleeve of her Minnie Mouse-themed scrubs. Minh would have loved this woman.

She checked the monitors before turning back to him. "Why don't you go home for some food and a shower?"

Gus couldn't form words. He stared at the nurse like a slack-jawed caveman.

She tilted her head as if engaged in a mental debate. After a moment, she nodded. "The day nurse will replace me in half an hour. I can give you a ride if you want."

Gus looked at Cathryn.

"You got a phone?" The nurse gestured with her head. "Leave your number at the nurses' station. No one's claimed her, so you're her only contact."

Gus nodded.

Half an hour later, he sat in the nurse's bright yellow VW Beetle. She turned off the radio as they drove, seeming to sense his need for quiet. When they reached his house, he mumbled his thanks and dragged himself into his mother's ambush.

"Gustaf! Where have you been? You think our attending an awards ceremony gives you leave to stay out all night? That a vague message 'not to worry' excuses your behavior?"

Gus trudged upstairs to his room. His mother shrieked like a banshee and followed.

"Do I smell smoke? I knew those *friends* were a detrimental influence. You are fortunate Miss Alycia can't see you like this. From now on, your social interactions are restricted to those your father and I—"

Gus slammed the door. He wrapped his bandaged hands in the plastic the nurse gave him and shuffled to the shower. When the water ran cold, he crawled into bed.

Chapter 23

Cathryn opened her eyes to a haze of spinning lights, or perhaps it was she who spun. She slipped back into oblivion.

Flames, suffocating heat. She tried to escape, but the flames dragged her to the floor. Her father growled in the shadows. She struggled against the fire's grasp.

Her eyes flew open. The room smelled like the disinfectant from her night job. Something beeped to her left. *What is Tony doing here? Where am I?* Her vision blurred.

She dipped back into darkness and dreamed of smoke and death.

* * *

Warren Jones took a final swig of apple juice before he entered the office. He'd never acquired his colleagues' taste for coffee. A little fruit sugar set his gears spinning better than a tankard of caffeine.

He knew he was in for a long day when his boss barreled toward him—bushy black beard untrimmed, suit coat half off, and manila folders in hand. "You hear about that fire by the library last night? One survivor, a teenage girl."

Warren accepted the file. "Why is this my case?"

"Nurse noticed half-healed bruises, predate the fire."

Warren skimmed as he walked toward his desk. "Hey, how many seventeen-year-old Caucasians named Cathryn Banks do you think live in Minneapolis?"

"No clue. Why?"

"My daughter's best friend spells her name that way, but she told us she was moving to Denver."

His boss threw a file onto his colleague's desk. "You need someone else to take the case?"

Warren shook his head. "Even if it is the same girl, she'd benefit from a familiar face."

"I'll trust your judgment, but Warren, if you can't handle it, you come straight to me. Understood?"

"Yes, sir."

* * *

Cathryn dragged herself toward consciousness, but her head sank into the pillow as though fighting extra gravity. She blinked her tired eyes open and peered at the bulky man who was checking the monitor beside her.

"Your son is a lot like you." Her voice emerged a raspy whisper.

He leaned over her. "What makes you think you know my son?"

"Your nametag. Tony laughed when I told him Pietro means rock. He said you're a softie." Her eyelids drooped, and her limbs weighed too much to move.

"You're a smart girl, Cathryn. I'm sure Tony will visit when you're more awake."

"Tony's dad is a nurse. Am I in a hospital?" She fell asleep before she heard the answer.

* * *

Warren examined the file. Cathryn Joy Banks, born to Beatrice and Jedidiah Banks, last known address 2319 Maple Leaf Avenue South, Minneapolis, Minnesota 55404. Mother died in the fire. Father's whereabouts unknown.

Warren typed JEDIDIAH BANKS into the police database and found a list of misdemeanors and DUIs. Plausible case.

He listened to staticky hold music as the hospital transferred him to the nurses' station.

"Hello?" a man answered.

"Hello, this is Detective Warren Jones following up about a report of bruises on your patient, Cathryn Banks. Have you contacted the family yet?"

"We don't even have a number."

"If someone shows, let them in. Without proof, we cannot legally keep a parent from their child, but keep an eye on Cathryn's reactions and write down anything suspicious."

"Okay. The night nurse talked to the kid who pulled her out of the fire. She didn't think he was our guy, but I suppose you're the expert."

Warren jotted that in his notes. "I'll look into it. Thank you."

"Sir? One more question."

"Shoot."

"Cathryn is my son's friend. I can switch her to another nurse, but I'd rather not. She's skittish, and she trusts me. Will that be a problem?"

"Shouldn't be. What is your name?"

"Pietro Giordani."

Warren's hand stiffened around his pen. "Your son's name is Tony?"

"Yes, sir. How did you know?"

Warren sighed. *Looks like this case will hit close to home.* "I'm Minh Jones's father. I wasn't sure it was the same Cathryn."

The hospital intercom garbled in the background. "That a problem?"

Warren thought of the girl who'd been best friends with his daughter for nearly twelve years. "I won't make it one if you don't."

* * *

Cathryn winced as fluorescent light assaulted her eyes. She tried to turn over and regretted it. Her body ached. Parts of her itched painfully.

Take stock. She wiggled the toes on her right foot. *Still working. Now the left.* She flinched, but something restrained the movement—a cast or a splint. *Okay. Right hand.* Fine. She tried her left fingers. *Don't panic.* She inhaled the scent of starched sheets and fluttered her eyes open.

She wore a loose gown. Monitors beeped beside her. *Hospital.* She rubbed the bandages that encased her left arm and tried once more to move her fingers.

"Morning, sunshine. Remember me?" A man in pale-blue scrubs stood at the end of her bed.

Cathryn shook her head, but she had to steady it with her hand when the room spun. She squinted at the man's large nose and round head. "Are you Tony's dad?"

"Right three times in a row."

"I don't remember the first two."

"Don't worry. Confusion is normal when you first wake." His Tony-esque grin reassured her. "Can you tell me where you are?"

Cathryn scanned the room. A whiteboard dominated one wall.

"Ogden Medical Center," she read.

"Good. Now, how about the date and time?"

The clock above the board said 10:00. *A.M. or P.M.?*

"The board says Friday. The clock says 10:00. I'm guessing by the light from the window that means 10 a.m." Cathryn rubbed her temples. "That information would be more helpful if I remembered when I got here."

Mr. Giordani laughed. "We'll get to that. Any pain right now?"

Cathryn shook her head. *Nothing more than usual.* "I can't move my left fingers."

The nurse frowned and put his fingers into her left hand. "Squeeze."

Cathryn grimaced with effort, but her fingers didn't even twitch.

"Don't worry. We'll have the occupational therapist check you out." He sat beside her. "Cathryn, now that you're more awake, I'm going to ask you to do a hard thing, okay?"

Cathryn nodded.

"Tell me what you remember."

Searching her memories was like hunting for something at the bottom of a pitch-dark pool. "I . . . I remember being sad . . . then my dad came home, but he . . . and then everything was burning. It was so hot. I couldn't breathe . . . Mom." She grabbed the nurse's arm. "My mom was upstairs. Is she okay? Can I see her? Is she okay?"

He put his hand over hers. "Cathryn—"

"No. Please, no. I promised I'd be there when she—" Her voice cracked. "Please. Tell me she's okay."

"She's gone, Cathryn. I'm sorry."

Chapter 24

Minh wheeled toward her locker after school, but she halted when she saw Gus. When he hadn't showed this morning, she'd assumed he'd finally gotten sick like a normal human being. By the looks of him, he caught more than the flu.

His hair sprang in all directions as if he'd slept on it wet and not bothered to comb it. His eyes were puffy; his clothes, slung on haphazardly. He walked in an uncoordinated shuffle so unlike his usual confident stride that Minh did a doubletake to confirm she was looking at the right person. *He looks like hell chewed him, swallowed, and barfed him back up.* She wasn't the only one to notice.

Tony grimaced. "What happened to you?"

Gus leaned against the wall of lockers. He started to say something, stopped, and started again.

"Cathryn is not in Denver. Her house burned to the ground last night. She's in the hospital."

"What is this, a sick joke?" Minh said.

Gus's eyes snapped toward her like a whip. "Is there any humor in my expression?" His voice dripped venom, but within seconds his face drained of anger, as if he didn't have the strength to maintain it. "I was there, Minh." He whispered the words and held up his bandaged hands.

The friends battered him with questions.

"I have no other information. As far as I know, Cathryn hasn't even regained consciousness."

Minh strummed her fingers on her thigh as she absorbed everything he'd said. "Let me call my dad. He might have heard something from his coworkers." Gus nodded, evidently too tired to argue. *Now I know he's telling the truth.* Gus was never too tired to argue.

Minh's father answered her call, but she didn't trust the discomfort in his voice. "What do you mean you can't talk about it? Unless—" Her vision darkened. "Dad, tell me she's not your case."

She knew the answer before she heard his vague dismissal. She bit her fist and inhaled. "I want to see her." She prepared to argue, but her father understood. "Okay. I will. Love you too." She hung up and addressed her friends. "He offered to drive us to the hospital tomorrow morning."

"What is the significance of Cathryn's being your father's case?"

Damn. Gus wouldn't let her gloss over her reaction. Her fingernails stabbed her palms.

"My dad specializes in cases of domestic violence."

The silence that followed might have stretched into eternity had Tony not punched his fist into a locker, denting it beyond repair. Minh met Gus's eyes, and in them, all the pieces to the puzzle that was Cathryn fit together into a cohesive whole—and shattered.

Gus slid to the floor. "We had all the evidence."

Minh stared at nothing, her thoughts filled with every time she told her father to "leave work at work." She should have told him to work harder.

"How could we be so blind?"

* * *

Warren sank into his desk chair and brushed his fingers over the picture of his wife and kids. He'd spent the rest of the day searching for Jedidiah Banks. Banks's former boss reported he'd been a decent employee until a few months ago when he started showing up to work hungover or still drunk. Mr. Fifer hadn't seen Banks since he fired him, so Warren inquired at the bars whose addresses were listed in the misdemeanor reports. One owner threw Jedidiah out yesterday afternoon for fighting. That was Warren's only clue to where the man was hiding.

Poor Cathryn. He was used to cases like this—worse than this—but he'd never had one hit so close to him. *How did I miss it?*

"Sir, back away from this desk. Now." Marlys's warning carried through the entire office. It took a tough woman to be a receptionist for police officers. They'd be in trouble when the old bird retired.

"That bitch took my little girl!"

Warren moved closer to the lobby in case Marlys called for backup. A middle-aged white man paced in front of her desk, reeking of alcohol and vomit which the secretary didn't seem to smell. *Maybe there are benefits to old age.*

"Ninety-eight percent of missing persons cases resolve within twenty-four hours. Fill out this paperwork, and we'll see how we can help."

"She followed the damn neighbors, burned everything to shit." The man's words slurred around his swollen lower lip. "You have to find her."

"Calm down, or I'll call someone with a gun to make you calm down." Marlys's tone was more intimidating than any weapon.

Warren followed his hunch. "Sir, was your residence 2319 Maple Leaf Avenue South?"

"Yes, sir. See, I knew I'd get to someone in charge." He glared at Marlys, who glared back.

"Jedidiah Banks?"

"Yes, sir. Now how do we get my daughter back?" The man swayed on his feet.

"Mr. Banks, your wife and daughter were inside your house when it burned. Your daughter Cathryn is in the hospital."

"You found her? Where is she? I'll pick her up."

He didn't ask if she was okay. Warren's gut twisted at the possessiveness in the man's eyes. He'd seen that look too many times.

"Why don't I drive you myself?"

* * *

Warren walked close enough to Jedidiah to grab him if needed, but far enough away to breathe without choking on his stench.

"Hey, how much will this cost me?" Jedidiah's eyes darted around the hospital lobby.

"Mr. Banks, I have a feeling it won't cost you a penny." Warren wanted to pull out his cuffs right then, but he knew the law. Nothing but Mr. Banks's less-than-charming personality suggested he gave Cathryn her bruises.

They rode the elevator to the third floor and walked to the nurses' station.

"Excuse me, we're looking for Cathryn Banks. This is her father, Jedidiah."

The young woman looked up from her computer and wrinkled her nose. "Cathryn is Pietro's patient. I'll find him for you."

Warren needed no introduction to recognize the nurse who appeared minutes later. He was a large-nosed version of Minh's friend Tony.

"Nurse Pietro, I'm Detective Jones. This is Jedidiah Banks, Cathryn's father."

Pietro threw Warren a worried look and addressed Jedidiah. "The occupational therapist is with her now. You have a strong daughter, sir."

"Course she's strong. I raised her. Where is she? I'll take it from here."

"I don't think you understand," Pietro said. "Cathryn won't be ready to go home for at least a couple of days."

"Where is she?" Jedidiah's tone darkened. Pietro appealed to Warren, who nodded.

"Room 304," the nurse said, defeated.

Warren followed Jedidiah to where Cathryn sat on the edge of the bed. As soon as she saw her father, the color drained from her face, emphasizing the contrast between her pale skin and the dark zigzag of stitches in her forehead.

The therapist who knelt in front of Cathryn must have noticed her reaction too. Warren couldn't see her face from behind, but the folds of the woman's dark blue hijab shifted as she tilted her head. She took a strange device out of Cathryn's left hand.

"Cathryn, do we need to call your nurse?"

Cathryn stared at her father.

Jedidiah's hand twitched at his side. "You going to answer that?"

"I'm fine." Cathryn's words had no power behind them, as if she'd said them without enough breath support. Judging by the way her chest moved in shallow bursts, Warren guessed she had.

Jedidiah jerked his head toward the door. "We're leaving."

"What?" The therapist spun and stood in one smooth motion. Apart from the creases that appeared when her almost-black eyes widened, her warm brown skin was smooth. She must have been fresh out of graduate school, never encountered this situation.

Pietro appeared, sparing Warren the explanation. "A patient's guardian may refuse medical treatment, Amiina." He offered Cathryn a set of sweats, but the therapist snatched them.

"I'll help her change." She closed a curtain around Cathryn's bed, and the rest of them waited in a tense silence.

Warren cleared his throat. "Mr. Banks, have you thought this through? Your house is a pile of ashes. Maybe Cathryn should remain in the hospital until you find better lodging."

"No doctor or occu-whatever can take care of my daughter better than me."

On cue, the occupational therapist whipped open the curtain. She looked ready to tell Jedidiah exactly what she thought of his caregiving, but Pietro asked her to find a wheelchair for Cathryn. *Smart man, that nurse.*

Warren pushed past Jedidiah and knelt in front of Cathryn, took her pale hands in his own.

"Cathryn, if you don't feel ready to leave, just say so. It's okay not to be okay."

Cathryn's lips parted. Her eyes screamed, "help," but no sound emerged from her mouth.

"Stay away from my daughter." Jedidiah grabbed Warren's arm and pulled him away.

"He's just doing his job, Dad." Cathryn's voice was a hoarse whisper. "Police officers have to check."

She caught Warren's eye, and her barely perceptible headshake answered all his questions—why she was pretending not to know him, why she wore long sleeves in summer, why she never invited Minh to her house. Her father was abusing her, and unless Warren came up with some hard evidence fast, he'd go right on doing it.

"Mr. Banks, I'm not convinced your daughter wants to go with you."

Jedidiah lowered his voice. "My daughter does as she's told." He turned to Cathryn. "You ready, kiddo?"

Cathryn blanched. She took a strangled breath and broke into violent coughs. Pietro grabbed an inhaler from her bedside table and made her inhale a few puffs. He patted her back and spoke in a soothing tone, but Cathryn's eyes remained fixed on her father.

"I'd say that's answer enough." Warren straightened to his full height, a good five inches taller than Jedidiah. "Cathryn, stay with Nurse Pietro for a minute. I need to have a chat with your father before you leave." He gestured to the door.

Jedidiah's bear-like frame swelled as his muscles tensed. "No cop can tell me how to care for my own kid. You don't know—"

"I know her favorite color is blue. I know she memorizes the dictionary for fun, works at the library, and has a crush on a guy named Gus." He took a step forward. "A father ought to know those things about his daughter, but judging by the look on your face, you didn't, so you tell me which one of us knows best?"

Warren was ready for the punch. He'd provoked it, needling the scumbag until the white-knuckled fist hurtled toward his face.

He hadn't counted on Cathryn.

He hadn't known how fast she could move, that even with one bad ankle she could close the gap between them, but she did. Cathryn threw herself at her father, grabbing his arm mid-swing. His subsequent backhand left her sprawling on the floor.

Cathryn grabbed the computer on wheels and pushed it between herself and her father's next blow. It fell to the ground in pieces. Warren launched himself at Jedidiah, but the shorter man slipped around him. Taking his cue from his daughter, Jedidiah grabbed another wheeled stand. Cathryn raised her left arm to block the blow. He swung.

A loose screw, a sharp edge—that's all it took to rip through her stitches and tear open her arm. Cathryn cried out as blood spurted from the wound. Pietro shouted orders to the other nurses. Warren lunged at Jedidiah, but he fended him off with an uppercut to the gut. Two hospital security guards helped drag the raging man to the floor.

"Cathryn, let me help you." Pietro reached for Cathryn's arm, but she jerked away, splattering his scrubs with blood. A flurry of hospital personnel invaded the room, but Cathryn evaded them, eyes wild.

Pietro held up his hands. "Cathryn, we need to stitch up your arm before—"

Jedidiah roared and struggled against his captors. Cathryn screamed. She kicked one of the nurses and scrambled toward the door, but Pietro another nurse caught her before she further injured her arm. They held her still while a woman in a white doctor's coat injected something into her triceps, and within moments she fell limp. The nurses loaded her onto a cart and rushed her out of the room.

Warren pulled out his cuffs. "Jedidiah Banks, you are under arrest. You have the right to remain silent . . ."

Chapter 25

Minh snarled as her father helped her over the bump. *All these people in wheelchairs, and no one thought to properly bank the curb?*

Tony told them hospitals prefer only a few visitors at a time to avoid overwhelming patients. He'd volunteered to wait until this afternoon, which left Minh stuck with Gus for company. Fortunately, Gus hadn't said a word the whole drive. He followed them into the elevator with the same lost-puppy demeanor with which he'd followed Cathryn at the beginning of the year.

If the school's elevator compared to her dad's rusted Chevy, the hospital's ranked as a Mercedes. Minh was a connoisseur of elevators. This one *almost* made up for the curb.

"Nurse Pietro," her father said when they reached the nurses' station, "I think you've met Minh and Gus?"

"The hero!" Mr. Giordani grinned at Gus. "You certainly impressed Nurse Albie."

Minh raised an eyebrow, but Gus ignored the comment. "How is Cathryn?"

"She was up a while yesterday, but she . . . she had a difficult afternoon. They started her on some heavy-duty pain meds last night, so she might be a little confused."

Minh's dad elected to speak with Mr. Giordani while they visited. Minh thought she'd prepared herself to see her friend swallowed in pillows, but her breath caught as soon as Gus opened the door.

179

Cathryn's battered body looked like it might fall apart without the bandages holding it together.

Gus strode into the room. Minh shook herself and wheeled in after him. Cathryn stirred, and the corners of her chapped lips turned upward.

"Minh," she wheezed.

"Hey, Cat."

"I missed you so much."

Minh swallowed her emotions. "I missed you too."

Cathryn broke into coughs so violent Minh was certain she heard her bones rattle. The tissue Cathryn used to cover her mouth turned black with soot.

"Hey, Cathryn. Use that inhaler like I showed you," Mr. Giordani called from the hall. Gus shook the dark blue inhaler and handed it Cathryn. She inhaled twice, and her coughing slowed.

Cathryn sank into the pillows and looked at Gus. "Were you guys fighting?"

Gus cocked his head. "What do you mean?"

Cathryn's fingers wavered as she reached for Gus's hands. "Sometimes I worry about leaving you two alone."

Gus snorted. "I'm not sure whether to be flattered by your concern or insulted by your assuming I would be injured while Minh would emerge unscathed."

"Don't be silly, Cat," Minh said. "He'd have bandages on more than his hands after I was through with him." Her joke didn't penetrate the pain medications. Cathryn's look of concern deepened, and she moved to sit upright.

Gus eased her back. "Neither of us has engaged in physical hostilities in your absence."

Cathryn blinked her eyes open wider, but they drooped back to half-closed. "Then what happened to your hands?"

Minh leaned forward. She hadn't yet heard the specifics of Gus's injuries, and she couldn't imagine why the nurses referred to him as "the hero."

Gus cleared his throat. "It's too lengthy a tale for now. You rest. I promise to regale you with the details once you've recuperated."

Cathryn's eyelids finished their downward course, and she fell asleep.

Minh thought of Gus as a coin flip between anger and arrogance, but the way he looked at Cathryn gave her pause. He brushed a stray hair away from Cathryn's face with such tenderness that Minh was forced to consider that she might be wrong.

Gus brushed a stray hair away from Cathryn's face, wishing he'd crashed his car sooner.

* * *

"I never liked you." Minh had mastered the art of weaponizing her tone and facial expression. Her current demeanor read, "Take no prisoners."

"Is that opinion likely to change?" Gus had learned from experience that arguing with Minh was like chiseling rock with a piece of cooked spaghetti.

"I haven't decided yet." The fluorescent light flickered, giving Minh's narrowed eyes an even more menacing gleam. "Are you in love with her?"

"Love is nothing more than a conglomeration of hormones and chemical reactio—"

"I didn't ask if you believe love exists. I asked if you were in love with Cathryn."

Leave it to Minh to make the distinction. Gus told himself he didn't believe in love. He'd collected ample evidence against it while observing his parents. Then he met Cathryn. She was evidence for a lot of things he didn't believe.

"Only Cathryn would lie half-conscious in a hospital bed worrying how *I* hurt *my* hands." *I don't deserve her.*

"How did you hurt your hands?"

Gus opened his mouth, but he wasn't ready to relive that moment. "I explained earlier. I was there."

His terse reply did nothing to dissuade Minh. She looked like a CEO waiting for an unfortunate intern to explain why he sold half the company for a pittance.

Gus rubbed his temples. "I saw her on the bus, and—"

"You saw her, and you didn't tell us?"

"I had to confirm"—*small words*—"I had to make sure I wasn't hallu— going crazy. When I returned the next day, her house was engulfed in flames. I injured my hands pulling her out."

Minh seemed in no hurry to release him from her glare. Gus sensed she was evaluating more than his words. After an uncomfortable silence, she gave him a half-smile.

"So much for not rescuing damsels in distress."

"I'd rather this damsel had skipped to the happy ending."

Minh touched Cathryn's bandaged arm. She wore a vulnerable expression Gus found disquieting on her.

"Why didn't she tell us?"

Good question. Cathryn and Gus discussed everything from Noam Chomsky's theory of universal grammar to Murray Gell-Mann's study of subatomic particles. Only one subject never entered their conversations—their homelives. Since Gus didn't want to talk about his either, he hadn't thought much of her omission, but now he wondered. With all the polysyllabic words that flowed between them, why had she neglected a simple "help?"

"I don't know."

Minh's familiar sass returned. "You, admitting you don't know something? Have aliens invaded your brain?"

"Possession by extraterrestrials is one hypothesis. I for one suspect I still suffer from carbon monoxide poisoning."

Minh laughed. "You know you spend too much time around geniuses when you understand their dark jokes." The laughter fled her face as Cathryn wheezed softly. "I can't imagine the hell she lived."

Gus stared at the floor. *I should have figured it out.* Cathryn shouldn't have needed to ask for help. What kind of scientist can't see what's right in front of him? What kind of friend?

Tears stung his eyes. He blinked them back lest Minh catch him, but the fiery artist was wiping her own cheeks dry. Gus thought of Minh as an armored tank, but the way her lower lip trembled forced him to consider that he might be wrong.

They both looked away.

Gus grasped Cathryn's fingers and felt them warm in his grip. He wished he'd dared to take her hand the day they walked across the Stone Arch Bridge.

"Yes."

Minh shook herself and glared at him. "Yes what?"

"Your question regarding my feelings for Cathryn. The answer is yes."

* * *

The last place Tony wanted to spend his Saturday morning was the library, but this was for Cathryn, so he forced himself through the entrance.

He inhaled a smell both too clean and too dusty, like a freshly vacuumed carpet. He preferred the pungent odor of engine grease. With a car, he could get his hands dirty, muck around, and if all else failed, smack it with a wrench. Books were delicate, easily torn and stained by his sausage-sized fingers.

He could see why Cathryn liked it, though. The library was quiet yet filled with words—like her.

Tony rolled his shoulders and proceeded to the front desk, where an elderly man greeted him.

"Hello, young sir. How may I help you?"

"You Mr. Z?"

"I am."

Tony twisted the hem of his shirt. "It's about Kitten, er, Cathryn."

Mr. Z grabbed a pencil. "Has she sent a forwarding address?"

"She never left." Tony related everything he knew, which wasn't much.

The librarian shook his head as though filling in the blanks himself. "I suspected life in her home was no paradise, but I never imagined anything so dark. How can I help?"

Tony gestured to Mr. Z's notepad. "I got a few ideas."

Chapter 26

Warren marched toward the hospital elevator.

"Would you slow down?" Liz dug her polished fingernails into his coat. "I have to take three steps to every one of yours."

Warren snorted. "Might be only two if you didn't wear those ridiculous heels."

Liz fluffed her auburn ringlets. "Just because I'm not going out on the town today doesn't mean I can't *look* like I have a life."

They entered the elevator, and Liz used the mirror at the back to apply another layer of ruby red lipstick. She always wore floral dresses and costume jewelry, contrasting her pasty complexion with bright colors.

"Thanks for coming on a Saturday, Liz."

Liz blew a kiss to the mirror. "I owed you one. Now we're even." She gave him a wicked smile. "How's Beth? Kicking law-school ass?"

"Straight A's so far."

"That's my girl. The rest of the brood good too?"

Warren nodded.

"How you feed all those kids on your salaries is one of life's great mysteries."

Warren chuckled as the elevator door opened. "My wife doesn't mind shopping at thrift stores."

They approached the nurses' station just as Pietro popped out of another patient's room and cleaned his hands with a squirt of sanitizer.

"Nurse Pietro, this is Elizabeth Finestock, the department psychologist I told you about this morning."

"I wish we were meeting somewhere else, Ms. Finestock." Pietro shook her hand and turned to Warren. "The doc cut back on her pain meds, so she should be alert. She's tougher than she looks, but she's in a heap of hurt, and not all of it physical."

"The sad but necessary evil in our jobs is that we must bring that hurt to light to heal it," Liz said. Pietro nodded grimly.

* * *

Cathryn squinted at the newspaper, but a noise at the door distracted her. Minh's father entered; a petite woman trailed him.

"Cathryn, this is my friend Liz Finestock. She wants to ask you a couple questions."

Cathryn's mouth went dry. Cops asking questions never led to anything good. Her hand shook as she tried to close the newspaper. *How do right-handed people do this?* After fumbling for a minute, she shoved the whole bedside table away.

Ms. Finestock shut the door with an all-too-familiar thud. Cathryn reached for a ponytail that wasn't there with a hand that couldn't fidget with it anyway.

Ms. Finestock cocked her head. "Should I leave the door open in case you need to call Nurse Pietro?"

Cathryn nodded, disturbed she'd been so easily read.

Ms. Finestock sat next to her, crossing her legs at the ankles. "You like to read the paper?"

"I like to read anything with words on it." *Where is she going with this?*

"I was sorry to hear about your house, Cathryn."

"Far more important was the person in the house, Ms. Finestock."

Ms. Finestock shifted in her seat. "You're right. I'm sorry. You and your mother were close, weren't you?"

Cathryn nodded.

"What did you do together?"

"Mostly housework. Sometimes she'd volunteer at the library with me."

"What do you and your father do together?"

Cathryn fixed her eyes on the wall calendar. "He likes to watch TV. He tells me about his day over dinner."

"Cathryn, can you look at me?" Ms. Finestock's face invited trust the way bait invited a mouse into a trap. "Do you remember what happened with your father yesterday?"

Cathryn touched her bandaged arm. Yesterday's "incident" was hazy in her mind, but she didn't need a photographic memory to fill in the details.

"Cathryn?"

She squirmed and looked at Minh's dad. "Do I have to do this?"

"No, but you'd help a lot if you did."

"W-what are you going to do?"

Ms. Finestock answered. "Cathryn, what your father did was wrong. The more we know about other wrong things he's done, the more likely we are to make sure he never hurts anyone again. You can tell us, Cathryn."

Cathryn wanted to believe in a world where she didn't dread 6:00 p.m., hide bruises, or panic at the sound of a door closing, but she knew better. She'd been nine the last time she and her mother tried to escape.

They ran to the neighbors' house to hide, but her father discovered them. She hid in the closet with her mother, suffocating in the record-high heat while her father pounded on the front door. His screams cut through the charged air of an impending storm.

He chopped down their neighbors' door with an ax as the first rumbles of thunder reached them. Señor Maldonado tried to stop him, but Cathryn's father knocked the shorter man unconscious. Fifteen-year-old Diego tried next, but soon he lay sprawled on the front step next to his dad.

Cathryn clung to her mother and watched through a hole in the door as her father hacked up furniture. He brought the ax down on the coffee table, but a bang louder than anything Cathryn had ever heard drowned out all other sounds. The first droplets of rain splattered against the window, but the lightning had done its job.

Señora Maldonado and ten-year-old Joaquín rushed down the stairs, fleeing the smoke in the attic.

Cathryn's mother burst from the closet. "Don't hurt them."

Her father dragged her mother out to the lawn and beat her. Cathryn sprang out of the house.

"Dad, stop!" Her father's eyes burned like those of the monsters from her storybooks. He hit her. When she woke, she was locked in her bedroom with her mother. She never saw the Maldonados again.

It took seven years to summon the courage for another escape attempt, but this time it was their house that burned, and their escape money burned with it. Her father always won.

"Cathryn?"

Cathryn blinked back to the present.

Ms. Finestock leaned forward. "Cathryn, we can help you. We can —"

"No. You can't." More than her voice trembled. "You'll only make it worse."

"Make what worse, Cathryn?"

Cathryn scooted away. She looked at Minh's dad. "I don't want to do this anymore. I-I don't want to answer any more questions."

Mr. Jones looked at Ms. Finestock, who shook her head.

"Okay. No one will force you, but Cathryn, if you ever want to talk, you call me. Can you promise me that?"

Cathryn nodded. Anything to make them to go away.

* * *

Warren rubbed his temples as he emerged from Cathryn's room. "That could have gone better."

"She's built her father into an invincible force in her mind," Liz said. "I hate to say this, Warren, but her behavior indicates an extended history of abuse."

"We need her to confirm that. We're holding her father on the assault charge, but unless Cathryn talks, that's all we have."

They found Nurse Pietro at the center station. He grabbed a blue file and handed it to Warren.

"The report you asked for this morning. Her dad nearly finished what the fire started. Sliced veins, severed nerves, torn muscles—she could have bled to death. Surgeon did the best he could, but the occupational therapist will have to reevaluate to see if she'll regain the use of her fingers." He shook his head. "I worry about that arm. The stand hit her in the exact wrong spot." A light turned on above the room opposite them. "If you'll excuse me, that's one of my patients calling."

"Thank you." Warren leafed through the report. Nurse Pietro was both efficient and thorough. Amidst paragraphs of medical jargon were photographs of Cathryn's forearm. It resembled Frankenstein's monster. Burns covered the backside, but the inside was worse. The blow from the stand not only widened her original puncture wound, it carved a new fissure that extended from her wrist to her elbow. The swollen flesh pulled against the stitches, red and angry.

Warren's throat tightened. "I need to take myself off this case."

"Technically, it shouldn't have been yours in the first place." Liz hopped to sit on the counter. A nurse gave her a sidelong glance before moving out of earshot. "Should you have provoked that stinking pile of llama puke? No, but if you hadn't, that poor girl would be in a crappy hotel with him right now. You wouldn't see her again until you had to identify her body."

Warren ran his finger over the photograph. "They can assign another agent."

Liz snorted. "Carmen and Sue are up to their necks in cases, which leaves Bob Davis. In case you've blocked his ugly mug out of your mind, he's the same age, shape, and color as the man who ripped open Cathryn's arm yesterday. If that gorilla takes charge, I'll have to do 90% of the work, and you know how I *love* working on Saturdays."

"Liz, I'm being serious."

"All right, let's talk serious." She snatched the report out of his hands. "When my questions got uncomfortable, where did Cathryn look?" She smacked Warren with the folder. "At you. That girl just lost her mother. How many other safe adults do you think she has? On this case, I'll take an emotionally compromised Warren Jones over the ape-man. I'll sweet-talk the boss. You focus on getting Cathryn to talk."

"Thanks, Liz."

"Thank me by treating me to lunch." She hopped down from the counter and started toward the elevator. "While we're out, let's buy flowers for that wife of yours. You're going to put in some serious overtime with this case."

* * *

Cathryn's whole body trembled. *They'll tell. They'll try to help, and he'll find out. I should have pretended to be asleep.*

A knock at the door interrupted her panic. "Hiya, Kitten."

"Tony? What are you doing here?"

Tony and his mother carried several bags into the room.

"I got a present for you." He handed her a package that looked like a tribe of kindergarteners wrapped it.

Cathryn fingered the ribbon. "A present? I haven't done anything."

Mrs. Giordani laughed. "That's why it's called a gift, kiddo."

Cathryn set the package in her lap and used her right hand to unwrap it one piece of tape at a time. Underneath the paper lay *The Fantastic Flying Books of Mr. Morris Lessmore.* She stroked the raised letters on the cover. "How did you know?"

"That's part two." Mrs. Giordani's eyes glimmered.

"There's a part two?"

Tony grinned. "You didn't think we'd let you get stuck eating hospital food, did you?" Tony unloaded containers of food from his nonna, including several cannoli.

Cathryn smiled for the first time all day. "Thank you."

"We're not done yet," Tony said as he reached into another bag. "I stopped by the library. There was a gal there—short, black hair, spoke Spanish with a lisp . . ."

"Pilar?"

"Yeah, that's it. She wanted to give you this." He handed her an envelope. Inside was a get-well card written in Spanish:

From now on, may we only see each other at the library,
because you belong in school.

Take care,
Pilar and Rosa María

Tony handed her a tissue. "The kids wanted to write cards too. This one is my favorite." He cleared his throat. "'Dear Miss Cat, I am sorry you lost one of your nine lives. I hope you don't come back as a psychopedia because I would miss your stories. From, Jordan.'"

Cathryn laughed. "I think he meant encyclopedia."

The three of them alternated reading the cards while they ate, with Cathryn translating the Spanish ones. Cathryn hadn't laughed so hard since she went to the state fair with the Joneses, and Minh picked a fight with a clown. Soon the children's colorful scribblings covered every spare surface in the hospital room. Cathryn had never understood the expression "weeping tears of joy," but that didn't stop the tears from streaming into her smile.

Chapter 27

Mark Ostergaard had known Warren Jones for years, so when the detective offered to take him and Laurel out for lunch, he didn't hesitate to accept the invitation. As soon as they shook hands, however, Mark's instincts told him this was more than a lunch date. Years of negotiating business contracts had sharpened his ability to read people, and Warren Jones behaved like an incompetent con artist.

"So, how are you two?" A controlled innocence infused Warren's tone.

Laurel answered. "Well, I'm as good as I'll get." She laughed at her own dark humor. "Really, I am well, and Mark just closed another big deal. This lunch was good timing."

"Glad to hear it."

Enough with the distraction tactics. "I take it you invited us out for more than small talk, Warren."

Warren sipped his water, an amateur's way of buying time. "Actually, I did have ulterior motives. I want to run an idea by you."

"I'm listening." Acquaintances and even strangers presented Mark with terrible business ideas every day—an annoying side effect of success—but this surprised him. Warren didn't strike him as the type for get-rich-quick schemes.

"Well, I know before"—Warren gestured to Laurel—"everything, you went through the approval process to be adoptive or foster parents."

Mark dropped his fork. "You want to give us a baby?"

"A teenager actually. I know what you're thinking, but this girl is nothing like Jeremy." The Bentrigaards' teenage foster son featured in many church group discussions. "I'd take her myself, but we have a full house, and frankly, it wouldn't be best for her. Our place is too chaotic. She needs someplace quiet, someplace safe."

Mark's head spun. "I don't know, Warren. I mean—"

"I want to take her," Laurel said.

"Honey, we—"

"Come on, Mark. We have a huge house all to ourselves. We may as well put it to good use. Besides, it would be nice to take care of someone else for a change." Laurel's mouth set in a determined line. For too long, life had brought her nothing but pain. Maybe company would be good for her. Caring for someone else might help her feel useful again, assuming this girl wasn't a troublemaker.

Mark pushed his plate aside. "Why don't you tell us more about her."

* * *

Cathryn grimaced as she tried to make a fist. The occupational therapist had learned the best way to motivate her was to teach her new Somali words after every task, but her hand didn't share her enthusiasm for vocabulary.

Cathryn stared at her noncompliant fingers as if her eyes could communicate the signal her nerves failed to transmit. Nothing.

"Will I ever be able to use my hand again?" Her voice emerged a whisper.

Amiina's face softened. "We can't make predictions, but let's focus on the positives. The swelling around your stitches has decreased, and you can bend and straighten your elbow." She set her notes aside. "I know that answer is frustrating and maybe a little frightening, but be patient with your body. I promise to write a thorough report for your outpatient therapist."

Cathryn fixed her gaze on the whiteboard where the night nurse had taped one of her get-well cards. "I don't have money for therapy."

"Don't worry. If all else fails, the university clinic charges on a sliding scale, which for you would be zero."

Zero. Cathryn had never owned much, but now even "the clothes on her back" were sweats printed with the hospital logo. How could she pay for these treatments? What would her father do when he received the doctor's bill?

"Cathryn? You look a little sick, should I call your nurse?"

Cathryn shook her head. "I'm fine."

Amiina furrowed her brow. "Don't give up, Cathryn." She said goodbye in Somali and headed out the door.

Cathryn pulled the hospital bed's starchy blankets around her shoulders, but she couldn't help shivering. The nurses, doctors, and other professionals who poked, prodded, and questioned her said she was "going home" today, but they later caught themselves and mentioned a foster placement.

Cathryn held her stomach as her anxious thoughts triggered nausea. She knew kids who'd gone into foster care. Their lives were horrific, and the placements weren't always an improvement.

Before the fire, she'd acquired jobs, contacts, and a stockpile of money. Now, her assets included a children's book and a handful of get-well cards. She knew nothing about these foster parents. At best, her staying with them would provoke her father to extremism.

He'll hurt everyone I love. Then he'll lock me in a windowless room for the rest of my life. Cathryn's stomach revolted. She rushed to the bathroom, but the walking cast on her left ankle hindered her movement. She managed to vomit mostly in the toilet, but some of her chicken and gravy lunch splattered onto the floor. Hospital food was even less appealing when regurgitated.

"Cathryn?" Mr. Giordani appeared, his purple scrubs already stained with something.

Cathryn grabbed a handful of paper towels and tried to clean her mess. "I'm sorry."

"Hey, don't worry about that. I'll take care of it." He crouched beside her. "Amiina said you looked queasy."

Cathryn scooted away from his attempt to feel her forehead. "I'm fine."

The lie squeaked out of her tight throat. She'd lost her home, her hand, and her escape plan. How could she be fine? She was alone.

Her lower lip trembled. "I miss my mom."

Mr. Giordani sat across from her. "It's okay to cry, Cathryn."

For years, Cathryn had trained herself to contain her emotions, but once the tears started falling, she couldn't stop them. Her entire body shook as she wept.

Mr. Giordani spoke in a soothing tone, but her sobs muffled his words. Cathryn tried to dry her eyes, but she couldn't push her left fingers against her face, which instigated another round of tears. She gulped air and forced herself to release it slowly.

Someone knocked, and her attention snapped to the bathroom door.

Mr. Jones surveyed the scene. "Nervous?"

Cathryn drew her knees into her chest and nodded.

Mr. Giordani stood. "Why don't we get you cleaned up, and then you and Detective Jones can discuss what's bothering you."

He helped her to her feet and started cleaning the bathroom floor. "I can—"

"Nope." He waved away her protests.

Cathryn washed her face, swished mouthwash, and limped into the room where Mr. Jones waited for her.

"I arranged for you to stay with friends of mine," he said as she sat on the edge of the bed. "I've known them for years. You'll be safe there."

So he says. "And my dad?"

"In jail until the trial." He leaned forward. "He'll stay there a lot longer if you testify."

Cathryn shook her head. "You'll just make him mad." *They're making it worse.*

"Cathryn, do you trust me?"

Cathryn fidgeted with the tissue box on her bedside table. She trusted Mr. Jones, but he didn't know her father.

Mr. Jones took the tissue box from her and set it aside. "Why don't we tackle one thing at a time? Let's get you settled with the Ostergaards, and we'll discuss the trial later. Deal?"

Cathryn nodded. Not like she had much choice.

"Great." Mr. Jones stood. "We finished the paperwork, so as soon as you gather your things, we can head out."

Cathryn grabbed *The Fantastic Flying Books of Mr. Morris Lessmore,* which had the get-well cards tucked between the pages. "There's one more card on the whiteboard."

Mr. Jones handed it to her. "What else can I help carry?"

Cathryn shrugged. "This is everything I own."

"Right." Mr. Jones looked at his shoes and rubbed the back of his neck, but Mr. Giordani emerged from the bathroom. He rummaged through a cupboard and handed a loose bundle to Cathryn.

"I know hospital sweats are the height of fashion, but if you want more variety, I brought some of my daughters' and nieces' old clothes. Not sure if they'll fit, but hopefully they'll tide you over."

Cathryn's tepid smile stretched her cheeks, as if her face had forgotten the expression. "Thank you."

After Mr. Giordani helped her tie the laces of her hand-me-down right shoe, Cathryn followed Mr. Jones to his car. It felt like an eternity since she'd seen the outside world, and she let herself stare out the window the entire ride. *Step one: assess foster situation. Step two: form new escape plan.*

Mr. Jones parked across from the Lake of the Isles. "Here we are."

Cathryn's jaw dropped. "You mean people actually live here?" She'd always thought the mansions along the lake shore were historical relics maintained to add ambiance for tourists.

Mr. Jones chuckled as he opened the door for her. Cathryn clutched the plastic bag containing her belongings and hobbled up the walkway. *Dad would never search for me here.* The thought did nothing to calm her nerves. A nice house didn't guarantee nice people. Gus's family proved money couldn't buy parenting skills, and her own father demonstrated that monsters hid behind charming smiles.

Just as they reached the front step, a handsome couple opened the door. They were short of breath, as if they'd run to answer it, though the man appeared as fit as her father. Even if he weren't, Cathryn couldn't out-maneuver him in a walking cast.

The man cleared his throat. "I'm Mark." He held out his hand, but Cathryn flinched, bumping into Mr. Jones behind her.

He steadied her with a hand on her shoulder. "Cathryn, this is Mark and Laurel Ostergaard. I'll leave you to get acquainted, but if you need anything, call me."

He handed her his card. Cathryn shifted her bundle to beneath her arm to accept it. The Minneapolis Police logo glinted in the afternoon sun. *How bad must your life become before a cop gives you his card?*

He turned to leave, but Cathryn called after him. "I don't have a phone."

"We have a landline you can use," Laurel said. She wore her hair tied beneath a scarf like Amiina, but the gold cross hanging from her neck suggested she was Christian. "Come on inside. I'll show you."

"I can take that." Mark reached for her bag, but Cathryn jerked away.

"I-I got it."

His smile twitched. "Right. Uh, come on in." He held the door open for his wife and waited for Cathryn to follow.

Cathryn held her breath as she crossed the threshold. As soon as she had enough space, she stepped out of Mark's reach and waited for him to pass.

"There's the kitchen," he said, pointing directly ahead to the state-of-the-art appliances that would make a celebrity chef envious. He gestured to the right. "The living room is through there. Warren, er, Mr. Jones said you like to read. We have a window seat you might like for reading or doing homework."

"I get to go back to school?" Cathryn fumbled her bundle and scrambled to catch it one-handed.

"Of course," Laurel said. "We're out of district, but we explained the situation to Principal Evans, and he was happy to re-enroll you."

They have enough money to ensure the rules don't apply to them. The arrangement unsettled Cathryn, but the prospect of seeing her friends encouraged her.

"Your room is upstairs." Laurel led the way. The stairs didn't creak, but Cathryn tested each one anyway, hoping they'd mistake her tentativeness for clumsiness. Stairclimbing in a waking cast wasn't exactly graceful.

Mark opened the first door on the left, but Cathryn hesitated, unwilling to enter an enclosed space that may not have an escape window. Mark backed away, and both adults eyed her expectantly. Cathryn clenched her right hand over her bag and thump-limped into the room.

"If you don't like the colors, we'll replace them." Laurel babbled as she flitted about rearranging things that weren't crooked, but Cathryn didn't hear a word after her eyes landed on the bed. An ache sank into her chest as she thought of her own iron-framed bed and lilac bedspread. She hadn't slept in it since the night she shared it with her mother. Soon after, her mother had forgotten who she was.

"Cathryn, is something wrong?" Laurel asked.

Cathryn swallowed. "No, it's just . . . I got used to sleeping on the floor."

* * *

Mark exchanged a glance with his wife, certain his expression mirrored hers.

They weren't prepared for this.

Laurel cleared her throat and gestured to Cathryn's bag. "Why don't we put your things in the dresser?"

Cathryn pulled a shirt out of the bag, but it unfolded in her hand. She struggled to re-fold it in the air before laying it on the bed and using just her right hand.

Laurel neatly hid a grimace as she unloaded three mismatched outfits that were too wide and too short for Cathryn. "We can shop for clothes that fit later."

"I can adjust these, and I'll wear them more than once before I wash them." Cathryn added a pair of socks to the drawer. "I'm good at cleaning, and organizing, and, um . . ."

"You don't need to earn your keep, Cathryn," Mark said.

Cathryn started at his voice. Laurel slide the dresser drawer closed with a frown.

197

"We're happy to buy you clothes. I'm a shopaholic anyway." She put on her best hostess smile. "It'll be fun. We can get to know each other."

Cathryn looked like she'd rather be a test subject for an acupuncture student, but she nodded obediently.

The last item from the bag was a children's book. As if by instinct, Cathryn held it to her nose and inhaled. Her face lost its pinched look—until she caught them staring.

"Sorry." She dropped the book. "I-I like the smell."

Okay, she's a little bizarre, but there are worse hobbies than book-sniffing.

Laurel picked up the book and whispered, "I do the same thing with my spice jars."

Her comment earned a small smile from Cathryn.

Better quit while we're ahead. "We'll leave you to settle in," Mark said.

Cathryn straightened like a soldier in line for inspection. "I'll be quiet as a library."

"Or you could listen to music." Mark gestured to the stereo on her desk.

Cathryn's face fell as if she'd given the wrong answer to a teacher. "Oh."

I've been a foster father for less than ten minutes, and I've already messed up. Mark opened his mouth, but Laurel took his arm before he could retract his comment.

"We'll be in the living room if you need anything." She pulled him into the hallway. They closed the door behind them, but within seconds it flew open again.

Cathryn's frantic eyes widened. "It opens."

Mark exchanged a glance with Laurel. "Would you rather lock—"

"No." Cathryn rubbed her burned arm. "Does the window open too?"

Mark nodded. "It's a funny crank. I'll show you how it works."

He knelt on her bed and pulled up the drapes. "Like this." He paused mid-demonstration. "Can you see from over there?"

Cathryn inched closer, eyes flitting to the door.

Mark pointed to the latch. "Make sure you lock it at night. This is a nice neighborhood, but occasionally some punk thinks it's funny to graffiti these old houses. If you hear something, come get me."

Cathryn nodded vigorously. "Thank you."

The bed creaked as Mark stood. Cathryn shifted away from him as he padded across the carpet toward the door.

"Mr. and Mrs. Ostergaard?"

"Yes?" Laurel said.

Cathryn gestured to the entire room. "Thank you."

"You're welcome, Cathryn," Mark said. "Let us know if you need anything."

He resisted the reflex to shut the door on his way out, and a heavy silence followed them to the living room couch. In his years as an entrepreneur and investor, Mark gained ample experience with introductions, but he'd never encountered one that surreal.

"She seems . . ."

"Terrified." Laurel filled in the blank.

Mark nodded. Warren had described the girl, but nothing prepared them for the female Tiny Tim who limped up their walkway. He'd heard plenty of horror stories about friends' teenagers—sarcasm, eye-rolling, sneaking out, smoking. It sickened him that Cathryn needed the door wide open while other teens slammed it in their parents' faces.

Laurel rubbed her thumb along her palm. "That arm . . . she's so young."

"Are you having second thoughts?"

She met his gaze. "Not for a second. You?"

"No. It's just . . . I hope someday we can talk without her flinching."

To Mark's astonishment, Laurel scooted close and rested her head on his shoulder. "I'm still mad at you, but let's try to focus on her, okay?"

Mark wrapped his arm around her. "Deal."

Chapter 28

C athryn inhaled the familiar scents of locker room and cheap perfume. She never thought she'd set foot in school again, but here she was.

"Hi Tony."

Tony paused his wrestling match with his backpack to grin at her. "Look who's back in town." He patted her locker. "You shouldn't have to hit it anymore. I fixed it for you."

"How did you know my combination?"

"Gus." Tony pointed with his thumb to where Gus was entering through the front doors.

Figures he would know. Cathryn opened her locker—without hitting it—and placed her backpack inside. The new canvas was stiff, and the zippers hard to operate. *At least I don't have to worry about the strap breaking.* Still, she missed her old one.

She reached for a notebook, but it slipped through her left hand and clunked to the floor. Cathryn shifted her gaze to her mangled forearm. Her eyes acknowledged it as part of her body, but her brain couldn't accept that it no longer worked. She tried to clasp her hand, but her fingers mocked her. *This will be harder than I thought.*

"Allow me." Gus retrieved her fallen notebook. "Why don't I carry your things today?"

Cathryn squinted. "What happened to your hands?"

He yanked them out of her reach. "Slight miscalculation with a chemistry project. My mother was irate."

"Yeah," Tony said, pounding Gus's back with a nervous grin. "Dr. Boom here is lucky we have a vacant lot out back."

"Dr. Boom?"

Gus squirmed as if clothes didn't fit. "As it happens, Tony shares my interest in pyrotechnics. Apparently, that warranted a new nickname."

"Oh." Cathryn hadn't imagined that while she'd been gone, her friends had built new lives that didn't include her. *Do they even want me back?* She reached for her ponytail, but her hair was down, and her hand found the singed edges where part of it had burned.

Cathryn jerked her hand down. She gave Gus a tentative smile, but she stiffened when she caught sight of the crowd of students who stared at her as if she'd sprouted tentacles. Attention was dangerous.

At least, it always had been.

School should have represented a return to normal, but instead, she'd entered a parallel universe where things only appeared familiar. What was safe in this new reality?

"What are you waiting for, a song and dance?" Tony shouted at the onlookers. "Scram." The gawkers glanced at one another.

"You heard the man, beat it." Minh rolled through the crowd, and the spectators scattered like a flock of pheasants before a hunting dog.

Tony pulled his friends into a huddle. "All right, Kitten, we're gonna get you through this. Me and Ink will handle crowd control, and Gus will be your caddy. Okay? Come here."

Tony enveloped her in a gentle hug. Cathryn hung on longer than necessary, letting his warmth sink into her. When she released him, she managed a shaky smile.

"Thanks, guys."

* * *

The walking cast on Cathryn's left ankle thumped as she limped to the living room. Her backpack dropped to the window seat with a thud, but the zipper refused to cooperate. She worked hard in occupational therapy, but she still couldn't even touch her fingers to her thumb. With a grunt of frustration, she tossed her backpack aside.

A warm breeze slipped through the open window, rustling the embroidered curtains. Cathryn wondered if she would ever stop feeling like an intruder in the Ostergaards' home. Their "house" resembled a palace from a storybook. It reminded her of Gus's, except lonely instead of haughty. It was a house filled with longing, as if it were always waiting for someone to come home.

A casual observer would miss the tension between the Ostergaards, but Cathryn had spent her life monitoring the ebbs and flows of her father's anger. She didn't trust their smiles. They were laced with pain.

Cathryn braced her backpack against the floor with her left elbow and pulled the zipper with her functional right hand. *Just needed a little elbow grease.* She grabbed her English book. She knew she should be focusing on crafting a new escape plan, but she couldn't think about that right now. Not with a book in her lap. *Just one chapter.*

The clang of pots and pans woke her. *Not again.* The doctor warned her she would tire easily. Cathryn had ignored her warning, but she couldn't ignore her body's demands for rest.

The kitchen soon smelled of delicious things Cathryn couldn't identify, and Laurel called her to the table. Cathryn had eaten her usual huge lunch and wasn't hungry, but she knew better than to violate dinner rituals, so she limped to her seat.

The tablescape could have been in *Good Housekeeping*—spring-themed without being tacky. Sprigs of lily of the valley poked out of an intricately etched crystal centerpiece, and lavender napkin-irises rested on a seafoam green tablecloth.

"Let's pray," Mark said. Cathryn kept her eyes on his closed lids as he continued. "Heavenly Father, we thank you for providing for us. Thank you for our health, the roof over our heads, and the food on our plates. Teach us to use these blessings to the benefit of others. Bless our time together tonight. Amen." Mark opened his eyes and gestured to the food. "Ladies first."

Ladies first. Four days in a row. *This is so backward.* Cathryn watched carefully as the three of them dug into a meal large enough to feed eight people.

"Cathryn, you look like you're dying to ask a question," Laurel said.

Cathryn's face flushed. She hated to admit ignorance, but she needed to know the rules of this house.

"Um . . . does this happen—I mean, like this—does it happen like this every night?"

"Does what happen?"

"Dinner."

Laurel furrowed her brow. "Well, sometimes we have leftovers."

Mark frowned. His eyes sharpened into focus as he grasped what prompted her question. "Cathryn, look at me." His intensity commanded her attention. "As long as you are with us, you will have a roof over your head, clothes on your back, and food on your plate. Do you understand?"

No. "Yes, sir."

Cathryn filled the awkward silence that followed by stacking the plates, but she had trouble picking up the stack one-handed.

"Don't worry about that, Cathryn. I'll clean up," Laurel said.

"You cooked, honey. I'll do the dishes," Mark said.

Laurel's eyes widened. "Really? Don't you still have to draft that report?"

"I'll get up early." He gathered the silverware with gusto, as if taking energy from Laurel's surprised smile.

"I guess I'll finish laundry." Laurel gestured to Cathryn. "Did you put your clothes in the hamper?"

"Yes, but I can wash them."

Laurel waved away the suggestion. "I'll just add them to my load. You get back to your homework."

Cathryn shook her head as she limped back to the living room. Before the fire, she'd spent her nights scrubbing machinery and her days manning a cash register. In between, she made dinner for her father, kept the house spotless, and cared for her mother, but the Ostergaards expected nothing of her. *This is so backward.*

She plopped into the window seat and pretended to do homework while she strategized. The trial would fail. Her father would ensure she returned to his custody. She should disappear before then, but she had no money, and with her bum ankle, she couldn't even travel on foot.

Cathryn doodled a dollar sign in her notebook. Earlier, she'd contemplated robbing the Ostergaards—they wouldn't miss the money—but she couldn't do it. Their behavior may be baffling, but they fed her, clothed her, and paid for her school supplies without asking anything in return. Cathryn's mother would never forgive her if she stole from them.

She crossed out the dollar sign. The Ostergaards supervised her too closely for her to slip out and earn her own money. She'd have to wait until she returned to her father. Winning his trust might take years, but at least no one would get hurt.

She rubbed her left arm. No one but her.

A breeze blew through the window, making her shiver. The afternoon warmth had chilled in the evening. Cathryn reached for the window crank with her left hand, sighed, and switched to her right. The crank turned, but the window didn't budge. She pushed the crank down as she turned, and the window responded. Two inches from closed, the windowsill split with a loud crack. Cathryn froze.

"Window break?" Mark strode over from the kitchen.

Cathryn pressed herself against the wall. None of her muscles responded to her pleas to run.

Mark inspected the damage. "That's the problem with these old houses. Stuff breaks. I'll get some plastic to keep the draft out, but in the meantime, you might want to study in your room." His expression shifted as he faced her. "Cathryn, are you okay?"

"I-I'm sorry." Whatever force had held her still now set her shivering.

Mark moved toward her. She squeezed her eyes shut.

"Cathryn, it's just a window."

She cracked an eye open. "I'm sorry."

Mark took a deep breath. "Once is enough, Cathryn. I'll fix the window. You take your books to your room."

Cathryn scurried to her room. She sat with her back to the bed and stared at the open door.

No one closed it.

* * *

Cathryn's Diary

I keep waiting for bruises, but instead come questions. They ask about my day, my friends, my favorite books. What does that mean? The thought of giving the wrong answer makes me sick.

The front door has only one lock, and the stairs don't creak. If something breaks, they fix it. They spend more money on one dinner than my father gave us for a week. Every night, Mark gives God credit for everything his money buys. Then he asks the women who did nothing to earn that money to eat first. What sort of man is that?

Is this real? I can't make sense of anything. I wish Mom were here.

* * *

Laurel suspected Minh was the real instigator of this outing, but she didn't care. After their shopping trip ended with Cathryn hyperventilating in sticker shock, she'd jumped at the second chance to connect with her foster daughter. Warren said Cathryn needed to feel safe before she'd agree to testify, but despite their best efforts, she rarely spoke, and she studied them with haunted eyes. Minh's presence seemed to reassure her, but she still scanned the sidewalk for threats as they approached the museum.

Laurel hadn't set foot in the Minneapolis Institute of Art since she herself was in school. The entryway loomed just as large as it did then. She could almost hear the enormous glass sun taunting her as she passed.

Stop being silly. You're a successful adult. No one is grading you. Laurel dismissed her buried demons, dropped a twenty in the donation box, and forced herself to walk calmly onward.

Cathryn, however, might have skipped if not for her walking cast. A smile lit her face, and for once, she moved ahead of Laurel. Her posture opened as if she were inflating, and she gestured emphatically as she chattered. Historical facts and quotes poured out as if her words had burst free of a dam.

This was a good idea. This "human encyclopedia" contrasted sharply with the terrified scarecrow who first limped up the walkway. A charming young woman emerged from the cloud of fear —quirky and smart, friendly and good-humored. Laurel felt she was meeting the real Cathryn, and the more she saw, the more she liked the eccentric bookworm.

They moved to a gallery featuring Rembrandt's paintings, and Minh became the delighted child. She babbled about color contrasts, perspectives, and other art terms Laurel forgot long ago. *Be honest, you never learned them in the first place.*

"She sounds like your friend Gus," Laurel whispered.

Cathryn covered her chuckle. "If they ever realize how much they've picked up from one another, they'll erupt."

Laurel's heart warmed at Cathryn's smile. After their disastrous trip to the department store, she'd almost given up, but shopping was *her* passion. Bonding with her foster daughter required her to leave her own comfort zone and enter Cathryn's.

After learning more about Rembrandt than they'd ever wanted, they dragged Minh through the remaining galleries. While nothing like the girls' days of her youth, Laurel admitted she'd enjoyed herself.

"Thank you for bringing me," Cathryn said as they waited for Minh to get out of the bathroom.

"If my parents could see me now, they'd accuse someone of body snatching." Cathryn furrowed her brow, so Laurel clarified. "I wasn't the best student when I was your age, much to my parents' disappointment."

Something in Cathryn's eyes—whose color defied categorization —made her want to continue. *"Trust builds trust,"* the social worker said.

"They wanted me to go to college, but I knew I'd never have the grades. When I enrolled in culinary school instead, they stopped speaking to me. I tried to reconnect when . . . later, but they never answered my calls."

"That's awful."

"You are the last person I can complain to about parents."

Cathryn shook her head. "'No one's pain is lesser simply for being different.'"

"Who said that one?"

Cathryn stared at her hands. "My mother. She used to say, 'God holds the tears of a frightened child as close to His heart as those of a sobbing widow.'" Cathryn smiled sadly. "My mom supported whatever I wanted to do, even when I declared myself the world's first astronaut-princess. For a couple weeks, we referred to the library as space command."

Their laughter bounced among the sculptures. *She's finally letting her guard down.*

"I'd love to hear more about your mom—if you're up to sharing of course." Laurel kept her tone nonthreatening. "Maybe we could picnic by the lake sometime, just the two of us."

Cathryn met her eye. "I'd like that."

* * *

Cathryn's Diary

Mrs. Laurel Ostergaard is stronger than she looks. I admire her, though I doubt she would believe me if I told her. Even now as I watch her dance around the kitchen in choreography only she knows, I can't help smiling.

She insists the right food can solve any problem. As a girl who has always been hungry, I cannot disagree. A former caterer, she is incapable of making anything without using every one of her copious pots and pans. She wields her kitchen knives with the precision of a samurai, and manages a half dozen simmering, searing, and sautéing dishes with the same ease with which she strolls around Lake of the Isles each morning.

Despite her devotion to good food, she resembles a recently liberated POW—recovered from emaciation, but still bearing strain. Her hair is wiry and thin, gray despite her relative youth. She hides it beneath silk scarves, and her strategically applied makeup covers the ends of a scar.

She once confessed to the bathroom mirror, "I wish someone had warned me it doesn't grow back the same." I can picture how her hair used to be based upon the hole left by its absence—voluptuous honey-brown waves combed to glossy perfection. I'd wager somewhere in the bathroom remains a bin filled with elegant pins, combs, and curlers—like an altar to a lost loved one.

That day as I was snooping, she sighed at her reflection. Then she put on her scarf, smiled, and said, "I do love this color on me."

I wish I had her resilience.

My mom and I dreamed of escaping together, but our plan burned to ashes. Now I live with strangers who have troubles of their own. They think I don't notice how they hide beneath an immaculate house and expensive car, but I do. I guess it takes one to know one.

I've learned the world is full of broken people pretending to be whole. Some pray and wait for God to heal them, but I've never seen that work. If God exists, perhaps it is He who waits for us to heal each other.

Chapter 29

Cathryn tried to tune out the doorbell as she studied, but her legs were getting stiff. She repositioned herself in the window seat and tucked a strand of hair behind her ear. She'd tried a ponytail, but she couldn't tighten it enough without her left hand. *I'll get it eventually.* Right now, she'd rather enjoy school while it lasted.

"That book must weigh more than you." Mr. Jones smiled at her from the other side of the coffee table, evidently the source of the doorbell. Cathryn liked Mr. Jones, but he was wearing the smile people showed her when they wanted to "talk." She kept her textbook open, hoping he'd take the hint that now was a bad time, that any time was a bad time.

"How are you holding up?"

"I'm fine. The Ostergaards treat me well. I have more homework than I ever thought possible." Cathryn lifted her textbook.

"Well, take a break," Mr. Jones said as he sat beside her. "Cathryn, they set a date for your father's trial. Your testimony would go a long way."

Cathryn stroked the scars on her left forearm. Nothing good ever arose from talking to the police, even if the cop was your best friend's dad. This trial was doomed to fail like her first-grade teacher's call to social services. At least if she kept quiet, she might spare herself a beating.

"Do you remember the night that punk with the piercings asked after Minh?" Mr. Jones said.

Cathryn blinked at the sudden shift in topic. "Um, yeah. Minh's more into tattoos, but she's a sucker for piercings too."

Mr. Jones frowned at that but continued. "Do you remember what happened next?"

"You showed him your badge and gun and said, 'Do you want to ask that question again?'" She chuckled. "I'm sure he wet himself. I'd never seen anyone run so fast."

Mr. Jones grinned, but his eyes turned serious. "I made that kid leave because I protect my family Cathryn, and that includes you. I know you're scared, but I'll be there. Me, the Ostergaards, your friends—we won't let anything happen to you."

His family includes me? Cathryn admired the Joneses. Even in kindergarten, Minh had feared nothing. Who could hurt her if her daddy scared away the bad guys? Cathryn feared everything. Her daddy *was* a bad guy. Family for Cathryn had always meant danger, but maybe she needed to broaden her definition. She liked the idea of a family like Minh's—bound by love if not by blood.

"You don't need to go back to him, Cathryn."

"Could I stay here?" Cathryn liked this house. It was quiet as a library, complete with a comfy window seat, a full fridge, and unlocked doors.

"Mark and Laurel won't let you go without a fight."

Mark and Laurel. They seemed friendly, but Cathryn saw the stress cracking their marriage. "What if they decide I'm too much trouble? What if my father finds out?" *He'll kill me.*

Mr. Jones leaned forward. "We'll handle your father. You just tell the truth. I know it's hard, but you're a strong young woman."

Cathryn grabbed a strand of her hair and wrapped it around her finger. She didn't feel strong. "I have a photographic memory. I remember everything about that night. Everything." Her voice cracked. "I remember that the front rug was crooked, that we needed to change the light bulb, that one of the kitchen chairs wasn't pushed in all the way . . ." She squeezed her eyes shut, and a single tear fell. "My dad's face, the door slamming, the smell—I just want to forget."

"To move on from something, you must acknowledge that it happened."

Acknowledge it happened. Her life was a tapestry of lies. If she pulled one thread, the entire weaving might unravel.

Cathryn shook her head. "I'm scared, Mr. Jones."

His eyes softened. "Being scared doesn't mean you can't do this."

Cathryn had heard him use the same tone when his son Ghost hid under their basement stairs. If there was one police officer she could trust, it was Mr. Jones.

"You can put him in jail?" Cathryn whispered.

"*You* can put him in jail."

Cathryn fingered the pages of her textbook. *Mom wanted me to finish school.* Her mother's sacrifices would be in vain if she returned to her father's custody. Deep down, Cathryn knew she wouldn't survive long enough to attempt another escape, much less graduate. If she wanted to control her own destiny, she'd have to defeat her father in court.

"Eleanor Roosevelt said, 'Do one thing every day that scares you.'" Cathryn met Mr. Jones's eye. "I'll do it."

For Mom.

* * *

Other girls complained, but Cathryn had always preferred to wear robes for choir concerts instead of formal clothes. Confined by the stiff pencil skirt she wore now, she struggled to mount the courthouse steps with her friends. *At least I upgraded to a thinner ankle splint.*

Pilar and Minh's sister Beth tried to prepare her last night. They claimed court was nothing near as dramatic as TV. The lawyers submitted everything in writing ahead of time, so in theory, the proceedings shouldn't take long. "Short and sweet," Beth said. Cathryn's stomach felt anything but sweet.

The nausea worsened as she navigated the regal halls. In other circumstances, the building's history would have fascinated her. She and Minh might have discussed the architectural style of the period. Now, Cathryn struggled to keep her knees from buckling.

They entered a room that seemed far too mundane for a dispensary of justice. The faded padded chairs and scratched wood furnishings reminded Cathryn of an old church. Her pulse quickened when she spied the back of her father's head. He turned, and his hurt look paralyzed her.

Sound ceased. Unable to break eye contact, Cathryn watched his expression shift into a snarl. The walls erupted in flames. She smelled whiskey and heard her mother scream.

Cathryn bolted.

* * *

Minh and her father reacted first, calling Cathryn's name and darting after her. They returned moments later, breathless and shaking their heads. The judge allowed them fifteen minutes to find her.

"Where would she go?" Tony asked.

"Someplace safe," Laurel said. A chorus of suggestions followed.

"A library."

The group quieted and turned toward the speaker.

Gus addressed the judge. "Which room contains the most books?"

* * *

Cathryn collapsed between two bookshelves and bawled. She'd wanted to march into the courtroom and expose the monster behind her father's smile, but she was no heroine. One look from her father and her courage crumbled.

She sobbed until her head spun from the effort. First, she'd failed to save her mother, and now she failed to get her justice. Her chance at freedom slipped away, and she was as helpless to prevent it as she had been to stop her mother's illness.

The edges of her awareness sensed someone sit beside her, but the rest of her mind drifted through a mire of fear and failure. A smell reached her first: a mix of crisp detergent and Old Spice that didn't quite mask the boy beneath. She rested in the scent, allowed it to draw her back to the present. When she lifted her head, Gus's blue eyes met hers.

"We decided only one of us should approach you. I proposed we establish who via rock-paper-scissors." He shrugged. "Tony always leads with rock, and Minh, predictably, cheats."

Cathryn's laugh emerged a strained hiccup. "Thanks, Gus. Winston Churchill said, 'One always measures friendships by how they show up in bad weather.'"

"He also said, 'If you are going through hell, keep going.'"

Cathryn rubbed her left wrist. "I tried, Gus. Even when Mom got sick, I kept trying. I failed."

"You were alone then. You aren't now. 'Failure is not fatal, it is the courage to continue that counts.'" He grinned. "I read Winston Churchill's biography."

Cathryn leaned into him, and he wrapped one arm around her shoulders. She breathed him in, and for a moment, the world stopped spinning.

I have to do this. If she wanted to determine her own future, she had to confront her past.

Cathryn pushed away. "I think I'm ready."

Gus helped her to her feet, but she yelped when she took a step. Her ankle throbbed.

"Guess I shouldn't have run on it."

Gus put her arm over his shoulder and led her to where the others waited.

"I'm sorry I panicked. I'm okay now, aside from a sore ankle."

"Here Kitten, take this." Tony slipped his crucifix over her head. "Good luck charm."

"Thanks." She hugged him, let his bulk warm her for a moment before pulling back. "Can we try this again?"

* * *

To an outside observer, the proceedings were less exciting than filing taxes. To Cathryn, they were torture. She squeezed Gus's hand as she listened to bar owners, coworkers, and Nurse Pietro relate their interactions with her father. Nothing they said hinted at the man her mother married, but they described to perfection the one who left her to die alone.

Cathryn reached the stand despite her wobbly knees and throbbing ankle. The judge allowed her to sit as she swore to tell the truth, but her gaze slipped to her father. His eyes burned with the promise of pain, and she missed the lawyer's first question. She tried to answer the second time, but she couldn't breathe.

Handcuffs bound her father's hands. Fear tied Cathryn's. She'd glimpsed freedom with the Ostergaards. Could she learn to live a normal life, or was her father's twisted love the only kind she'd ever know?

Her father and his lawyer sat to her left. Memories filled the rows behind them: bedtime stories, goodnight kisses, ice cream dates as his "little princess." Intermingled with them were beatings, screams, locked doors, and untasted dinners.

On the other side of the courtroom sat her friends, the ones she'd fed lie after lie. The falsehood should have poisoned their friendship, but there they sat. Cathryn fingered Tony's crucifix and remembered Gus's words. *"You were alone then. You aren't now."* Maybe fear wasn't a monster she needed to slay by herself.

The lawyer repeated her question for the third time. Cathryn took a shaky breath, and out of the darkest places in her heart came the words she'd spent a lifetime suppressing. Her mother's broken arm, the Maldonados' house, the fire—she told the story of her life as it was, not the fanciful version from Story Time. One by one her knots of lies unraveled.

Jedidiah Banks was found guilty of felony charges for aggravated assault, repeated battery, and child abuse and neglect. He was sentenced to fifteen years in prison. Cathryn was free.

At least, she hoped she was.

Chapter 30

Cathryn pulled her knees into her chest and tried to tune out the argument that raged beyond the bedroom wall. *I'm not home. Mark's not Dad.* She pressed her fingers into her ears, but the Ostergaards' shouts reverberated inside her skull and collided with memories.

Cathryn forced herself to breathe. The lingering smell of their chicken dinner soured in her nostrils, so she grabbed her English book and inhaled through its pages. *All couples argue.* She clenched her good hand. *I'm not there. He's not him. I'm not there. He's not him . . .*

The screaming continued, and the present to which she clung gave way before the onslaught of the past. The room melted around her and re-solidified as her old living room. Laurel's shouts became her mother's screams. Mark's voice twisted into her father's.

* * *

Mark tried and failed to control his tone. "We've been over this. The doctor said you can't return to work." He pulled his hair. "I know you feel better on these new meds, but what about your bad days? Canceling last-minute is no way to run a catering business."

"I just want to do something useful." Laurel slammed her fist on the desk.

"Laurel, it's a miracle you're even alive." *Isn't that enough?*

215

"What's the point of being alive if you're not living?"

"You—"

A scraping sound interrupted Mark's reply. He and Laurel exchanged a glance. *Cathryn.* They dashed to her room, their argument forgotten.

Laurel stepped inside. "Cathryn?"

"Cathryn, are you in here?" Mark scanned the room. Cathryn's desk was bare apart from a mug of pens and her picture book. The chair was pushed in, the carpet clean, and the bed made. The only sign of Cathryn's inhabitance was the trashcan full of papers.

Mark's mouth went dry. Did she run away?

Laurel held a finger to her lips. After a minute, they could hear Cathryn hyperventilating under the bed. "Cathryn? It's okay, sweetie. Nothing's wrong. No one's hurt. You can come out."

Mark lifted the bed but dropped it at Cathryn's cry. He saw his own panic mirrored his wife's face. *What have we done?*

They left Cathryn alone in the hopes she would come out on her own. They fell asleep on the couch waiting.

* * *

Mark rubbed his temples. "Do you ever stop feeling like a total incompetent?"

"Nope." The entire church group answered in unison.

Warren put a hand on his back. "Welcome to parenthood."

* * *

Cathryn's Diary

You can put a man in jail, but how do you stop his spirit from haunting you? I feel his gaze on the back of my neck when no one else is in the room. My stomach sinks every time I hear keys jingle. I flinch when people hand me things.

Every minute past six, my heart beats faster. He never comes, but in some ways, he never left.

Is this freedom? How long until it feels like it?

Chapter 31

Tony finished his last bicep curl and winked at Cathryn. She still bumbled through gym class, but now that the Ostergaards ensured she ate, she'd filled her skeletal frame with lean muscle. As Minh described it, she was "a line drawing someone finally colored."

Whoever it was drew dark circles beneath her eyes, too.

Tony switched to his other arm as Cathryn finished with her right hand. She returned the weight to the rack and yawned.

"You think this is nap time, Banks? No slacking off in my weight room." Coach Karne's face approached purple.

Cathryn's paled, as if the blood were rushing from her face into her teacher's. "I can't grip the weights with my left hand. I have a doctor's note."

"Stop milking for sympathy."

The last time Tony saw Cathryn so still, she fled the courtroom, but she this time she held her ground. "I-I can give you the number for my occupational therapist."

"I already excused you from two full units. You can't expect to pass without doing any work."

Cathryn shrank beneath her teacher's harsh tone. Tony grit his teeth. Standing up for herself must have taken a lot of courage, but Coach Karne squashed it. How was she supposed to recover if no one supported her?

"I got this, Coach." Tony trotted to Cathryn, but when he placed a hand on her shoulder, she yelped and raised her mangled arm in self-defense. The image hit Tony like a battering ram. He'd seen that posture before, the night he startled her at the shop. Why hadn't he recognized it for what it was?

Coach Karne scowled at the gawking class. "This is gym, not drama."

Tony ignored his teacher. "It's okay, Kitten. Breathe. In and out. Atta girl."

Cathryn took several gulps of air before she peered at Tony through the curtain of her arms. She blinked, as though waking from a dream, and lowered them.

"Sorry."

Tony tried to reassure her with a grin. "You game for something crazy?"

She hesitated before nodding.

"Sit tight. I'll be right back." Tony retrieved a strap and tied the lightest weight to Cathryn's left arm. The color returned to her face as she lifted it.

"You really can fix anything, can't you?"

"You should see me do an oil change."

"I'd rather watch you build a bike. Too bad mine didn't make it."

Coach Karne cleared his throat. Tony moved to block his line of sight and started doing squats. The gawkers returned their attention to their own weights.

Cathryn resumed her bicep curls with a grin. "You've always been my gym-class guardian angel." She froze mid-curl. "I know you would've helped. I—"

"Don't worry about then. Focus on now."

"Now isn't going so hot." Her eyes grew distant. "I can't even get through gym class without panicking."

Tony's gut clenched as her face fell. He wanted to pummel her good-for-nothing father, but Minh taught him there was more than one kind of help. Cathryn didn't need his flying fists right now. She needed a heart-repairing wrench.

Luckily, he had one sitting in his garage.

* * *

Minh drew a line, but no ink marked her paper. "Demarius! Cap my pens after you borrow them." She chucked the dried-out pen into the trash. *Brothers.*

Voices from her parents' church group drifted through the hall. Minh caught Cathryn's name and crept closer to the living room. A woman, maybe Laurel Ostergaard, was speaking.

". . . not impressed with the school counselor. She's even tenser the days she sees him."

"You should have seen her face when the window broke." Minh recognized Mark's baritone.

"Give her time. It's early yet." No mistaking Nichole. The child psychologist's voice reminded Minh of a buzzing insect.

"Every kid is different," Minh's dad said. "Demarius, he acted out when we first adopted him. Minh rolled right in like she owned the place, and Ghost . . . well, we're still figuring him out."

"It's not that she's any trouble." Mark's voice again.

"Not at all," Laurel added. "If anything, we have the opposite problem. The one time she didn't come home from school on time —remember Warren, how we called you in a panic?—she went to the library."

"She does nothing but study," Mark continued. "I find myself wishing she would talk back to us so I know she feels comfortable."

A pause followed. Minh suspected Laurel was nodding.

"Aside from school, she discusses only happy memories with her mom. If we mention what she said in court, she puts her nose in a book and shuts us out. I wish I could put her at ease, but I'm a caterer, not a counselor."

After several rounds of "give it time" and "trust builds trust" from Nichole, the conversation shifted to Ghost's latest exploits. *These are good people, Cat.*

Throughout their friendship, Minh had been the strong one. She'd mastered the art of cajoling her introverted friend into mischief-making, but they were older now, and life was more complicated than covering their tracks after sneaking into Beth's room. Flashbacks weren't bullies Minh could tell off. She couldn't save Cathryn from trauma that already happened.

Maybe she didn't need to. Minh taught Tony that helping didn't mean doing things for her but supporting her doing them herself. For twelve years, Minh had been strong *for* Cathryn, but now Cathryn needed *inner* strength. Minh may not be able to protect her friend from her own fear, but she could support Cathryn as she conquered it herself.

Minh put the rest of her pens away, transferred to bed, and stared at the ceiling, strategizing. *May as well start with that school counselor . . .*

* * *

The office door clicked shut. Cathryn tightened her one-handed grip on her textbook.

"Mr. Olson, I have a lot of homework. Do I have to give up study hall today?"

The counselor frowned. "Cathryn, you can't keep using school an excuse not to process what happened."

"I'm not."

"Then why do you bring your textbook? It's a safety blanket, Cathryn."

Cathryn clutched the book to her chest.

"Your mother died, you almost burned to death, and your father attacked you in the hospital. You can't tell me you feel nothing."

Cathryn fixed her gaze on the bobble-headed Pit Bull on the desk. It seemed to growl. Mr. Oslon squatted in front of her. She scooted her chair back until it hit the wall behind her.

"I know it's hard, Cathryn." He reached to place his hand on her arm.

"Minh!"

"What?"

Cathryn swallowed. "Minh Jones, my friend. Can she come?"

Mr. Olson stood. "Would that make you more comfortable?"

Cathryn nodded. *Minh will know what to do.*

"Okay, let's try it." Mr. Olson made the call, and agonizing minutes later, someone knocked at the door.

"Hello, Minh. Cathryn asked you to join her counseling session today."

Minh glanced at Cathryn. "Probably to tell you you're an idiot."

"Excuse me?"

"You put her behind a closed door with a guy who's the same age and appearance as her abusive father? Brilliant, Dr. Phil."

"Cathryn needs—"

"Bullshit. Cathryn can decide for herself what she needs."

Mr. Olson straightened. "Ms. Jones, you are heading for detention."

"No." Cathryn stood. Her legs shook, but she forced herself to meet the counselor's eye. She *did* feel everything that happened, every second of every day. Her failure to save her mother was an ache that greeted her each morning she awoke in a strange house with people she still didn't understand. Her stomach revolted when the clock struck six, and she jumped every time a door shut. Even buttoning her jeans became a trial for her one working hand. Cathryn lived in a miasma of grief, confusion, and terror, but Minh was right. She hadn't planned an escape, survived a fire, and testified in court to have someone else tell her what she needed. She could decide for herself, and being trapped with this man wasn't it.

"If you're going to send someone to detention, send me. I don't want to be here, and I'm not staying." Cathryn marched out of the office, but her defiance drained the instant she reached the hall. She leaned her head against a locker and closed her eyes.

"Atta girl, Cat."

"Thanks, Minh. I was dying in there."

"Next time call Tony. I'd love to see him punch that guy's face in."

Cathryn managed a half-smile before sobering once more. "I'm sorry I lied." Twelve years of guilt in four words.

"None of this is your fault."

"It isn't yours either." Cathryn watched her best friend's tough façade crack as her words hit their mark.

Minh spoke her next words carefully. "You should talk to someone, Cat. Just not that bozo."

People knew Minh as the tough girl with a vocabulary as colorful as her ink-stained fingertips, but what Cathryn admired most about her friend was her selflessness. In one sentence, Minh had offered to listen while also giving Cathryn the freedom to seek counsel elsewhere.

Cathryn trusted no one more than Minh, but seventeen years' worth of lies was too heavy to drag up her throat at once. The best she could manage was a weak smile.

"I know."

* * *

Mark entered the kitchen as the grandfather clock struck 1:00 a.m. He opened the liquor cabinet, grabbed a bottle of brandy, and poured it down the sink. After tossing the bottle into the recycling bin, he proceeded with a bottle of rum. The ritual calmed him, as if he were pouring his frustration out with the alcohol. *Beats lying awake all night.*

A tap drew his attention. Cathryn poked her head around the corner.

"I'm sorry about the noise," Mark said. "I didn't mean to wake you."

"It wasn't the noise." Dark circles carved channels beneath her eyes, and her nightgown was soaked with sweat.

"I'm sorry, I—"

"It's not your fault I have flashbacks." Her brow furrowed. "What are you doing?" She took a half step into the kitchen.

May as well tell the truth. "I had an uncle growing up who was an alcoholic. I promised myself every time I was tempted to look for answers in the bottom of a glass, I would upend it over the sink instead."

"A wise promise." Cathryn warily approached the counter. "You fought with Laurel again."

No use hiding anymore. Cathryn had seen through their white lies from the beginning. *What did Nichole say, trust builds trust?*

"I don't enjoy being the bad guy. I want to support my wife, but she can't do everything she wants anymore. Just months ago, she was drooling in a hospital bed. I . . ." He'd visited every day, seen the love of his life cut apart, flooded with toxins, and irradiated. For months, his wife's frail body had been more bandage than skin, more machine than human.

Mark emptied another bottle of rum.

"'The loneliest moment in someone's life is when they are watching their whole world fall apart, and all they can do is stare blankly.' F. Scott Fitzgerald."

Mark nodded. Something in Cathryn's expression made him want to keep talking, as if she were reaching into his heart and pulling the words out. "It was a rollercoaster from hell. We thought the chemo and radiation had taken care of everything; then they told us the cancer had metastasized. She needed brain surgery." He pressed his shaking hands into the counter. "I thank God every day she's alive."

"My mother thanked God too." Cathryn's voice was soft, as if she weren't sure whether she were speaking or thinking. "She had this prayer candle. It became a talisman for her. She couldn't walk, couldn't talk, had no idea who I was, but she knew what that candle meant. I often came home to find her asleep with it in her arms like a child with a stuffed animal."

Cathryn shook her head. "To the end of her days, she loved a god who gave her a death sentence. It was beautiful, in a way. I know that's an oxymoron, but if anyone could make death beautiful, it was my mother."

Mark held his silence and kept his distance. She rewarded his patience by continuing.

"I'm glad I didn't go through what you did. All the ups and downs, I don't think I could have handled that. With Mom, it was like . . . like taking a long walk to the bus station and sending her off. I knew she was going to die. I just"—her voice broke—"I just wanted to hold her hand when she did." Cathryn covered her mouth and ran back upstairs.

Mark stared after her, knowing a piece of his heart had broken off and followed.

* * *

Cathryn had been staring at her science book for ten minutes without reading a word. *I'm so close to caught up. Just a few more weeks.* She scanned the page, but to her exhausted eyes, the words may as well have been alien pictographs. *Fine.* She wandered to the kitchen where Laurel stood at the island and chopped vegetables at a speed that gave her whiplash just watching.

"Can I help? I could use a break."

Laurel's surprise gave way to a smile as she handed Cathryn a pan. "Why don't you sauté these onions?"

Cathryn placed the pan on the burner, but her hand hovered over the knob. She backed away until she bumped into Laurel.

"Cathryn?"

Cathryn tried to swallow, but her mouth went dry. "Maybe I'm more of a chopping person than a sauteing person."

Laurel frowned.

Cathryn rubbed her scarred forearm. "It's just . . . last time I turned on the stove . . ."

"Oh." An awkward silence stretched into the space between them. Laurel pursed her lips. "Has anyone ever taught you to cook?"

Cathryn shook her head. Her culinary experience consisted of eggs, sandwiches, and things she could reheat on the stove.

"Okay. Let's start with the basics, and we'll work our way up to the stove."

Laurel showed her how to chop vegetables, though it took some troubleshooting to figure out how to keep her injured fingers out of the blade's way. She didn't mention the fire, which Cathryn appreciated. When Minh advised her to talk to someone, she hadn't expected to confide in her foster parents, but they proved trustworthy confidantes. They knew the poison of unsaid words, but they also understood that some days, she just needed to chop vegetables.

After a half hour, Cathryn felt more comfortable with knife work. The small accomplishment gave her hope for future lessons in sauteing. Just as she finished the last carrot, the doorbell rang.

Laurel gestured for Cathryn to answer it. "I'll finish cooking."

Cathryn opened the door a crack before flinging it wide. "Tony? What are you doing here?"

"Come on out. I'll show ya." Tony led her to what appeared to be a conglomeration of various discarded bikes. Whatever its origins, the gears gleamed, and the indigo paint sparkled.

"You said you needed a new ride." He beamed. "I hooked the left brake line in with the right. Try it out."

Cathryn squeezed, and both sets of brakes tightened. She may not have made progress on her homework today, but now she could chop vegetables and ride a bike. One step at a time, she would reclaim her life.

Cathryn tackled Tony in a hug. "It's the most beautiful bike I've ever seen."

Chapter 32

S *moke scorched Cathryn's lungs. She raced up the stairs toward her* *mother's cries, but no matter how fast she forced her legs to move, stair after stair disintegrated beneath her feet. Her father's howls pursued her.* I have to save Mom. *The staircase disappeared, and she fell.*

Cathryn gasped and flung off her drenched sheets. She stumbled to her desk. Her sweat chilled as she leaned against it and took deep breaths.

I'll never be free. No matter how hard she fought to retake her life, her father still dominated her mind.

Cathryn clutched *The Fantastic Flying Books of Mr. Morris Lessmore* to her chest and cried herself back to sleep.

* * *

Cathryn resettled herself in the window seat's plush cushion. It had been stiff when she moved in, but her frequent study sessions had worn it to a comfortable softness. She stifled a yawn. Too comfortable.

"Can you walk me through this problem again?"

Gus nodded and repeated his instructions. Good thing she was a quick study because Gus was a lousy tutor. Cathryn stopped him periodically to ensure he taught one step at a time. In a way, she was teaching him.

"How goes the studying?" Laurel asked.

"Okay." Cathryn rubbed her temples. She'd committed to honoring her mother by finishing school, but no matter how hard she pushed herself, she never seemed any closer to catching up.

"We've covered over a week's worth of material in the past hour and a half. You're doing substantially better than 'okay.'" Gus gave her his you-can-be-so-illogical look. Cathryn bit her tongue to keep from laughing. *What would I do without him?*

"Since we have company, I've decided to give you a pop quiz in lieu of having you help with dinner," Laurel said. "Question one: how do you tell whether a pineapple is ripe?"

"If it's heavy, yellow, smells nice, and the inner leaves are easy to pull out."

"Correct. Question two: why do we sear meat?"

"Because brown food tastes good. I still don't understand that one. Why would the color change the flavor?"

"I believe she is referring to the Mailliard reaction," Gus said.

"What?"

In an odd role reversal, Gus translated. "The Maillard reaction is a chemical reaction between amino acids and reducing sugar that occurs above 140° Celsius. The reactive carbonyl group of the sugar interacts with the nucleophilic amino group of the acid, producing distinctive flavor compounds."

"Oh, I get it now."

"I'm glad one of us does," Laurel said with a wry smile.

* * *

Laurel kept one eye on the living room as she scrubbed a sticky film of spilled vinaigrette off the counter. Not surprisingly, Cathryn had fallen asleep on the window seat. Gus zipped his backpack and sat for a moment, observing her. When Laurel met the genius teen, she found his calculating gaze disturbing, but now she understood.

One afternoon, Gus had watched Mark carry in the groceries. The next day, Gus insisted on carrying Cathryn's books. Mark surprised Laurel with flowers; the following weekend, Gus brought a chocolate bar for Cathryn. He'd sputtered something about glucose and brain function, and Laurel swore he blushed.

Laurel wondered what—or who—prompted Gus to study Mark, but she realized with a twinge of guilt that he couldn't have chosen a better model.

After a minute's contemplation, Gus threaded one arm under Cathryn's knees, wrapped the other around her back, and lifted her from the cushion. Laurel led him upstairs to Cathryn's room. Gus lay her in bed, and together they covered her in quilts.

Cathryn murmured, grabbed Gus's arm, and pulled it into herself. Gus paused, calculating again. He squeezed her hand and slipped his arm free.

Laurel walked Gus to the door. "Thank you."

"For boring Cathryn to sleep?" Gus's scowl drooped.

"She fell asleep because she feels safe with you. You don't realize how much that means." Gus didn't hear Cathryn wake from nightmares every night—every night except the ones she spent studying with him.

"My parents are neuroscientists. I know how trauma affects the brain." Some of the edges of his face softened. "Cathryn is the most intelligent girl I know, but I-I wonder how much more brilliant she would be if she'd been born an Ostergaard."

"Better to be grateful for what is than to lament what might have been." Laurel cringed at her hypocrisy. She was still learning that lesson. *I owe Mark an apology.*

Gus scanned the entryway as though searching for the route home. His eyes landed on the staircase. "Last fall my only concern was my grades."

"Sometimes God leads us down unexpected paths."

"That's—"

"I would know."

Gus's scowl hardened. "You're saying it was divine providence Cathryn almost burned to death because of her abusive father?"

"I'm saying God had a role in your being there to pull her out."

Gus shook his head. "If only I'd—"

"Stop. Gus, there was nothing else you could have done." Laurel put a hand on his elbow. "Chance, fate, divine intervention—it doesn't matter what you call it. The important thing is you got her out." Gus's jaw clenched over any emotion that might have broken into his face. *He's a boy trying so hard to be a man.* "Why don't you want her to know?"

"I don't want her to feel indebted. I— It's silly, but"—he rubbed the back of his neck—"I just want to see her smile again."

"That's not silly; that's selfless."

The boy's eyes filled with an emotion Laurel doubted even Cathryn could define. "Did you mean what you said, about Cathryn feeling safe around me?"

"I wouldn't have said it otherwise."

Gus smiled awkwardly, as if his face didn't know how to form the expression. "Good."

* * *

Cathryn trailed Laurel and the grocery cart. Her cooking lessons had extended to ingredient sourcing.

"Do we have everything for that recipe you wanted to try?" Laurel asked as she examined an apple for bruises.

Cathryn consulted her list. "We still need cinnamon."

"We'll grab that last. The baking aisle is near the check-out lines."

They circumvented meandering elders and lollygagging children with military efficiency, but when they reached the frozen section, Laurel's lips dropped into a frown.

"We'd better avoid the chocolate ice cream if we're making a fried dessert. Mark had a minor midlife crisis when his swim times got longer."

Mark seemed fit enough to Cathryn, but she didn't know much about triathlons.

"Laurel? Laurel! Oh, how good to see you." The woman who joined them looked like she'd stepped out of a magazine. From her coiffed chestnut hair to the manicured toenails poking out of her stylish sandals, her appearance was flawless.

"Amber, what a pleasant surprise." Laurel's smile looked like Minh had painted it on.

"I usually only shop at the Lunds on Hennepin—better service and more . . . exclusive clientele. What a marvelous coincidence to catch you when I happen to pop in here. How are you? You look . . . alive."

Laurel's knuckles whitened around the cart's handle, but her smile remained plastered on her face. "I am well. Thank you for asking."

"You're welcome. You know I adore you. Oh, Laurel, we miss you so much at the salon. I see you've salvaged . . . something with that scarf. Anywho, got to run. Kiss kiss dear." The woman fluttered past like a hummingbird in pursuit of sugar.

Laurel's smile disintegrated as she strangled the cart handle.

Cathryn set the list in the cart and faced her foster mother. "Losing your hair teaches you who your true friends are, doesn't it?"

"Yep."

"She isn't one of them, is she?"

"Nope."

Cathryn glanced at the freezer. "Do you want to buy that chocolate ice cream?"

"Absolutely."

* * *

Girlish giggles and the smell of something sweet greeted Mark after work. Towers of mixing bowls rose from the sink, syrupy pots piled on the stove, and messy baking sheets littered the counter.

"When did the sugar factory explode?"

Laurel eyes twinkled. "Cathryn wanted to try— What was her name?"

"Rosa María," Cathryn answered.

Laurel nodded as if she should have remembered. "She wanted to try Rosa María's recipe for buñuelos." She checked her pronunciation with Cathryn. "They're a type of fritter drizzled with syrup."

"They're a mess," Cathryn said. Both gals dissolved into another round of giggles. Laurel handed Mark a fritter.

He chewed the crispy, sugary, sticky bite. "You may have to hide the rest from me."

Laurel beamed. "I worried following Rosa María's smudged handwriting would be impossible."

"'Impossible is a word to be found only in the dictionary of fools,'" Mark said. He'd bought a calendar of famous quotes, and so far, he considered the investment worthwhile. Cathryn still kept him at arm's length, but she no longer flinched every time he spoke.

"Napoleon Bonaparte," Cathryn said. She turned to Laurel. "You should write a food blog."

"Me?" Laurel's smile vanished. Mark braced himself for acidic words, but Laurel looked forlornly at the mixing bowls. "I don't know if I can."

Mark hadn't believed his heart could break into smaller pieces, but the pain in Laurel's voice ground it to dust. He'd thought she resisted her limitations out of stubbornness, but with the anger stripped out of this oft-held argument, Mark saw her shift from denial to grief. She'd lost a career she loved, and he had insisted she be grateful. *Oh Laurel, I'm so sorry.*

Cathryn shifted her weight as though assessing the risk before wading into the ocean of unsaid words between them. "The internet is flexible. You wouldn't need to post every day. I can help with the writing, and I'm sure someone in Minh's family can teach you photography."

Laurel looked at Mark. Here was an opportunity to make their new normal something she loved.

"I think it's a fantastic idea."

Laurel gifted him the brightest smile he'd seen in a long time.

* * *

Gus recorded one last note on systematic desensitization before putting away the book. He hoped Cathryn would try the technique someday, but for now, she needed to feel secure in her new environment.

He'd tried to explain his plans to Tony, but the mechanic gestured erratically and said, "Just tell me what to do." When Gus explained they needed to shower after working with fire because smells triggered Cathryn's flashbacks, Tony grinned and said that would please "his goddess," which confused Gus. He knew Catholics venerated their saints, but he'd never heard of a Catholic goddess with an interest in personal hygiene. Without Cathryn to translate, however, their conversation went no further.

Gus added his papers to the pile, aware of the irony of storing his notes on trauma recovery with his research on how to ask a girl to a dance. He hopped in the shower. His experiment for science club hadn't involved smoke, but he figured overcaution was best. Cathryn felt safe around him. He wouldn't jeopardize that for anything.

Once clean, he returned to his room, but the sight of his mother perusing his notes sent tiny pinpricks shivering across his wet skin. *How much has she read?* His father sat beside her, smiling.

Nothing good ever came from his parents' smiling.

"I see you've taken an interest in psychotherapy," his mother said.

"Yes." Gus forced the word out of his clenched teeth.

"Wonderful," his father said. "You'll get along well with Georgia."

"We're moving to Georgia?" *I'll never see her again.*

His mother laughed dryly. "No, dear. Georgia is the granddaughter of the esteemed and recently retired Dr. McPhearson."

Gus's stomach roiled as if he were digesting his last chemistry experiment. *Don't wealthy scientists ever have sons?*

"Put on your blue dress shirt," his mother continued, setting his notes aside. "We're meeting them tonight."

"No."

"No?" his father said, tone threatening.

"I have a date tonight." Gus didn't know whether helping Cathryn with her homework qualified as a date, but he needed to send a message.

"I see." His father drummed his fingers on his thigh. "Gustaf, your behavior of late has been unacceptable. You will accompany us to the McPhearsons' or face the consequences."

Gus squared his shoulders. "No."

His mother's face twisted into the smile she'd given their last maid before firing her. "You turn eighteen this fall. Are you sure you're ready for the independence, for life without your parents providing you with nice things like food and clothing?" She gestured to the towel around Gus's waist.

The walls closed in around him. This was no idle threat. They would toss him to the streets the second he turned eighteen if he didn't cooperate. He'd never been more than a "networking asset" to them.

Graduating high school would be difficult if he were homeless, and getting a scholarship would be impossible if he didn't graduate. His future depended on one more year of their support, but he couldn't take part in their scams anymore. He couldn't pretend to be the quiet-but-good-looking guy those girls wanted him to be after he'd found someone who liked him for the opinionated person he was.

There was another way. Gus hated himself for resorting to it, but he had no alternative.

He cleared his throat. "Very well. Your loss." He moved to his dresser and fished out his blue dress shirt.

His father took the bait. "What do you mean?"

Gus shrugged. "I would have thought you'd encourage my relationship with the Ostergaards, but—"

"The Ostergaards?" His mother stood. "As in Mark and Laurel Ostergaard?"

Gus nodded. "Cathryn's foster parents. They seem to appreciate my helping Cathryn with her studies."

His mother brightened. "Well, you didn't say your 'date' involved tutoring." She grabbed a pair of dress slacks and handed them to Gus. "I hope you told the Ostergaards your charitable instincts run in the family."

Gus nodded stiffly, as if his neck operated with rusty hinges.

His father rubbed his hands together. "I'm sure the McPhearsons will understand. After all, that poor girl is depending on you."

His parents left with greedy grins on their faces. Gus collapsed onto his bed and waited for his stomach to stop revolting before getting dressed. By the time he reached the Ostergaards' home, he was so exhausted he worried he might fall asleep before Cathryn did.

Mark answered the door. "Hi Gus. Cathryn is in her usual spot." He gestured toward the living room.

"Mr. Ostergaard? Mrs. Ostergaard?"

Mark turned around, and Laurel joined them in the entryway.

Gus opened his mouth, but no words emerged. He swallowed his thickened saliva and tried again. "If my parents invite you to a charity ball, you should refuse. They are . . . aggressively pursuing additional income." Gus hung his head. He'd never been more ashamed to bear the name Hein.

Laurel put a hand on his shoulder. "I understand complicated parental relationships."

"Thanks for the heads-up," Mark said, "but we can handle scammers."

Laurel ushered him into the living room, where Cathryn's smile calmed his stormy stomach and erased his exhaustion. In Cathryn, he'd found everything his parents claimed didn't exist—friendship, forgiveness, trust, compassion . . . love—virtues his parents scorned, but Gus learned were more valuable than a hundred research grants.

Gus sat beside Cathryn and dared to drape his arm across the couch behind her. She scooted closer and shifted her textbook between their laps. He knew his freedom would last only until his parents realized they couldn't con the Ostergaards, but for the next few hours, life was perfect.

Chapter 33

Cathryn forced her right hand to unclench. *It's just a mall. I can do this.* The light rail rolled to a stop, and she followed Minh, Mrs. Jones, and Laurel into the Mall of America. Cathryn had lived in Minnesota her whole life, but she had never ventured into "The Mall." Bright lights and the smell of fast food assaulted her senses. Delighted squeals echoed from the amusement park in the mall's heart.

Cathryn craned her neck to take in each floor, but Laurel left no time for gawking. They were on a mission to find Cathryn a prom dress.

Without Laurel's expert navigation, Cathryn would have been lost amidst the endless racks of clothing. She trailed her fingers over the soft, satiny, and sequined fabrics, but her mind wandered back to the science homework waiting for her at home. She was thinking of questions to ask Gus when a man to her left yelled something in Spanish.

Her hand froze on a dress covered in pink tulle. She shivered, and when she exhaled, she saw her breath. The room darkened until she saw only the flickering light by the gas station and the shadow of the fugitive who'd pursued her that night after work. Her skin crawled.

"Cat!" Minh threw her purse at her. "You okay?"

Cathryn shook off the flashback and searched for the voice. Behind her, a man she didn't recognize argued with a woman in Spanish. He didn't appreciate her dragging him along to buy "a few little things." Though his voice sounded similar, he didn't look anything like the fugitive. He was a normal guy out shopping with his wife on a normal day. *When will life be normal for me?*

"Cathryn?" Mrs. Jones eyed her from across the clothing rack.

"I'm fine." Cathryn faked a chuckle. "You know how I am about eavesdropping."

Laurel frowned. Cathryn hated that frown. It crept onto people's faces whenever they realized she wasn't making as much progress as they thought.

"Why don't you wait in the dressing room with Minh and Mrs. Jones, and I'll bring you dresses to try?" Laurel said. Cathryn nodded and allowed the Joneses to lead her away.

The dressing room contained the type of stiff, generically upholstered chairs found only in hotels and department stores. Cathryn sat between the Joneses and fidgeted with the end of her loose hair. Minh had found a how-to video on one-handed ponytails, but Cathryn still struggled with the technique. *Yet another way I'm failing.*

"Don't you worry, honey." Mrs. Jones wrapped her arms around her. The deep-voiced poet always knew how to make her feel at home. Maybe mothering all those kids gave her mind-reading powers.

"Thanks for this. I'm not particularly gifted in the fashion department."

Minh snorted. "I'll say. Girl as pale as you, light yellow is not your color, and don't even get me started on long sleeves on those skinny arms. You leave the fashion to Laurel and me, and we'll make sure Prince Not-So-Charming can't take his eyes off you."

At least half the blood in Cathryn's body migrated to her cheeks. "He hasn't asked me. I can't assume he will."

"Oh, he's done enough to prove how he feels about you." Mrs. Jones's smile had the mischievous twinge Minh's took on when she was plotting something behind her parents' backs.

"What do you mean?" Cathryn searched her memories, but she got lost in the fog surrounding the fire. *I'm missing something.*

Minh's expression was the facial equivalent of elbowing her mother in the ribs. "She means that blue-eyed egghead has followed you around like a lost puppy since the day he set foot in the land of the ten thousand lakes. He'll ask."

Before Cathryn could question them further, Laurel burst in with an armload of dresses. She held one up to Cathryn.

"Violet? On Cat? Really?" Minh said.

"Ignore the color. Just look at the style. I like the A-line cut on her."

Minh cocked her head and reassessed, reminding Cathryn of when she met Gus's mother. The other half of her blood rose to her cheeks.

"Agreed. Now let's try a color that doesn't make her look like a snow sculpture at a Vikings game."

Laurel shifted the dresses in her arms and held out a blue-green one. "Try this one."

Cathryn entered a stall and slid the silky dress over her body. She scrunched up her face as she pulled the zipper up her back. *Good thing I shut the door. Minh would never let me hear the end of it if she could see this.*

She emerged from the stall to three smiling faces.

"Perfect," Mrs. Jones said.

"That was easy," Minh said. "Let's go get ice cream."

Cathryn stepped to the wrap-around mirror. "Is that me?"

"You look lovely, Cathryn." Laurel smiled behind her.

Cathryn gaped at her reflection. She'd always known she was an ugly duckling, but she never expected to become a swan. True, her left arm looked as though it had passed through a woodchipper, but aside from that, she could almost describe herself as pretty. Her hair was clean and free of tangles; her face was clear of bruises, and her skin shone with a healthy glow. She looked like a normal teenage girl.

Cathryn swallowed a lump in her throat. *I wish Mom could see this.*

* * *

Minh drummed her fingers on her thigh while she waited for a lanky senior to finish speaking with Gus. Judging by the way his calves outsized the rest of him, he was a lacrosse teammate. After a minute, Gus nodded, the senior left, and Minh swooped in for the ambush.

"Have you asked Cat to prom yet?"

"I have not had the opp—"

"Gus! You have to ask her. We already bought a dress." *She's going to blow his giant brain to smithereens.*

"If you would allow me to explain, I made preparations to—"

"Hey, guys, what's happening?" Tony strolled to them with even more swagger than usual. *Things must have gone well with Ariadne.*

"Gus hasn't asked Cat to prom yet," Minh said.

"What? Have you learned nothing this year?"

Gus dodged Tony's swat to the back of the head. "As I was just explaining to Minh—"

Tony and Minh interrupted in a chorus of exasperated squawks.

"Guys!" Gus put one hand out like a police officer controlling traffic. "I got this."

Minh and Tony exchanged shrugs as Gus strode to Cathryn, who had just walked through the door. He bowed with a flourish.

Minh's jaw dropped. "Oh my God. He's reciting Shakespeare."

Tony beamed. "I taught him everything he knows."

* * *

Cathryn rehearsed Somali vocabulary in her head to keep from fidgeting.

"One more pin and done." Laurel released Cathryn's hair and admired her handiwork. As Cathryn suspected, she'd kept her box of hairstyling tools.

"You look great, Cat," Minh said. "You could even say you're glowing."

Cathryn laughed. "With good reason. As of last night, with two weeks to spare, I am, officially, caught up."

"That's wonderful, Cathryn. I'm so proud of you." Laurel gave her a quick hug before she got to her feet. "Minh, you tackle her makeup. I'll see if any of my jewelry matches her dress."

Cathryn scooted into Minh's reach but burst out laughing before the makeover could begin.

"What?"

"This reminds me of the time you convinced me to be your 'living art' project." Fourth-grade Minh painted half of Cathryn's face before Mrs. Jones caught them.

"Ha. Mom grounded me for months." Minh pulled brushes and powders out of a canvass bag that was as big as she was. She grabbed Cathryn's face. "Hold still."

When they were—Cathryn hoped—halfway through the makeover, Laurel returned. She opened a wooden box with a loon carved into the lid, pursed her lips, and held a silver necklace near Cathryn's sleeve.

"This one. The spinel stone matches the blue-green of your dress, and I have earrings to match."

"It's beautiful." Cathryn held the pendant up to the light for a closer examination. It was the same color as her mother's eyes. Her mind drifted back to her mother's amused smile when she'd loaned Cathryn her dress for her movie date.

"Cathryn? You don't have to wear them."

"No. It's not that." Tears blurred her vision. "It's just, my mom would have loved this." Laurel put an arm around her shoulders.

"Don't cry, Cat. You'll ruin the masterpiece I'm creating on your face."

Cathryn laughed the tears back into her eyes. "Thanks, Minh. Mom left me in good hands." She passed the necklace to Laurel. "Will you help me with the clasp?"

Despite months of therapy, Cathryn never regained full use of her left hand. She'd accepted that, but she wasn't going to let her father's parting gift stop her. For the first time in her life, she was going to a dance—with a guy she liked. She would stay out past six knowing two loving people waited up for her, and tomorrow, she'd practice that one-handed ponytail until she could do it in her sleep.

"Wow, this is quite the operation," Mark said from the doorway.

"Shoo!" Laurel waved him away, but her smile expanded. The tension between them had eased after a publisher asked Laurel to turn her blog into a cookbook.

"Go keep watch," Minh said. "I don't want to miss our first glimpse of the goddess."

"The goddess?" Mark and Laurel asked in unison.

"Tony's girlfriend, Ariadne," Cathryn said.

"Apparently, she fits the Greek stereotype as well as he does the Italian one," Minh said.

Cathryn continued. "He's never lasted so long with one girl, and he's *never* introduced us to any of them. They must be serious."

Cathryn related how Tony, taking Minh and Cathryn's advice, went to Ariadne's house and offered to fix their dishwasher. After repairing the dishwasher, dryer, and lawnmower, he punched out a teenager who had been vandalizing their fence. In turn, Ariadne brought Tony's family a batch of homemade baklava. Their hard work earned them a meeting between their parents, which naturally expanded to include the extended families. To ensure success, the young lovers incorporated copious amounts of food and drink into that evening. After a night of riotous festivities, Tony had a prom date.

Mark shook his head. "Remind me to think twice before celebrating New Year's with the Giordanis."

* * *

Mark smiled as Sylvia Jones adjusted her camera and directed the prom-goers to shift into the fading sunlight by Lake of the Isles. The next shot was a girls-only photo with Cathryn, Minh, and a shorter girl with dark curly hair—the goddess. Cathryn looked stunning. More important, she looked happy.

Mark couldn't believe how quickly she'd worked her way into his heart. He and Laurel had agreed to foster as a favor to Warren, but Cathryn was no charity case. She'd forced them to confront their pain even as she dealt with her own, and the pieces of their three shattered lives melded into something new. Mark couldn't be prouder of the kind-hearted young woman who stood smiling beside her friends, but his contentment dissolved as he remembered his high-school dance days. Cathryn wasn't ready for such juvenile chaos.

"If it will alleviate your apprehension, I can assure you I will have her home on time with her virginity intact."

Mark jumped as Gus appeared beside him. "Excuse me?"

"Your expression resembles Tony's before he threatens to punch my face in. I assume you've developed paternal instincts toward Cathryn, but you needn't worry. I would never force her to do anything that made her uncomfortable."

Mark was about to retort that he was a hormone-controlled teenager likely to do exactly that, but Gus's expression gave him pause. There in the eyes of the strangest guy Mark had ever met was the same emotion Mark felt the day he realized he'd do anything for Laurel. This young man pulled Cathryn from a burning building, tutored her in math for countless hours, and carried her to bed after she fell asleep. Somehow, Gus kept the nightmares away.

"Sorry."

Gus shook his head. "Don't apologize for being a good father."

The girls called Gus over for another picture, leaving Mark to ponder the label the teen so readily assigned to him. Throughout his life, Mark had earned many titles—Manager, Director, CEO—but he liked the sound of father best.

* * *

Cathryn tripped for the third time in one song. "I'm glad the waltz isn't part of public-school gym class. I'd be doing even worse."

Gus returned Cathryn's left hand to his shoulder and took her right in his own. "Try again."

Think of it as an exam. Breathe and focus on the task. The breath Cathryn inhaled only pumped more tension into her muscles. She hadn't expected prom to be so loud. And crowded. People popped in and out of her peripheral vision so fast she couldn't keep track of them all. Her skin tingled as if preparing for impact. She stumbled again.

"You're too stiff to follow the rhythm. Relax and follow me." Gus's eyes held hers. "I won't lead you astray, Cathryn."

She sensed he was talking about more than the waltz.

Forget the task. Focus on Gus. Cathryn concentrated on the warmth of his hand on her shoulder. He nudged her backward, and she followed. Her overstimulated senses calmed, and the rest of the room melted away until it was just her and Gus. Step after step he guided her along until they moved as one.

"You would be the envy of every academy girl." Gus surprised her with a smile. Cathryn liked the way it softened his analytical gaze. She caught herself staring and blushed.

"Three seconds before breaking eye contact. That must be a record."

Cathryn shoved him affectionately and glimpsed the rest of their friends past his shoulder. Tony's crooked-toothed grin was so large it squished the rest of his face, and Minh twirled near her mountain of a boyfriend.

"Minh teased me for 'glowing' earlier, but she could light a solar system with that smile."

Gus frowned. "A smile on Minh's face that isn't laced with vitriol is disquieting."

"Now you know how she feels whenever your face is missing its derisive sneer."

The music switched to a booming pop song. Cathryn's body tensed like a cat arching its back. Her father used to blast that song every year when he changed the locks on their house. The beat hit her like a fist, and the vocals clawed her nerves. Gus frowned. Her fingernails were digging into his hand. She released it and reached for her ponytail, only to remember Laurel had done her hair.

"I, uh, I'm going to the bathroom. Try not put the venom back into Minh's expression." She ditched her date and scurried to the bathroom as fast as her dress permitted.

Cathryn scrubbed her hands until she was sure the song was over. Even from prison, her father was keeping her from attending a school dance. She blinked back tears as she rubbed lotion into her burn scars. Every time she thought she'd freed herself, something triggered her panic response.

She put her lotion back into her purse, but smoke invaded her nostrils. Her good hand clenched the sink. *Not now.* She didn't hear the girls' giggles, didn't register whose voices they were. The smell hijacked her mind and hurled it back to her burning kitchen.

"Seriously? You're copying the internet's dumbest pyro in *the school bathroom*?" Shuffling sounded behind Cathryn. "Take your cigs with you. No one wants to breathe your exhaust."

The girls filed out on command. Cathryn's brain sputtered. She tore it loose from the flashback and focused on the present threat.

A pair of heels clicked across the dingy tiles. The junior class president stepped in front of the sink next to her. Cathryn had seen little of her since the backlash from Gus's rejection.

"Who did your makeup?" Belinda asked as she dug into her clutch purse for lip gloss.

"What?"

Belinda addressed Cathryn's reflection. "Your makeup. We both know you didn't do it."

"Uh, Minh."

"Huh. She deserves a medal." Belinda's lip gloss hovered in front of her face. She spoke to the mirror. "My dad came home from overseas. I don't know if house fires are anything like car bombs, but he can't stand the smell of smoke either."

Cathryn released her grip on the sink. "Thank you, Belinda."

"Yeah, well, even freaks deserve a junior prom." She finished applying her lip gloss, fluffed her glossy curls, and sashayed toward the exit. "Later, Cathryn."

Cathryn took a deep breath, but she coughed on the lingering smoke. *Just get out of here.* Shaking from the encounter but bolstered by the unexpected kindness, she marched into the gym.

A blast of sound overwhelmed her already battered senses. Her ears rang, her heart pounded, and her stomach roiled as the stench of sweaty hormones mixed with the smoke in her nostrils. She scanned for Gus amidst the dancers but saw her father's form disappear into the crowd. Droplets of sweat beaded around her hairline. She blinked as one dripped into her eye, and the dancing figures before her flickered like flames.

Someone touched her elbow. Cathryn yelped and jerked her arm free.

"Cathryn, are you all right?"

"Gus." Cathryn's relief stole the strength from her legs. Gus steadied her, but she untangled herself and stumbled back.

She cleared her throat to force the words out. "I'm fine. You-you startled me."

Gus's brow furrowed.

"I'm fine."

Gus pressed his lips into a thin line as he calculated his response. "May we step outside for a moment? This music is giving me a headache." He held out his arm.

Is it wrong to love someone for lying? Gus listened to heavy metal. No way mainstream pop gave him a headache.

Cathryn linked her elbow through his and allowed him to lead her to the parking lot. She breathed in the moonlight, counting through each inhale and exhale as, of all people, Tony had taught her. He used the technique when his sisters irritated him. After a few minutes of fresh air, Cathryn's head regained its center of gravity.

"Would you like me to drive you home?" Gus asked.

"No. I've always wanted to go to a dance. It's just"—she studied a crack in the sidewalk—"sometimes I hear or smell something, and I'm back there." She shook her head. "I'm sorry. You shouldn't have to deal with a crazy date."

"The only one trying to expedite your recovery is you, Cathryn."

"For an atheist, you have the patience of a saint."

"Some things are worth the wait."

Cathryn leaned against the railing and gazed at the junkers that littered the parking lot. Pinpricks from the chill air tickled half her skin. The other half bathed in Gus's warmth. His proximity should have made her nervous, but instead, it was a pillar of support—steady, strong, safe.

Cathryn faced the friend who'd become so much more than her trivia partner. Their classmates called him an arrogant cyborg.

Perhaps they were right, but he was also a tutor, an encourager, and a fail-proof remedy for nightmares. He was her hero.

"Thank you, by the way."

"You're welcome." The smallest of smiles cracked his stony facade. "For what, precisely, am I receiving your gratitude?"

"For saving my life."

The smile vanished. "Who told?"

"I'm not stupid, and our friends are terrible liars." Cathryn took his hands and rubbed her thumb along the burn scars. "Why didn't you tell me?"

"I didn't want you to feel indebted. My role was irrelevant."

"It's not irrelevant to me." Cathryn's comment brought a rosy tinge to Gus's cheeks. "Now who can't make eye contact?"

They laughed.

"Why don't we look at the stars instead?" Cathryn said. She filled her vision with the twinkling lights. "I never tire of stargazing. The night sky is so beautiful."

Gus made an affirmative noise, and Cathryn glanced his way. "You weren't even looking."

"You are more beautiful than any constellation." He reached for her, but at the last second, he retracted his hand and placed it on the railing. He gave her an awkward smile and turned his gaze to the stars.

Cathryn's chest ached. *He's afraid.* Afraid she'd flinch away from his advance. He was always so careful around her, but Cathryn was tired of being fragile. She wasn't going to let fear ruin this moment.

"Gus"—she moved his hand to her waist—"just kiss me."

Chapter 34

Mark lounged on the Joneses' couch, his arm around Laurel. She leaned into him, and he caught a whiff of tarragon from her afternoon in the garden.

"Lovely couples both," Nichole said as she handed the photos of Minh and Cathryn back to their respective guardians.

"We can't exactly complain about the guy who rescued her from a burning building," Mark said.

Michael, Nichole's husband, laughed. "Guess not. I'm glad Jillian isn't at that stage yet. I don't know how I'd handle it."

"That's where a badge and a gun come in handy." Warren passed the photo of Minh back to his wife. "Cathryn seems to be doing better."

"She is," Laurel said.

"But?" Nichole said. *How does she do that? Psychologists.*

Mark and Laurel exchanged a glance. Mark answered first. "We've had some great conversations—she's come a long way—but she still positions herself with an obstacle between us and keeps a clear path to an exit. I don't think she even realizes she monitors my every move."

"It's not just Mark," Laurel added. "Most of the time she's fine, but she gets fidgety around unfamiliar men, especially middle-aged white men." Laurel shook her head. "She has trouble in crowds too. I catch her scanning faces as if she expects her father to jump out from among them."

"Give it time," Nichole said. "She's still processing the trauma."

Mark nodded, wondering how much Nichole charged parents for telling them to wait and see.

* * *

Mark set the last dish in the sink, hugged Laurel from behind, and kissed her. Her cheek pressed against his lips as she smiled.

"I'd hug you back, but my hands are full of dish soap."

"I—

The phone cut off his reply. He released his wife.

"Hi, Warren."

"Is Cathryn there?"

Mark checked the grandfather clock. "She should be heading back from the library about now. Why?"

"Go get her. Now. Her father escaped."

* * *

The straps on Cathryn's backpack cut into her shoulder as she unlocked her bike. *Maybe I was too ambitious with my summer reading plans.*

"Cathryn."

Cathryn froze as her nightmares became reality. "Dad."

He stepped out from the shade of a maple tree, and the sunlight fell flat on his dingy, oversized windbreaker.

"Let's find your mother and go home."

Cathryn trembled. "Mom's dead."

"She's not dead! She took you away, but I found you. We'll find her too."

"You're not supposed to—"

"We're a family!" He pulled a pistol from his waistband, shielding it from prying eyes with his coat. "You're *my* daughter."

"Dad, please—"

"Walk."

If I go with him, I'm dead. He gestured with the gun. She obeyed.

Her mind raced as her legs took her toward the woods. *No witnesses.* She stopped at the edge of the asphalt. The gun's barrel pressed into her back. *Think.*

Cathryn faced him. "I know where Mom is. We can get her together." She took slow steps backward. "We can be a family again. Just put down the gun. Daddy?"

Her father stepped forward, but another man tackled him.

"Cathryn, run!" Mark shouted.

She raced toward the library. A shot fired, and Mark cried out.

"Get back here," her father screamed. A bullet pinged off a nearby dumpster, and Cathryn's legs cemented into the ground. She turned back to the scene. Mark lay clutching his right arm.

"You find a new father?" Her father snarled as he stomped toward her.

Mark looped his foot around her father's ankle and yanked. He hit the ground face first. The pistol clattered to the asphalt and slid toward Cathryn.

Mark kicked her father's ribs. He responded with a punch to Mark's face and grabbed his bloody triceps. Mark screamed and kneed him in the stomach.

The two men wrestled: her father, and the man who'd taught her everything she knew about fathers was wrong. If she didn't act soon, she may never get a chance to thank him.

Her father rolled into a crouch and reached into his pocket. The sun glinted off a knife.

Cathryn picked up the gun. Her father raised his arm. *Feet set. Line up the sights.*

She pulled the trigger.

An inhuman growl silenced birdsong. Blood dripped from her father's side; rage spewed from his eyes. Mark kicked him in the head, and he crumpled.

Cathryn stared at the gun in her trembling hand.

"Cathryn?"

She ditched the weapon and rushed to Mark's side.

"Cathryn, are you all right?"

"Am *I* all right? You took a bullet for me."

He winced. "That's a father's job, right? I'm still new at this."

Cathryn shook her head as tears welled. "Most dads just barbecue."

His laugh gurgled into a groan. "Any of those books cover first aid?"

"It's different in person." She bunched up the hem of her shirt and pressed it into the fountain of blood that poured from Mark's wound. Sirens wailed in the parking lot.

Cathryn held Mark's gaze. "Thank you."

Chapter 35

C athryn unbuckled her seatbelt after Mark parked.
"Are you sure you want to do this?"

"How's your arm?" Cathryn gestured to his sling.

"I won't be swimming triathlons for a while, but at least I'm left-handed."

"You be my left hand; I'll be your right." Her chuckle died quickly. "They added twelve years to his sentence."

"I heard."

Cathryn stared at her hands. "I shot my own father."

"He'd have killed us both if you hadn't." Mark's tone softened. "Cathryn, are you sure you're ready for this?"

Cathryn grabbed the flowers from the backseat and nodded.

They walked past the library and through the trees. A plot of ash met them on the other side, a stain of death in woods teeming with summer life. The squirrels' chittering clashed with the solemnity of the moment, but Cathryn barely heard them. She stared at the ruins.

"What do you do when your life is reduced to ashes?"

"'God's story never ends with ashes.'" Mark had acquired a knack for indulging her love of quotes.

Cathryn sniffed. "Who said that one?"

"A missionary named Elisabeth Elliot."

Cathryn's gaze shifted from the ruins to the lilies in her hand. "Smart lady."

She took a shaky breath, drifted to the center of the rubble, and knelt in the soot. This was her life—tense dinners, locked doors, and bruises, but also bedtime stories, hot chocolate, and laughter. All of it shaped who she was, but none of it dictated who she would become.

She would decide which parts of her past to carry into the future. Her father's anger would remain in the ashes, but her mother's strength—the love that overcame fear—that, she would take with her. No matter how many nightmares jolted her awake or how many flashbacks plagued her daylight hours, Cathryn would keep fighting, keep living.

A single tear ran down her cheek as she placed the bouquet onto the soot. "I love you, Mom."

Cathryn rose. She'd taken her first steps here. Time to take the next ones.

Mark put his good arm around her shoulders as they returned to the car and drove home.

* * *

Cathryn's birthday party resembled an eclectic international festival. She'd been "in Denver" on the actual date, but Tony decided she needed a belated celebration. Once Laurel took hold of the idea, the guest list grew so long they had to rent a pavilion at the park.

Tony and Ariadne tumbled in with an assortment of relatives, each carrying enough food to feed three small countries. Not to be outdone, Pilar and Rosa María brought a mountain of tapas and tamales. Between them and Laurel, they could feed half the city.

For their contribution, Minh's family provided the entertainment. Demarius strummed a tune on the guitar, and his mother's deep voice resounded through the park. Ghost showed off his acrobatic dance moves.

Pilar's oldest wrestled with Tony, and her youngest sat on Minh's boyfriend's massive shoulders. Rosa María's spunky five-year-old played catch with Minh while her toddler enjoyed Mr. Zabinski's rendition of *The Very Hungry Caterpillar.*

Near the drink cooler, Gus's parents engaged in an awkward conversation with one of Ariadne's uncles, eyes flitting to the Ostergaards every few seconds.

Cathryn fingered her perfectly formed ponytail, enjoying the warmth of the summer sunshine on her bare arms. People stared at her left arm, but for her, the right one was more jarring. After a lifetime hiding beneath long sleeves, exposing her skin—now clear of bruises and glowing with health—felt like a victory cry. Let them stare. She was done wearing lies.

"Only you would spend your birthday by yourself, writing." Gus smiled more often now, as if the brick-by-brick dismantling of his tower of ego left him free to enjoy life.

"Just stopping to smell the roses before you launch your rocket," Cathryn said.

Gus frowned. "Are you—"

"I'm sure I can handle a little smoke. I've been using the stove for a few weeks now."

Gus pressed his lips together into a flat line, likely thinking of Tony's ill-fated s'mores night, but Cathryn wouldn't give up. She'd even started seeing a new counselor.

She gave him her most mischievous smile. "If all else fails, we can dunk you in the lake afterward to wash out the smell."

Gus stared blankly for a moment before he realized she was joking. He chuckled and joined her on the picnic blanket.

"Mrs. Giordani and I have a wager regarding who will be the first to disrupt the peace: Tony, and the cousin who is incapable of taking his eyes off Ariadne, or my mother, and whoever happens to be nearest."

"Tough one, but my money's on Minh and Tony's cousin Katrina. Katrina made a snide remark about Patrick's tattoo. No way that goes unpunished."

Gus grinned. "We shall see."

The two watched as Tony gathered a group of the kids into a huddle. After a minute of whispers, he shouted, "Now!" The kids rushed Mark and tackled him to the ground. Tony roared with laughter, which Mark soon joined.

Cathryn smiled. "He's a good godfather."

"Godfather?" Gus asked.

"'Foster father' is too distant, but 'dad' . . . 'dad' has too many other emotions associated with it." She cast her gaze to the sky. "I think 'godparents' is what my mother would want me to call him and Laurel. She would have said they were the parents God sent to care for me after she couldn't." She met Gus's eye. "What? No lectures about unsubstantiated delusions?"

"I may not believe religion is factually true"—Gus looked at Laurel—"but I acknowledge the power of its influence." He put his arm around her. "Godparents is the perfect term." He kissed the top of her head, and she leaned into him, relishing feeling safe.

* * *

Cathryn's Diary

As I look upon the jubilant chaos of my birthday celebration, I am in awe of what grows out of the ashes of my past. I hid my pain beneath long sleeves, makeup, and lies, but now I know what Rumi meant when he said, "The wound is the place where the light enters you."

I once hungered through tense dinners and cowered behind locked doors. Now I feast at barbecues and dance beneath the stars. I traversed dark alleyways alone; now an entire park full of people support me. Real people, each with their own eccentricities, their own strengths, their own hurts. Is this what family feels like?

I am stronger now, being broken. I wanted to forget my past, but in my darkest memories, my mother held me closest. Whether her spirit now resides with the God she so adored, I cannot say, but her sacrifices taught me the power of love. I carry that power within myself, and with it, I can overcome anything.

Thank you

Thank you for investing your time in *The Lies She Wore*. Cathryn and the others have become like good friends, and I'm so pleased to share them with you. If you enjoyed my writing, please consider leaving a review. Even a two-sentence review is a fantastic way to support an author, and I would greatly appreciate your feedback.

Stay in touch!

Subscribe to my monthly newsletter for behind-the-scenes sneak peeks and exclusive content, like my short story *The Perfect Fit*, which features Tony. You can download the e-book at https://newsletter.ccthewordnerd.com/perfectfit, or by scanning the QR code below. I love connecting with readers, so don't hesitate to reach out!

The Perfect Fit

About the Author

C.C. Hansen has traded Minnesotan mosquitoes for Montanan mountains. When not writing, she either has her nose in a book, her hands in a ball of bread dough, or her feet on a trail through the backcountry.

Find Me Online

- Facebook: https://www.facebook.com/CCHansen3/
- Website: https://ccthewordnerd.com/

Acknowledgments

Many thanks to the beta readers, friends, and family members who read this way too many times and tolerated my endless brainstorming. I'd also like to thank all the wheelchair users who shared their experiences. I couldn't have done Minh's character justice without your insight.

Thanks as well to my editor for catching the errors that slipped past me after hours of writing made me go cross-eyed. My cover designer also deserves a medal for being able to transform the gibberish I sent her into the gem that bookends these words.

To my husband, thanks for letting me commandeer your standing desk whenever I want. Last but not least, I could not have finished this without my mother—my sounding board, cheerleader, and therapist rolled into one.

www.ingramcontent.com/pod-product-compliance
Lightning Source LLC
Chambersburg PA
CBHW011116100726
47898CB00011B/3108